And the Oaks Heard Them All

And the Oaks Heard Them All

A novel

Peter Karofsky

Kathryn Publishing
Middleton, Wisconsin

ISBN-13: 9780692636909
ISBN-10: 0692636900
ISBN 978-0-692-63966-5 (eBook version)
Library of Congress Control Number: 2016910552
Kathryn Publishing, Middleton, Wisconsin

And the Oaks Heard Them All is written for
my five grandchildren: Daphne, Logan,
Danny, Campbell, and McKerrah.

The book is dedicated with love to my favorite tennis
partner and my partner in life, Kathy.

Table of Contents

Introduction

AND THE OAKS Heard Them All journeys back and forth
between the summers of 1975 and 2006.

The novel has multiple references to tennis. Since some
readers may not be familiar with the game, I will use the
introduction to explain a few terms.

Tennis strokes. *Groundstrokes* refer to *forehands* and
backhands, shots hit after the ball bounces once. *Volleys* are
shots hit without letting the ball touch the ground. Every
point is initiated by a *serve*, which must land in the service
box diagonally across the net from the server. A *lob* is a ball
hit high in the air. An *overhead* is a shot that looks similar
to a *serve* but is used to return a lob.

Scoring of games. Four points are needed to win a
game, and there are two versions of scoring: *traditional* and
alternative. In *traditional* tennis, the scoring is 15, 30, 40
and game. A game tied at 40-40, which is termed *40-all*,
must be played out, with the victor winning by two points.
If at 40-all, the server or serving team wins the point, that
is called *ad-in*. If the receiver or receiving team wins that
point, the score is *ad-out*. When the player or team with

the *ad* fails to win the next point, the score is tied again and called *deuce.* Theoretically, a game can have an infinite number of ads and deuces.

In *alternative* or *no-ad* scoring, the points are scored 1, 2, 3, and game. If there is a tie at 3-all, a deciding point is played to determine the game winner.

Scoring of sets. The first player or team to win 6 *games,* wins the *set.* A set has to be won by at least 2 games (i.e. 6-0, 6-1, 6-2, 6-3, 6-4, or 7-5). If there is a tie at 5-5 (also called *5-all*) and one team or player wins the next 2 games, the set is won 7-5. However, if there is a tie at 6-6, a *7-point tiebreak* is usually played. A *tiebreak* is really an extended game in which players alternate serving. In a tiebreak, the team or player who wins must reach 7 points and win by at least 2 points. In most matches, the player or team who wins two *sets* is the victor. Sometimes a *10-point tiebreak* (as opposed to a 7-point tiebreak) is substituted for a third set to decide matches where players or teams are tied at 1 set apiece.

The court. *Baselines* are the lines furthest away from the *net.* Players must serve the ball standing behind these lines. The four squares on either side of the net are *service boxes,* where serves must land. Facing the net, the *deuce side* is on the right and the *ad side* on the left. On the far right and far left sides of the court are thin long rectangles called *doubles alleys.* They are not in play during singles matches but allow the court a greater area for doubles.

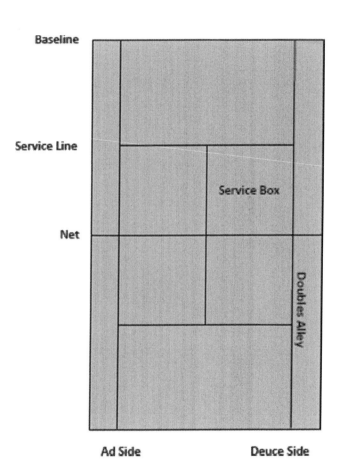

CHAPTER 1

Monday, June 19, 2006

ELLIE APPEL FELL asleep in the highchair and listed to the right. Her breathing was slow and shallow. An arm dangled by the tray. Sweaty blonde curls stuck to her forehead while small bubbles glistened between moist lips.

Brenda felt inside her purse to find the pliable plastic comb. She examined it, bent the comb backward, and let it snap sharply over the back of Ellie's hand anticipating a yelp or cry. Instead, Ellie's eyes opened wide...exceptionally wide. Stunned, her expression froze. She stopped breathing, both cheeks blanched, and her chin flopped down to her chest.

Brenda panicked. "Breathe. Dammit breathe! Oh, what did I do?" Was Ellie having a seizure? Should she dial 911? Desperately, Brenda looked around the room to see if anyone observed what had happened. She tapped Ellie's cheeks lightly trying to rouse her. The youngster began to move. She lifted her head, took a deep breath, then hollered. Covering the back of her right hand with the palm of her left, she rubbed the area slowly, bawling pitifully. Brenda wanted to comfort and quiet her. As she bent down to talk to Ellie, the infant's flailing arm struck her in the mouth.

Brenda retreated, confused by what she had done… alarmed by Ellie's response. It was Ellie's first day at the nursery. Why had she hurt her?

For almost twenty years Brenda had run the Few Hours A Day Nursery never intentionally harming a child. She scanned the other children in the room as they began to stir, then bent down to calm Ellie again. "There, there," she said with a serene voice. "You're OK. That a-girl. You're OK." But instead of picking her up, she gave Ellie a few crackers then watched the infant deliberately swipe them off the tray onto the floor.

Hearing a disturbance, two assistants entered the shaded room to help Brenda change the youngsters. White blinds prevented the sun from penetrating, but a few pinholes projected beams of light onto one wall. Cubbyholes were inlaid into another wall for the children's diapers, clothing, and snacks. All the walls were sky blue and some had pictures of animals. Six of the seven cribs in the room were occupied; a vacant one in the corner was Ellie's. Brenda had allowed her to stay in the highchair after Ellie fell asleep snacking.

As Brenda attended to Ellie, an assistant asked if everything was all right. Brenda said she thought Ellie had had a nightmare. Redressing her, Brenda looked at the back of Ellie's hand. It was red, but there was no swelling, and she seemed to move all her fingers normally. Brenda felt some relief.

Although the Appel children grew up in Oakbrook, Ellie was the first to attend Brenda's nursery. When Sadie's oldest daughter dropped Ellie off earlier, Brenda recognized Molly immediately. Years ago, Brenda had the misfortune of going to school with Sadie, Ellie and Molly's mother. When she was a teenager Brenda hated Sadie. As an adult, she still hated her, but that was no excuse for hurting her baby.

At forty-five, with two children in their teens, Sadie Appel surprised herself, her husband, and the community with the news of her pregnancy. "Everyone should have a child late in life," she advocated after learning her amniocentesis was normal.

Brenda surmised her pregnancy would give credibility to the weight gain that accompanied Sadie's approach to middle age, at least for a few months before and a few months after the baby was born. Brenda was always jealous of her schoolmate's lithe body during adolescence, even though Sadie was disproportionately thin at that age. Somehow, Sadie convinced her teammates that she looked better in her tennis uniform than the rest of them.

At 3:15, Brenda watched Molly Appel return to pick up Ellie. As Molly approached, her sister reached out with both hands, squealing with delight. Molly stared at the reddish square on the back of Ellie's right hand and at her red cheeks. She lifted her top to examine her tummy and back, then inspected her legs, too. She was unable to find any other splotches. Finally, she picked Ellie up, gave her a kiss, gathered the belongings from her cubbyhole, and carried Ellie outside.

After all the children left, Brenda trudged to her modest office. She pulled her chair back, sat down, and slouched over her seasoned wooden desk. A laptop computer, its dented lid closed, sat on a back corner. Both desk drawers on the right side fit unevenly into their sockets. Opposite the desk stood an old four-drawer beige metal filing cabinet etched with scratches.

At forty-three, Brenda Nelson Bjorkman looked her age. She had closely-cropped brown hair with a few gray strands; her nose had a slight hump at the bridge. She stood five foot five inches tall, weighed one hundred and thirty-seven pounds, and had a slight roundness to her belly.

Brenda stood up. Opening a drawer in the filing cabinet, she removed some folders. Each was dedicated to a child in the daycare center, and Brenda entered information every day from Room One into each of her children's logs. She opened another drawer to remove a new folder. Taping a clean label on the tab, she wrote *Appel, Ellie*.

Brenda chastised herself again for hurting Ellie. Last Friday, her partner, Marie, had mentioned that a new child would join her room. Had Marie revealed her name, Brenda might have had the weekend to think about Ellie Appel, and maybe she would not have reacted so rashly or maybe she wouldn't have allowed Ellie to attend Few Hours A Day Nursery at all.

Still, she had genuine remorse and wondered how long she was going to be angry with Sadie for events that were decades old. After all, they were both young at the time. But recollections of being bullied had never receded in Brenda's mind. She had not forgiven Sadie for making her adolescence more difficult.

Brenda collected herself. On a legal pad, she began writing notes she would save in the folder.

Monday, 6/19/06. Ellie Appel came to daycare for her first day. She is 9 months old. She was brought by her older sister, Molly. A note from Mrs. Appel accompanied her and is included in this folder along with information from Dr. Paul Farber of Oakbrook Family Clinic. Ellie has no food allergies and is on a regular diet. Her immunizations are up-to-date. She is a healthy girl except for one ear infection. She seemed happy around the other children and ate the lunch her mother packed for her. She fell asleep eating and it was decided to leave her in the highchair instead of moving her to a crib. She awoke after having a nightmare followed by a brief breath-holding spell.

Brenda paused. She could not decide whether to include a statement about the blotch on the back of Ellie's hand. What possible excuse could she provide? An insect bite? A bee sting? Clearly, her sister already noticed it. She could always say she didn't see anything happen to Ellie, but if she didn't document something in Ellie's chart, she was being derelict and could be subject to an investigation and perhaps even lose her daycare license. As she was debating what to do, Marie called her from another room. Brenda remembered immediately she was supposed to help her partner chair an after-hours staff meeting.

"Brenda?" Marie called again.

Brenda scurried from her office to a small conference room where Marie and their three assistants gathered. "Yes, here I am. Sorry I'm late. I was trying to catch up on some paperwork."

"No problem. I was just informing the staff about our air conditioner. We're hoping to have it fixed by Wednesday. It needs a new part and they won't have it until then."

"Have we informed the parents?" Brenda asked.

"I didn't hear from the air conditioner people until after lunch, so I thought we could tell them tomorrow. In fact, I thought we could write them a memo and tell them about the video system tomorrow, too."

Brenda was confused, "We aren't ready to tell parents about the videos yet, are we?"

"Well first, let me explain to the assistants what's going on," Marie began. "Brenda and I decided to install a new surveillance system. Soon, parents will be able to access their children's rooms at any time by computer. The company installing our system has already tested the equipment and seem pleased with the dry runs. They could have it up and running in another week or so."

After the staff meeting, Brenda clutched Marie's arm, "I had no idea you already hired a company or that they had begun working. I thought you were putting the video thing out for bids and assumed workmen traipsing through here were just gathering information."

"I was going to interview several companies, but Billy Williams came in with a low bid and offered us the best hardware. I researched some internet reviews. He is number one. That doggy daycare in Deer Point had cameras installed months ago and wrote an excellent online evaluation. He already placed recording devices in the play area outside and in our rooms."

"Really? I didn't notice anything in my room."

"They are well-concealed."

"And you said they were already operating?"

"Yes, Billy began running them this morning and recording, so we could see what the cameras were capable of picking up."

"I wish you had talked to me before actually hiring him."

"We agreed that I would take on this project," Marie reminded Brenda.

"We did, but I thought you'd at least let me know our options so we could make a final decision together."

"I'm sorry. It just seemed straight forward to me, so I hired Billy. I'm sure he'll do a great job."

"OK," Brenda sighed.

"Changing the subject…how did the new girl do today?"

"Ellie? I think she had a nightmare of some sort during rest hour," Brenda lied. "It must have really scared her, because she awoke and had a breath-holding spell."

"Did you say anything to her mother?"

"No, her sister picked her up."

"I have a kid in my room that has those. They're frightening," Marie remarked.

"I didn't realize what happened at first. I wondered if it was a seizure. You know my daughter had seizures. She hasn't had one in over a year now. When she was little, she would just fall down on the ground limp and unconscious. As she got older, her legs stiffened and her arms jerked back and forth," Brenda confided.

"Breath-holding spells I've seen, but I have never seen a seizure."

"Believe me. They're more frightening than breath-holding spells."

"I'm sure."

"I know Ellie's mother, Sadie. I used to go to school with her."

"Yeah, I've seen her around, but I don't really know her."

Brenda thought about sharing her perspective on Sadie with Marie but decided against it. Her husband and mother were the only people Brenda talked to about Sadie, but both seemed less interested and empathetic lately. Besides, Brenda had other things to worry about—the videos. What had they captured in Room One this morning? And who was going to review them?

CHAPTER 2

·❖·

Tuesday, June 20, 2006

Sadie brought Ellie to Few Hours A Day Nursery the next morning at 8:15. As she carried her daughter toward Room One, she spotted Brenda in the hallway. Sadie was exuberant in her greeting and hugged Brenda tightly with one arm, holding Ellie with the other. While Brenda didn't recoil from her embrace, she didn't receive it enthusiastically either. Sadie never acknowledged the fence that separated them. Brenda not only sensed a fence, she felt it had never been mended. But daycare was her business and Sadie was a client.

The two women had encountered each other many times over the years shopping, in schools, at parties, and on the tennis courts in Oakbrook. Sadie, a stay-at-home mom, played a lot more tennis than Brenda did.

Sadie was an only child (her mother had difficulty conceiving and was one of the first women in Wisconsin to use a fertility drug). Her parents, Mr. and Mrs. Winetraub still lived in Oakbrook, where her father was a retired pharmacist and her mother a homemaker. Mr. Winetraub was well-liked and well-respected in the community. He was philanthropic with his money and his time, volunteering once a week in a free clinic he helped to sponsor. A village board member, he also chaired a committee that brought emergency medical services to Oakbrook and surrounding areas. Mrs. Winetraub served on several committees, as well, including the historical society, beautification committee, and senior citizen center. She doted on Sadie, ensuring her daughter had virtually everything she wanted (except a sibling). The Winetraubs were one of two Jewish families in a town of almost two thousand. They observed the high holidays by going to a synagogue forty minutes east of Oakbrook, but they were not a religious family.

Sadie married Stan Appel, who was also Jewish but grew up in Milwaukee. Like Sadie's father, Stan was a pharmacist. After pharmacy school, Stan worked for Sadie's father as an intern. During that time, Sadie and Stan dated. In less than six months after meeting, they were married, and Mr. Winetraub made Stan a partner in his drugstore. Molly was the oldest Appel daughter and Ellie the youngest. Their middle daughter, Sandy, was fifteen.

Each time Brenda saw Sadie, she was amazed at her transformation from anorexic teenager to obese adult. Sadie probably weighed one hundred and seventy-five pounds now. At five foot three, two inches shorter than Brenda, Sadie virtually waddled when she walked. Sadie's wardrobe was pricey, but Brenda could never understand why Sadie persisted in wearing dark tight-fitting clothes as if she were immune to her own imperfections.

Sadie asked Brenda if she had noticed a blotch on Ellie's hand yesterday, and Brenda said she had. Sadie said Ellie's father, the pharmacist, thought the child was probably sucking on it, because today the area looked bruised. "What she did," Sadie chuckled, "was give herself a hickey!"

Brenda smiled nervously. Her cheeks felt hot. She started to perspire and become light-headed. She could feel her heart pumping hard, just like it used to when she was around Sadie as a teenager. If Sadie noticed changes in Brenda's demeanor, she didn't say anything. Brenda thought of all the times she had been set up by Sadie and wondered if Sadie's explanation of the bruise was another ruse. Brenda told herself to make sure to record it in Ellie's journal.

Brenda moved towards Room One. As she fumbled in her purse to find the keys, a plastic comb fell onto the floor. She grabbed it quickly losing her grip on her purse. The contents exploded out and scattered over the floor. Quickly, Brenda stuffed the comb back and began picking up her wallet, loose change, and other spilled articles. Sadie bent down to help, still carrying Ellie in one arm and stepped on Brenda's finger.

"Ouch!" Brenda exclaimed.

"Oh, I'm sorry," replied Sadie. "I was just trying to help you."

"It's OK. Thank you. I've got it now."

"Here," Sadie said, handing Brenda her cellphone.

Brenda felt discombobulated. With her hands shaking, she unlocked the door to her room. Then she reached inside the doorway to turn on some lights.

"This is Ellie's room," Brenda explained, steadying herself.

"It's nice."

Brenda walked over to a window and lifted a shade. She pointed to the corner, "And this is her crib. She didn't use it much yesterday, because she fell asleep in her highchair while she was eating. She looked so peaceful and comfortable I decided to leave her there to nap."

"She's actually a really sound sleeper. I'm sure she wouldn't wake up if you took her out and laid her down in the crib."

"Another thing happened, I wanted to tell you about," Brenda began. "I think Ellie had a nightmare yesterday."

"What makes you say that?"

"Well, when she woke up from her nap, she had what looked like a breath-holding spell. She became pale for a few seconds—and got kinda limp, and then she hollered. I was able to calm her down, though… I just thought you should know."

"It doesn't surprise me. She's had them before but only when she hurt herself. I've never seen her wake up and have one. That's unusual. Last week when she caught her fingers in a drawer, she blanched, her eyes bugged out of her head, and she wouldn't breathe. None of my other kids ever had one. I spoke to Dr. Farber, and he said she'll outgrow it."

"Good."

"I meant to ask you—did Molly pick Ellie up on time yesterday?" Sadie inquired.

"Yes. She seems like a nice young lady."

"Sometimes. At that age, they are so full of themselves. But she is good with Ellie."

"Well, Ellie obviously loves her. She was very happy to see Molly when she came to take her home."

"Yes, she does. Sometimes when Ellie says 'Maw', I don't know whether the little one means Molly or Mom. Molly is very protective of her, too. She even reprimands me if she thinks I'm not doing something right or if she feels I'm ignoring Ellie."

As the women were talking, an assistant entered Room One offering to take Ellie to the play area. Before Sadie relinquished her, she gave Ellie a peck on her cheek. Ellie whined at first, but the assistant engaged her with some toys, and Ellie's separation anxiety quickly abated.

"I did want to say one thing to you, Brenda."

"Of course," Brenda responded anxiously.

"Thanks for allowing Ellie to attend your daycare. I know you are pretty full, and I appreciate your letting her in."

"To tell you the truth, we had a youngster leave a week ago and a slot opened up. Glad we could accommodate her…are you playing much tennis?"

"Just in the county league. Are you going to be able to play on our women's team this fall?" Sadie asked.

"I wish I could, but my hours are unpredictable, and as much as I would like to play more, I just can't."

"Well it looks like you are starting to fill up. I had better let you go. You look hassled already. Thanks, again, dear. Bye."

"Bye...oh, Sadie, I almost forgot. We are having air conditioner problems, but it should be fixed by tomorrow."

"Yes, I noticed it was a little warm. Thanks for telling me. See you later."

Brenda decided not to give Sadie a parental handout discussing the air conditioner and video cameras in the nursery. She didn't trust Sadie and providing her with information about the video system now only increased the chances that her child abuse would be discovered. "They didn't record it, please tell me they didn't record it," she said to herself dejectedly.

The remaining workday passed quickly and uneventfully. After her children were gone, Brenda decided to update their files in her office. But then she thought about the camera in her room. She still could not recall seeing one. She stood up from her desk and returned to Room One. Brenda surveyed the walls carefully and located a small glass lens peering over the cubbyholes. No wonder she hadn't noticed it. It was incredibly inconspicuous.

Brenda returned to her office, reread her notes on Ellie and decided to amend her initial entry. She added:

A small red mark was observed on the back of Ellie's hand. Her sister picked her up at 3:15.

Brenda followed Monday's note with a brief missive about Tuesday's session and left for home. As she drove past Oakbrook High, she thought about the day once more. Outside of her interaction with Sadie, which was terribly awkward, she thought it went well. She liked Ellie. The child was cuddly and seemed happy. Again, Brenda scolded herself for injuring her the day before. Sometimes that temper was still out of control.

When she arrived home, the rest of the immediate family was already there including her mother, Ellen Nelson. Brenda's husband, Henry Bjorkman a.k.a. Henrik, was a plumber and owned his own shop. Three years older than Brenda, he grew up in Oakbrook and attended the high school, too. A fine athlete, he lettered in three sports his junior and senior years. He was an offensive lineman in football, a forward in basketball, and threw the shot put and discus in track. After graduation, he left town to attend technical college, where he learned his trade while playing semi-pro football for another two years. Although the couple went to the same high school, they didn't date until Brenda attended the University. They married shortly after she received her degree in education in 1986.

Brenda and Henry had two kids. Their daughter, Joy, was moderately cognitively impaired but was mainstreamed through the school system. At fifteen years old, she was preparing to play tennis in the Special Olympics USA National Games. She had won state in her division the previous year. Their son, Ricky, also played tennis and was in eighth grade.

Brenda's mother, Ellen Nelson, lived with the Bjorkmans, an arrangement that worked well for everyone. She was home to greet their daughter, Joy, when she returned from school. She also cooked meals and organized the house during times Henry and Brenda were at work. Having lost her son, John, in Operation Desert Storm in 1991 and without a mate, she thrived on the family she had. She had warmed over the years and was much more affectionate towards her grandchildren than she had been to her own children when they were growing up.

Brenda's years of complaining to her husband and mother about Sadie had dulled their interest in her conflict, so Brenda was cautious about telling them about her. Both confidants had wanted Brenda to be more assertive in the past. Although they realized Sadie bullied Brenda, they also felt Brenda enabled Sadie by not sticking up for herself. The previous evening, Brenda told her family that Sadie was bringing her nine-month-old infant to the daycare center. She deliberately eliminated all details, of course. Tonight she thought she might tell them that she saw Sadie and talked with her briefly. Then again, she might not.

Joy welcomed her mother home with a hug and Brenda responded, placing a kiss on her daughter's cheek. "How's my big girl?" she asked smiling.

"Good."

At five foot four inches tall, Joy was mildly overweight. Her cheeks were furry from anti-seizure medication, and she had a bump on her nose like Brenda's. Joy's speech was nasal and difficult to understand at times. Somewhat fearful of strangers, she was shy until she knew people better; those close to her found her amiable and pleasant. The family was very supportive, and Joy seemed unaware of her disabilities. She adored Brenda yet had a good relationship with her brother, father, and grandmother, too. Joy was capable of working, but it was clear she would never be able to live on her own. During summers, she helped clean her father's plumbing shop and accompanied him during his house calls when she wasn't on the courts practicing.

Joy's proficiency in tennis was well-known and appreciated by Oakbrook's citizens. Brenda had both children playing at an early age. When Joy was ten, Oakbrook High tennis coach, Tom Carrabas, watched her and suggested she compete in Special Olympics.

Brenda turned to Joy, "The courts should be dry, and I think you have another lesson with Coach tonight, Sweetie. Are you ready?" Brenda questioned.

"Yes," replied Joy.

"What did you do today at Daddy's shop?"

"We did inventory."

"And how did that go?"

"Good. We also made some house calls, and I went with Daddy."

"Whose houses did you visit?"

"I don't remember."

"Were the homes in Oakbrook?"

"I think so."

"Is Henry home, Mom?" Brenda asked.

"Yes. He's upstairs."

"Where is his truck? I didn't see it in the garage or driveway."

"I think he dropped it off at the gas station to have new tires put on."

Walking towards her son, Brenda inquired, "And how are you, Ricky?"

"I'm OK."

"What did you do today?"

"Played baseball at the high school. A bunch of kids from my class showed up. It was a lot of fun until some older kids kicked us off."

"I'm sorry. That's too bad."

"Ya. But we got to play most of the afternoon."

"Good. Well, I guess I'll go upstairs and change. I'll be right down. What's for supper?" Brenda asked her mom.

"Chicken. Take your time, dear."

Brenda climbed the stairs and saw Henry in the hall-way walking to their bedroom. She asked about his truck and Henry confirmed her mother's story. He asked Brenda to pick it up with him after dinner. She agreed, providing he took her out for an ice cream beforehand. "I think I need a little alone time with you," she said placing a kiss on his cheek.

CHAPTER 3

Monday, June 23, 1975

AL ANDERSEN AND Carrie Archibald ran tennis clinics for middle school and freshmen students three mornings a week during the summer. Both were varsity athletes at Oakbrook High. Lessons lasted two hours, and Al and Carrie charged each player five dollars per day. There were no tennis clubs in the community, so summer sessions were the only real introduction to tennis that seventh, eighth and ninth graders had. It was traditional for Oakbrook High tennis players to run summer clinics, and this was Al and Carrie's second year as mentors.

At seventeen years old, Al was physically mature for his age. He had a pleasant face accentuated by a straight nose and long eyelashes. His smile was contagious and made his sky-blue eyes sparkle.

Carrie was the same age as Al. Despite a small frame, she had well-developed shoulders and muscular legs. She bore a flat red birthmark on her right temple, but green eyes and a small nose were her most striking facial features. Her full head of hair was blondish-brown, and Carrie liked to wear it in a ponytail.

Many girls in the summer session worshipped Carrie. She was their role model. If Carrie wore a tee shirt and shorts to clinic, the girls wore tee shirts and shorts. When Carrie changed from white to colored socks on the court, her admirers switched to colored socks, too. For many girls, she was a blend of mother and big sister. Both boys and girls tried hard to win Carrie's respect and receive her approval.

Al had a prominent role with the kids as well. Most girls had a crush on him and enjoyed teasing him about Carrie. Al handled the affection and taunting skillfully. The boys, of course, mirrored Al's mannerisms, always bouncing the ball three times before they served and wearing hats or visors, because Al did.

Sexism was a hot topic in the 70s, and Al and Carrie strove to be sensitive about the issue. A few years older than their students, both teens saw the bias that existed before and after title IX[*] and the Bobby Riggs-Billie Jean King match. So, they tried pairing players together based on skill level as opposed to gender. Al and Carrie were very aware of how the changes affected girls and boys, too. For girls, competing on a level playing field with boys instead of cheering for them on the sidelines was novel. For boys competing against girls was difficult; losing to them was unimaginable.

Of the clinic's sixteen students, twelve were returnees and four were new. Most returning players were older than the newcomers and had a distinct advantage over them.

_____

[*] A bill enacted by Congress in 1972 to prevent sexual discrimination.

Al brought the four novices onto Court Four to begin teaching them how to dribble a tennis ball with their racquets. Starting them at the baseline, he had them bounce a ball onto the court while advancing towards the net. There were two boys and two girls in Al's group. All of them had recently completed sixth grade. One of the boys and one of the girls seemed to catch on, but the other two students had difficulty. Instead of dribbling, Al had both less-experienced players balance a tennis ball on their racquets from baseline to net.

The girl who performed well was Brenda Nelson. She seemed like a serious and self-conscious twelve-year-old who sought approval after every exercise. Walking around the court averting eye contact, especially with other children, Brenda didn't initiate conversations with her peers but did respond when they talked to her.

Brenda's vulnerability prompted Al to react in an almost brotherly way towards her. He complimented her several times during the first clinic, buoying her up by his attention.

"Excellent!" Al exclaimed as Brenda successfully dribbled a ball to the net. "That's great!" he applauded when she completed the task again. He hoped for a smile and, to his delight, received one.

Brenda was at a stage where she did not feel comfortable with herself. Her body was neither feminine nor childlike any more, and it was difficult to find clothes that fit and looked attractive. Intentionally, she wore neutral colors so she wouldn't be noticed. She had pimples on her forehead and avoided mirrors unless she had to comb her hair, which was oily and shapeless.

While Al worked with the new players, Carrie took the other twelve onto Court One. "OK," she instructed, "let's begin with groundstrokes. Form two lines at the corners of the baseline. I will feed you balls and you'll hit forehands from one side and backhands from the other. Change sides after you hit a shot, so that you alternate between forehands and backhands. OK?" Six students went to the ad side and six to the deuce side. Carrie wheeled a shopping cart filled with tennis balls to the baseline on the opposite side of the net and began feeding balls to them. "I forgot you were a lefty," she smiled at a red-haired girl, who returned a forehand shot from the ad side. "Nice shot!" When they finished the drill, Carrie asked her players to help pick up the balls and return them to her cart. Next they worked on volleys. In this drill, kids formed two lines near the net and worked on punching shots over the net and back to Carrie who fed each ball to them.

A half hour into their lesson, Al called all players off the courts and invited them to sit in the shade of six old oak trees that spread out over wooden benches and tables adjacent to the tennis complex. He instructed them to drink lots of water to protect them from the heat, which was fairly intense. Some newcomers did not have water bottles, so Al suggested they drink from a bubbler at the shelter, which was about a hundred yards away. Brenda and two boys from Court Four walked to the shelter together. Al caught up and accompanied them to the bubbler.

"How are you guys doing?" he asked.

"Good," one boy answered.

A second one asked, "When do we get to play some games?"

"We'll play some before you leave today. But first, I want you to learn how to hit the shots you need to hit in games."

"Cool."

"How about you, Brenda? How's it going?" Al inquired.

Looking down at her shoes, Brenda replied shyly, "OK."

"You know, all of you are doing really well considering this is the first real tennis lesson you've had," Al complimented them.

"My mom's played tennis with me before. She used to play a little when she was younger," admitted one boy.

Al asked Brenda, "Have you played before?"

"I've hit against the wall at the high school some."

"That's a great way to start learning. OK guys, let's get some water and go back to the other kids."

"I'll be there in a sec," Brenda said.

Al and the boys finished drinking from the bubbler and headed back to the courts. Brenda ducked into the girls' bathroom before returning.

Once the group reassembled, Carrie announced, "Let's continue where we left off before our break. I will take the same twelve kids who began with me onto the first three courts. The four kids who worked with Al will go back with him to Court Four."

Carrie assigned her twelve players to their courts. She placed three boys and a girl on Courts One and Two and two boys and two girls on Court Three. "Let's play a few games to twenty-one," Carrie instructed. "Anyone can put a ball in play, but it has to be a good feed, then play the point out like you would in an ordinary doubles game. The first team to twenty-one wins, but you have to win by two points."

Carrie gave each foursome a few balls and monitored play by walking back and forth among the three courts. "Come on," she encouraged. "You recall how we did this last summer." She watched a bit longer then said, "That's it! Remember, we are trying to get to the net more. We want to move in from the baseline and play the game at the net. That's how doubles is played."

As Carrie walked to Court Three, she saw one girl chomping hard on a piece of gum. "Sadie, your gum, please. You're going to choke on it. You won't ever see a pro chewing gum on a court."

"How about tobacco?" a boy asked with a wry smile.

"Not in tennis," Carrie answered. "And baseball players aren't chewing tobacco as much as they used to either." Carrie turned back to Sadie. "Turn your body to the side more on your volleys. Move your feet into position. There you go. Good, Sadie."

Sadie scowled. She was annoyed that Carrie was instructing her instead of Al. She viewed Carrie as competition.

She wished she was as old as Carrie and could play tennis as well. But really, what made Carrie so special? She had that red mark near her forehead, and she certainly didn't have any boobs. Sadie just couldn't understand what Al saw in her, or could she.

Al worked with the novices, standing beside each one and dropping balls in front of them to hit over the net. He helped them with forehands then backhands. After another break for water and shade, Al allowed his group to play some games. The boys wanted to keep score, but Al suggested they just play out points.

C H A P T E R   4

— ⚜ —

Monday, July 7, 1975

Two WEEKS HAD passed since the first summer lessons at Taylor Park. The weather had been warm, ideal for tennis. The park was luxuriant with green grass and an oak canopy full enough to provide complete shade for people sitting at the benches and tables. A lake, visible from the courts, made the setting more enchanting. Pierce Lake was big enough to accommodate small motorized vessels, and residents could fish from their piers or boats for blue gills, perch and small-mouth bass. Sometimes bald eagles soared overhead whistling or screeching to one another. A deep brook ran through the park near the oak trees connecting Pierce Lake to a larger lake several miles south of town, hence the name Oakbrook.

Oakbrook High did not have a tennis facility. High school teams used the park courts for practice and matches. The benches, tables and grass served as bleachers for spectators.

During the first week of lessons, in-groups formed among players. A natural division of boys and girls existed, of course. Age was another criterion. But one clique of fourteen-year-olds developed well before summer tennis began. Sadie was boss and the red-haired leftie was one of her lieutenants. Rachel rounded out the threesome of ninth-graders. Intelligent and athletic, her tennis skills were steadily improving. Rachel and Sadie had been friends since third grade. Rachel liked Sadie but feared her, too. She watched Sadie demean and insult other kids her age, especially girls. She also saw Sadie as a good friend who took her side and was supportive when Rachel had conflicts with other girls. Dee Dee was a latecomer to the triad. She had moved to Oakbrook from Indianapolis two years ago. Sadie and Rachel adopted Dee Dee, because she was compliant and athletic with no other friends. Like Rachel, Dee Dee felt vulnerable, because her status among tennis players depended upon her relationship with Sadie.

As was custom before each session, students gathered under the oak trees to talk and stretch before their lesson. Their chatter was quiet, but everyone was eager to play.

"How about some doubles matches today?" Al greeted them.

"Yes! Yes!" someone shouted.

One boy suggested, "I'll be your partner, Sam."

"Sorry, I already told Alex I'd play with him."

Al interrupted, "Carrie and I will decide who plays with who, guys."

"All right," instructed Carrie, "here are the teams and here's who you play against. Listen carefully now."

Sadie and Dee Dee were paired together. As usual, Sadie dressed stylishly in a blue Fila top with matching skirt, the same color as the laces in her Tretorns. Her outfit contrasted with Carrie's tee shirt and shorts, and with Dee Dee's matching outfit which certainly was not Fila.

The two girls were selected to play two boys a year younger than they. The foursome set off together for Court Three with their bags and water bottles. "Aren't you going to give us new balls?" Sadie demanded. Carrie nodded tossing an unopened can of Wilsons to her.

Brenda and the other three novices were assigned to Court Four. Brenda's partner was a classmate Jamie, who was pretty nice, considering he was a seventh grade boy. "Let's go get 'em," he said to Brenda competitively. Brenda nodded in approval.

"Court Four," Carrie yelled after them. "Here are your balls, and you guys can serve off a bounce. You do not have to serve overhand yet."

The matches began. Al and Carrie peered through the chain-link fence at their pupils, making occasional suggestions and refereeing disputes, like the disagreement on Court Two.

"Hey, that ball took two bounces before you hit it."

"It did not!"

"I saw it. The ball bounced twice."

"I don't think so."

"Well, I'm sure it did."

"I hit it after the first bounce…hey, Al, what are we supposed to do here?"

"Well, tell me what happened."

"I saw the ball bounce twice on their side before he hit it."

"Unfortunately, it's not your call," Al instructed.

"What do you mean?"

"Well, even if you think you saw…," Al began.

"I did see it, though."

"I understand. But it's still not your call. In the case of a double bounce, the player hitting the ball has to make the call."

"Well, that's not fair."

"Them's the rules kiddo," Al said lightly.

"So, who wins the point?"

"If they don't call a double bounce on themselves, then you have to continue playing the point out. If you interrupt the point, and they don't acknowledge a double bounce, they win the point," Al confidently answered.

"Well that stinks."

"That's the rule. Sorry."

Al moved to Court Four and watched Brenda play her doubles match. He was impressed with her shots. Clearly, hitting against the high school wall had strengthened her groundstrokes. After flubbing a ball into the net, she swung her racquet angrily. Her partner reassured her. "It's OK," he said. "We're still up forty-thirty." Brenda nodded. Her partner served the next point, and the receiver lofted a ball high over the net. Brenda backed up and hit the ball before it bounced. Her shot landed between her two opponents for a winner.

"Wow," Al muttered to himself. "That was impressive."

Meanwhile, Carrie was watching players on Court Two when she heard yelling on Court Three.

"That ball was in. No question about it!" Sadie complained.

"I saw it out," one of her opponents replied.

"Well, your calls suck," grumbled Sadie.

"Shut up!" her opponent yelled. "Every match you play there's an argument."

"That's because you can't call the lines."

"She's right, you know," interjected Dee Dee.

"No, that's because you're no fun to play with," their opponent persisted, shaking his head.

"I like to play with her," Dee Dee defended.

"You would, because nobody else will play with *you*."

"Oh, really?" Dee Dee shrugged her shoulders.

"Ya, really."

Carrie wanted to let the players settle their own argument, but it was obvious that this conversation was at a dead end. "OK. Enough. Players can call shots in or out on their own side only. You can question your opponents' calls, but ultimately it's their call that counts."

"But he called it wrong," Sadie scowled looking across the net.

"And she argues calls in every match she plays in. Every one," retorted her opponent.

"I do not. You're full of it," Sadie defended.

"OK, guys," said Carrie firmly. "This is a game. It's supposed to be fun, remember? Enough arguing. Play tennis."

After each court had played at least one set, Al called for a break. "Let's sit down and grab some water, or do whatever else you have to do," he suggested. "We'll go back on the courts in ten minutes."

Brenda sat down on the grass alone to drink some water from her thermos. After a few minutes, she decided to go to the bathroom. She left her canister and tennis bag by an oak tree and headed for the shelter.

There were three stalls opposite three sinks in the bathroom. The walls were made of concrete blocks painted a monotonous tan. A small window peered through one of them. Brenda hadn't noticed anyone else walk to the shelter, so it surprised her to see three girls standing at the sinks washing their hands and talking. When Brenda entered, the other girls continued their conversation as if she was invisible. Brenda opened a door to the nearest stall quickly, walked in, and locked it. She felt uncomfortable taking her shorts and underpants down, so she sat on the toilet seat fully clothed.

"That kid has always been a jerk. He's such a baby. A girl at school told me his sister got pregnant last summer and had to get an abortion," one girl, most likely Sadie, stated.

"Seriously?" another questioned.

"That's what she said," Sadie replied.

"Wow," exclaimed a third girl. "How old was she?"

"Fifteen or sixteen."

"Holy shit. Did she come back to school?"

"I dunno," responded Sadie.

"How about those new kids on Court Four?" asked a third girl.

31

"Ya, pretty lame aren't they?"

"I'll say."

"Always kissing Al's ass."

"Pretty pathetic."

"They'll never play varsity."

"That's for sure."

"Well, we should probably get back, girls."

Brenda heard the water turned off and the three-some walk towards the exit. On the way out, one of them opened the stall door next to her and went inside. Brenda looked down to find out who entered it, but she couldn't see any tennis shoes. As she sat up straighter on her toilet seat, a cold splash doused her shorts and tee shirt. Startled, she looked up to see Sadie leering at her over the divider between stalls, holding an empty container of water.

"I just wanted to see if you were a boy or a girl," Sadie said sarcastically. "We can't really tell. And usually you're supposed to take your pants off to pee, you know… you're not going to go whining to your buddy, Al now. Are you?"

"Ya," a second girl added. "Maybe he'll help you change your pants."

Sadie jumped down from the toilet. "I'm sure he has some boy undies for you. See you later."

"Ya, see you later."

The three girls snickered, shut off the bathroom light, and left together. After they were gone, Brenda stood up. She was cold and wet, uncomfortable and infuriated. With minimal light from the window, she found paper towels to blot her clothes. When she turned on the bathroom light and examined herself in the mirror, Brenda caught the flowered pattern of her underpants showing through her wet shorts and began to cry. She banged her palm on a sink, spit at the mirror, then slid down onto the floor in frustration.

Triumphantly, the three girls returned to the oaks where other players were sitting. "That new girl peed her pants!" Sadie yelled to them. Everyone looked at Sadie skeptically. "Really. She really did." Sadie smiled, as her collaborators nodded.

When Carrie told Al she would go to the shelter, Sadie suggested that Brenda would probably prefer to see Al. Her remark prompted Al to turn towards her with a reproachful stare that bounced off Sadie like a ball from a tightly strung racquet. She could care less if he was angry with her.

Carrie found Brenda still sitting on the bathroom floor and asked if she was OK. Brenda didn't answer, nor did she look up. Carrie hovered over Brenda for a few minutes, deciding how to be helpful. Then she asked her if there was anything she could do. Brenda still refused to acknowledge her.

"I'm here, because some kids said you had an accident."

"That's a load of crap. I didn't have an accident," Brenda refuted.

"I'm sorry. That's what the kids said."

"Well they're a bunch of liars then."

"Do you want to tell me what happened?

"No.

"Can I do anything?

"You could shoot me," Brenda suggested.

Eventually Brenda told Carrie the real story. By that time, her shorts and tee shirt were starting to dry, and although she did not feel as vulnerable, she was not ready to come out of hiding.

Carrie left her and returned to the courts where Al was teaching. After Carrie interrupted him to relate Brenda's story, Al called a halt to the session and waved everyone over to join him under the trees. He repeated Brenda's version of the incident to them and said he was disappointed in the girls who poured water on her. Carrie echoed Al's reprimand and scolded the girls for lying about what actually happened.

"But it was just her initiation," Sadie said facetiously.

Al glared at Sadie again, then cancelled class for the day. After every student left, Al went down to the shelter and knocked on the girls' bathroom. "Hey, Brenda, it's me, Al. Can I drive you home? Everyone else is gone." There was silence. "Brenda? Are you still in there?" Al asked. Brenda opened the bathroom door and shaded her eyes from the sun. "I'm sorry you had to go through that. Looks like you've dried off. Come on, I'll drive you home," he said again, as they walked to the parking lot. "I have your racquet and water bottle. Give me your bike. I'll put it in my trunk."

In the car, Al shared his displeasure about the incident and with Sadie's remarks. Brenda remained silent. "Hey," Al said as he dropped her off, "some varsity and JV players have a lesson with Coach Carrabas tomorrow morning at ten. Why don't you come by and watch?"

C H A P T E R   5

Tuesday, July 8, 1975

TOM CARRABAS TAUGHT English and coached girls' and boys' tennis at the high school. A self-taught player, he was on the varsity Oakbrook tennis team all four years when he was a student. He went to state in singles his last two years. Although he didn't play college tennis, his skill level was way above average. At thirty-five years old, he still played state and Midwest tournaments in his age group. Tom was affable and organized—an excellent teacher in the classroom and on the tennis court. Almost all the parents and players liked and respected him.

Tom returned to Oakbrook after his first job. Many graduates of the high school left town to further their educations or join the service but eventually came back to their roots like Tom. He enjoyed the community he grew up in and looked for a teaching and coaching position at Oakbrook High after graduating from the University. With the Vietnam War winding down, he was not worried about being drafted. Unfortunately, there were no openings, so he taught tennis while substitute teaching in a town fifty miles away. He also began to play local tournaments. When Tom's former English teacher retired a few years later, her position became available. Tom applied for and was accepted as the new English teacher. He also became assistant to his past coach and began to supervise the boys' and girls' junior varsity teams. He became head tennis coach a few years later when his mentor passed away.

Tom married his high school sweetheart, Nancy, after they graduated from college. She worked in the Oakbrook School District office. The couple lived in town with their eight-year-old twin daughters.

Tom stood outside the chain-link fence waiting for his students to arrive at the park. During the summer, he taught tennis to the more advanced players, most of whom were on varsity or junior varsity teams.

As usual, Al was one of the first players to arrive. Spotting Coach Carrabas, he wandered over and briefed him about students he and Carrie were teaching. In particular, he thought two incoming freshmen, Dee Dee and Sadie, were good enough to play JV tennis. Coach lamented that the school was too small for a freshman team, where any ninth grader could play. He didn't like cutting students from high school teams before they had at least one year of competition.

Al looked over his shoulder and noticed Brenda engrossed in a book…at least she made it appear that way. A blue bicycle leaned against the wooden bench next to her. He excused himself and walked over.

"Hey, Brenda…what's up?"

"Nothing much."

"Glad you could come."

"Ya."

"Pretty nice day, huh?" Al asked.

"Yes."

"Well, today we drill with Coach Carrabas and Coach Ginger. Have you ever met them?"

"Not really. I've seen him around. I don't know her."

"She's a graduate student at the U," Al reported. "She coaches the JV teams part-time."

"Oh."

"So, we drill every Tuesday and Thursday, and then on Saturdays, we play matches. We really do a lot of the same things you guys do."

"Do the other girls from our clinic come here to watch?" Brenda inquired apprehensively.

"Very seldom. I think you're safe."

"Mmm."

"So, are you going to scout me?"

"Scout?"

"Do you know what that is?"

"No. Not really."

"A scout is someone who works for a university or a pro team and goes to see athletes play to see if they're good enough to play for the team that hired the scout," Al tried to explain.

"Huh?"

"Well, say I wanted to play for the University."

"Do you?" Brenda asked intrigued.

"No, but just say I did. OK? Then the University would send a person out to scout me and see if I was good enough."

"Oh."

"So, I was just teasing," Al smiled.

"I get it," she said.

"Well," Al sighed looking around, "I guess almost everyone's here. I'd better go stretch. Will I see you tomorrow?"

"Yup. Bye," Brenda said picking up her book again.

"So what are you reading?" Al asked.

"*To Kill a Mockingbird*."

"I loved that book, but I don't think I read it until I was in high school. How far are you?"

"I just started it a couple of days ago. I'm at the part where the two Finch kids meet Dill."

"Well, at least that explains why I thought you were a scout!"

"Funny," said Brenda, holding back a smile.

After Al left to stretch, Carrie arrived and waved to Brenda. Brenda waved back. She enjoyed watching the older kids interact as they showed up at the courts and marveled at the easy conversation between sexes. She didn't see the awkwardness she felt and observed with kids her age. She wondered if she would ever feel that uninhibited with boys, or girls for that matter. Brenda was certainly feeling less tension in her communication with Al. She wasn't used to talking to men or boys, except her brother, John. She came from a single-parent home. Brenda's parents divorced when she was six and her brother was only three. She hadn't seen her father since he left. Brenda and her mother had a decent relationship, but her mother was not very affectionate. Her brother could be a real pain, often barging into her bedroom or the bathroom she was using uninvited. Still, John looked up to Brenda and genuinely loved her. She was his best friend and confidant.

Brenda's mother, Ellen Nelson, worked in the city library. She went out with a few men after her husband left, none of them long-term. Some men were nice, but Brenda did not like the last man her mother dated. He took the family out to dinner one night and was very rude to the waitress. He called her "honey" and made her take his steak back a couple of times, complaining it wasn't prepared properly. During some exchanges with the waitress, he peeked at Brenda and winked as if she was a co-conspirator. In fact, he looked at Brenda often during the meal, making her feel uncomfortable. When he dropped them off at home after dinner, Brenda told her mother she thought he was a pervert.

Brenda turned her attention to the players. As they stretched under the oak trees, Coach Carrabas addressed them, "This is a very important time in tennis history, and I want to make sure you are all aware of the significance of the Wimbledon finals a few days ago. Can anyone tell me what happened?"

Al leaned forward. "Billie Jean King beat Evonne Goolagong-Cawley 6-0, 6-1. The newspaper said it was one of the most lop-sided finals in Wimbledon history…do you think Billie Jean will really retire, Coach?"

"I don't know. I hope not. She played a great semi-final against Chris Evert, eventually pulling out the third set. But losing only one game in a Wimbledon final is unbelievable! Anyone tell me what happened on the men's side?"

One girl answered, "Arthur Ashe beat Jimmy Connors."

"Correct!" said Coach. "Ashe's victory is special for a number of reasons. He is the first black man to win Wimbledon. He grew up poor in Richmond, Virginia. His mother died when he was very young, so his father raised him and his younger brother. Ashe learned tennis on segregated public courts. When he played tournaments, he had to put up with racial slurs plus other forms of bigotry. He beat Connors by outsmarting him. He knew Jimmy liked to wail on the ball, so instead of feeding Connors a steady diet of fast hard shots, he varied the velocity. He threw Jimmy's timing off causing him to make a lot of errors. Ashe won in four sets. He blew Connors off the court in the first two sets 6-1, 6-1. Lost the third set 5-7, then beat him 6-4 in the fourth. So, lots of take-home lessons from this victory, guys." Tom paused. "What did Arthur Ashe teach us about life?"

"The old 'sticks and stones can break your bones' theory?" someone suggested.

"What do you think about that theory?" Coach prompted.

"I think words can still hurt—a lot," one boy volunteered.

A number of players nodded in agreement.

"Other thoughts?" Coach encouraged.

"If you want something badly enough, and you work really hard, you can achieve it?" proposed another girl.

Someone next to Al disagreed "Not always."

"Two very good points," said Coach. "One of you is saying never give up. While another is saying no matter how hard you work and try, some things don't pan out... anyone else?"

Carrie raised her hand, "Using your head in athletics is just as important if not more important than using your body?"

"Would you agree that applies not just to athletics, but to life in general, Carrie?" asked Coach.

"Yes. I would."

"Very good...OK. Let's get onto the courts."

Coach divided his players into two groups. He took eight players with him on Court One, and Coach Ginger, took the remaining seven players with her to Court Three. Beginning at the corners of the baseline, each player hit forehands then backhands like the younger kids did in their drills.

Brenda thought it was strange seeing advanced players performing the same drills less experienced kids practiced. What impressed her, though, was how well the older students hit. Despite having more power, their shots still consistently stayed in the court. The tenor of instruction was different, too. She noticed that Coach Carrabas and

Coach Ginger were very serious and unafraid to chastise their students for mistakes.

Both Al and Carrie were on Coach Carrabas's court. Brenda focused on Al, then Carrie. She wondered if she could ever be as good as they were. Al was fast and moved effortlessly. He sprinted from one corner to the other after slamming balls diagonally over the net. Brenda watched his gray tee shirt darken under the arms with perspiration. When Carrie struck the ball, deep knee bends made her look like she was sitting down on the court. Brenda thought Carrie's low crouch helped generate the power behind her groundstrokes. Brenda also admired Carrie's tee shirt, which bore the high school mascot, an Acorn, and the words "We Are Nuts About Tennis."

After the groundstroke drill, drinking from their water canisters, Al and Carrie trudged over to a table near Brenda.

"How about that!" Al called to her.

"Pretty awesome," she replied.

"Pretty exhausting."

Al seemed more animated than usual. Brenda watched him hold his racquet up and reset his stance, probably showing Carrie something he had just learned. Carrie looked at him seriously. Then smiling, she squeezed his shoulder. Al took his towel and wiped something off Carrie's back, maybe a bug or a leaf. Before returning to the courts, he playfully snapped the towel at her backside and chuckled.

CHAPTER 6

Saturday, July 12, 1975

SATURDAY MORNING WAS match day at Taylor Park for junior varsity and varsity players. Coach Carrabas organized each session, often staying to watch his students compete. As tennis coach for the high school, he was not allowed to organize summer team practices, so the pairings he orchestrated were different from ones he designed for his high school teams. Besides, not all participants in the summer program attended Oakbrook High. A few players were from neighboring communities.

Mixed doubles was unique to summer tennis, as high school teams separated the sexes; girls played tennis each fall and boys played each spring. Everyone enjoyed mixed doubles, because it was not as competitive as all male or all female matches.

Coach Carrabas selected Al and Carrie to play against another mixed doubles team. Since the teens had been teaching at the park together over the past two summers, they relished the chance to be partners. Both were entering their senior year; both had spent most of their lives in Oakbrook. Since Al and Carrie played tennis and their class size was small (only seventy-six members), they knew each other well. Until recently, Al had dated a girl in the junior class, but their relationship had ended early spring. Carrie had never had a serious boyfriend but was part of a group of boys and girls who hung out together. As they spent another summer teaching, their relationship began to evolve.

Throughout the set, Al complimented Carrie on her play. Carrie's forehand was as good as any forehand Al competed against. It was flat and powerful. She surprised their opponents by hitting winners repeatedly. Al and Carrie won the first set easily, 6-1.

After the set ended, both doubles teams sat down on benches under the oak trees to rehydrate and socialize. No one noticed the brown and white puppy lying by the trees. Abruptly, Carrie sprang from her seat startled, as it began nuzzling her leg. "Oh, my gosh you scared me!" Carrie bent down to pat him (or her). The dog licked Carrie's hand and sniffed her shoes. Then he jumped up (it was a he!), placing his front paws on Carrie's shins. She looked for a collar but did not see one. "I wonder where he came from?"

Leaving Carrie, the puppy began barking. Al rotated around to face him and picked up a stick. The dog attacked it, trying to pull it away. A tug-of-war ensued for a few minutes accompanied by soft puppy growls. When the pup tired, he sat down on his haunches and stared at his new friends.

Al reached over, picked him up, and placed him on his lap admiringly. The dog was less than a foot and a half high with fuzzy light brown fur on his back. His belly was white. With big black eyes and a white stripe between them, he had an endearing face. He had four white boots for paws and a white tip at the end of a substantial tail. After patting him again, Al put him down so tennis could resume.

To the foursome's amusement, the puppy discovered an old tennis ball and played with it when they went back on the court. As the match continued, the pup appeared to referee points by barking and hopping along the chain-link fence like a rabbit. Before long, he lay down and went to sleep until the set concluded. Al and Carrie played well again, winning 6-2.

As Carrie returned to the tables and benches, the puppy jumped at her left tennis shoe to bite her laces. He growled and chewed ferociously. Carrie kept sliding her foot away, but the dog was relentless. She scratched his backside, "All right, you. That's enough."

"I think you're his favorite, Carrie," Al laughed, placing a hand on her shoulder.

"He is a cute little guy," she remarked. "Where do think he lives? He can't be very old."

"I agree," Al said, picking him up. "He looks a little skinny, but otherwise he looks healthy."

"Should we take him to the police station to see if someone lost him?" Carrie suggested.

"Ouch!" Al feigned as the puppy nibbled at him. "Those are my fingers, buddy. God, those are sharp. Now, that's better. I like your kisses. They're not as good as Carrie's, but they'll do."

Carrie slapped Al's arm, "Shh… how about my tennis?"

"It was awesome, partner," Al said to Carrie. "We kicked some serious butt today. What did you think young fella?" he asked the dog.

"So, should we take him to the station?" Carrie proposed.

"We probably should. He's too young to be out here on his own. Why don't you leave your bike. We can take him in my car. OK?"

"Sure. Give him to me. I'll hold him so you can drive."

After introducing the puppy around, the couple said goodbye to Coach Carrabas and a few other players, then drove to the police station. The building was only a couple of miles away, so Carrie allowed the dog to sit on her lap. With windows down, the summer breeze felt good and made the puppy's fur stand on end. They passed a few farms. It was a good summer for crops; corn stalks were waist high and soybeans were green and healthy. Even tobacco looked plentiful. The dog wiggled trying to climb up to the open window. "Oh, shit!" Carrie shouted. "Sorry," she quickly apologized.

Al looked over and saw a trickle of yellow running down Carrie's shorts. He pulled the car over and stopped. Leaving his seat, he went to the trunk to remove a towel, which he handed to Carrie.

"Good thing Sadie wasn't here to witness this," Al mused, taking the dog from her.

"Right. I'm sure she'd have something embarrassing to say. She sure is awful to Brenda and some of the other younger girls, isn't she?" Carrie responded drying off her clothes. "OK, you. That's enough of that."

Al handed the dog back to her, as they continued towards the police station. Entering town, they passed a gas station on the right, then took a left on Main Street and drove between the Chevrolet and Pontiac showrooms, past a jewelry store on the left, and the bakery and pharmacy on the right. They continued towards the golf course before pulling into a parking lot at the police station.

Taking the pup with them, they entered the building and began talking to an officer on duty, whom they didn't recognize. No one had called about a missing dog, they learned, and the station did not have a facility for feral animals. (Carrie took issue with that description but didn't say anything). The county humane society could be called if they wished, but if an owner was not found the dog could be euthanized.

The teens left with the puppy in Carrie's arms. "OK you little pisser, what do we do now?" Al asked. He knew his parents would never allow him to keep the dog. "Would your folks take him in?" he asked Carrie. Carrie told Al her big sister was allergic to dogs and cats but was away on a summer fellowship. Carrie thought she might be able keep him in the basement until they found the owner or a suitable home.

Carrie returned to the passenger seat in Al's car with her charge, as Al retrieved a piece of rope from his trunk to use as a collar and leash. "What else do you have back there?" Carrie asked.

"I have a blanket," Al said. "Want to take him by the lake?"

Carrie liked that plan. She had to retrieve her bicycle anyhow. They decided to stop at the A&W first for burgers, fries, and root beer. They thought they could eat their lunch in the car, but the puppy had other ideas. He whined and thrashed, obviously hungry, so they decided to take their meal by Pierce Lake.

After they parked, Carrie looped the rope around the puppy's neck and began to walk him towards the beach, but he dug his front paws into parking lot gravel and refused to budge. Carrie pulled gently on his leash but was unable to move him. Al gave the A&W bag and blanket to Carrie and took the rope from her. "Come on, little guy," he encouraged. "Let's go." But the puppy stood his ground. "OK. You win," Al conceded, lifting him and carrying him to the beach.

Carrie laid a blanket down. Al removed the rope allowing the dog to wander, hoping he would relieve himself so they didn't have to worry about that again. Carrie sat on the blanket removing food and drinks from the A&W bag. Al joined her with the puppy on his heels. "No," Carrie instructed, as the dog started to gnaw at a wrapped hamburger. "My God. He's impossible. If children are this difficult, I'm not having any!"

Al grinned, picked the puppy up, and placed him between his legs. Opening his sandwich, he plied a piece of hamburger away and fed it to the pup. Hardly chewing, the dog gobbled it and looked for another morsel. Al fed him a piece of his bun, which quickly disappeared, too. "He's just hungry, poor guy," Al said, then gave him a few more bites of food. "That's enough, pal. I don't want to make you sick." Al stood up with his sandwich and wandered over to the lake. The puppy followed, and when he reached the shore, dropped his head and drank eagerly.

Al returned to Carrie, and they quickly finished their burgers and fries. They were sipping their root beers when the dog returned to lie down near them. Al slid over towards Carrie. "He looks so innocent now, doesn't he?" he said.

Carrie smiled, and Al put his arm around her and kissed her on the cheek. She turned her head towards him and their lips met. They kissed tenderly then put their heads together and looked down at the puppy like proud parents. They snuggled for a short time enjoying the day, their surroundings, each other's company, and the dog. It was summertime in Oakbrook.

"So, I hate to break this up, but we need to talk to your parents to see if they'll let you keep this little guy until we find his owner or someone to adopt him," Al said. "I can put your bike in my trunk and drive you home."

Carrie agreed. Al took the rope that doubled as a leash to tether Carrie's bicycle to his trunk. Carrie placed the puppy on her lap, and they drove to her parents' home. When they arrived, Al removed the bike and handed Carrie the rope. The puppy did better on his leash this time, as Carrie maneuvered him towards her house.

"Are we still on for tonight?" asked Al.

"Of course," she answered. "See you around seven."

✦

At seven o'clock sharp, Al rang Carrie's doorbell. Carrie answered, thanked her parents for watching the puppy, and went to Al's car with him. She told him that she had to be home early. Her parents would allow her to keep the dog for a few days, but she had to take complete responsibility for him.

Al and Carrie agreed on an abbreviated date. They decided to drive ten miles out of town to a store that sold homemade ice cream. It was still light outside and the air was warm. With windows down, they smelled freshly spread manure. "Ah, that Wisconsin aroma!" Al bragged.

"You mean that dairy air!" Carrie laughed holding her nose.

They each had hot fudge sundaes at The Ice Cream Parlor before driving back to Carrie's. Al walked her to the door, where they kissed before he left. "I had a great day," he said.

"Me, too. Goodnight. Call me tomorrow?"

"I will. Pat Mr. Pooch for me."

CHAPTER 7

Sunday morning, July 13, 1975

AL'S FAMILY LIVED on the outskirts of Oakbrook and on Sundays attended a Lutheran church in the town of Raven. Carrie's family attended the more liberal of two Lutheran churches in Oakbrook. After Al returned from his service, he called Carrie to ask about her evening.

"Our buddy is fine, but I am *really* tired. I was up just about all night with him. We went out countless times to pee. Then he'd come back inside and whine. I stayed in the basement with him. Finally, in order to get some sleep, I brought him onto my cot.

"When you and I were out last night, my parents made some gourmet dishes for his royal highness, which he inhaled. I swear if my sister wasn't allergic, my folks would let me keep him."

"Well, why don't you let me have him for today?" Al offered. "I've got some mowing to do, but I could swing by your place and take him after that."

"Maybe I'll drive him over to the park and let him run a little. Do you want to meet us there?" she asked.

"Sounds great. Two o'clock?"

"Sure. See you then. Bye." said Carrie.

Al performed his chores then drove his family car to Taylor Park. It was another perfect summer day. Carrie and the puppy were already there. The couple embraced briefly, then walked closer to the water where the puppy was wading. He had discovered a school of minnows and was snapping at their silhouettes. When he saw Al, he bounded from the water to jump up on him with wet paws. Al didn't care and dropped to the ground to wrestle with the dog, mimicking his growls and barks with incantations of his own. "No biting," Al admonished, as the pup attacked his fingers again. "OK. That's enough, let's go for a walk."

The puppy explored the shoreline surrounding Pierce Lake. Al and Carrie walked behind him holding hands, intrigued by his energy and curiosity. He led them towards a small open area surrounded by trees and covered with grass. There was no sand, and the water was barricaded from land by a low rock wall. Lake traffic was light, especially for a Sunday afternoon.

The puppy began to tire, eventually plopping down. Al and Carrie joined him. Lying on their backs, they followed floating clouds together and listened to gentle waves slapping against rocks.

Carrie, exhausted from her vigilant night, closed her eyes. Al took a deep breath, shutting his, too. A relaxing breeze stirred leaves above them. Their grassy bed was comfortable and soon the teens and puppy fell asleep.

A pair of cardinals chitchatted from aloft, as squirrels played tag under leafy trees. Honeybees buzzed above wild flowers, and a rabbit, still as a statue, stood sentinel near the wall. Al and Carrie continued to nap, but the puppy awoke thirsty. As he wandered awkwardly towards the lake, the rabbit scampered into tall weeds. Rocks prevented the dog's access to water, so he sauntered farther away. When he attempted to scale the wall, a shadow abruptly overtook him. With wings outstretched and legs extended, a massive bald eagle lowered its talons into the puppy's coat and clutched his back before he could escape. The dog yelped with fright and howled with pain, as the eagle whistled. Al and Carrie awoke with a start to watch the scene play out. Carrie screamed. Al ran towards the wall, waving his hands and yelling, but the eagle's wings were already beating. With difficulty, the giant bird ascended with his prey towards Pierce Lake. The teens, helpless, listened to the puppy's anguished cries. When the bird was twenty or so yards over the lake, he suddenly banked to his left and began to fly back towards the grass. With the puppy still in his clutches, the eagle fell to the ground, overwhelmed by his burden. Immediately, he released the dog. Then he flapped his wings, cackled, and began his solo ascent over the water. Al continued running after the eagle ensuring his departure. Carrie ran to the dog.

The puppy was lying on his right side, trembling with fright and breathing rapidly. He had blood oozing from his back. Carrie bent over him and started crying. She talked

to him soothingly. His eyes were open, and he began looking around. She searched under the blood, trying to assess
the extent of injuries and found a puncture wound where
a talon had penetrated his skin. "He needs a vet," she told
Al, as he ran towards her after making sure the eagle was
gone. Al knew there were no veterinarians in Oakbrook but
recalled seeing Dr. Vogel at church that morning. He knew
the doctor had an office in Raven. It was a twenty-minute
ride, and he wasn't sure Dr. Vogel would even be home,
but it was the only option they had. Gently, he picked up
the injured puppy. The dog was still shaking, but he didn't
mind Al lifting and carrying him to the car. The trip back
to the parking lot seemed ten times longer than the stroll
to the secluded area where they had napped.

Before leaving town, the couple stopped at Carrie's
house. They explained what transpired to her parents and
returned their car keys. Al offered to drive Carrie's father
to pick up his vehicle at the park, but her dad declined.
Instead, Mr. Archibald encouraged Al to call ahead to
make sure the vet was home.

"But Raven's a long distance call," Al demurred.

"Don't worry about it. This is an emergency," Carrie's
father insisted, handing him a telephone book.

Fortunately, Dr. Vogel was home, and after hearing
Al's story, agreed to see them.

Mrs. Archibald provided a few towels and gave Al some
money for the visit. With little cash in his wallet, he reluc-
tantly accepted the offering.

Their trip went smoothly, as the puppy became increasingly responsive. He was no longer shaking, and his breathing was slower and less labored. By the time they arrived in Raven, the wound on his back had stopped bleeding. Al veered into a gas station to ask directions.

After parking in the driveway, Al helped Carrie and the pup out of the car. He introduced them to Dr. Vogel at his front door. They proceeded to the back of the house, where the clinic was located. Dr. Vogel took the dog from Carrie and placed him on an examining table. Before looking at his patient, he asked the teens what they knew about the dog. They explained to Dr. Vogel that they had found the puppy and didn't really know anything about him.

Focusing on the dog, the doctor performed his examination, petting and talking to him softly. Not only did he observe his wounds (there were a few of them on his back), but he looked at his eyes, ears, and mouth, too. Then he listened to his heart and lungs with his stethoscope and palpated his abdomen with his hands. Finally, he moved all four limbs to make sure there were no fractures.

"This little guy has been through a lot," the veterinarian started, "but I think he's going to be OK. I'll clean up his wounds and give you an antibiotic for him. He's really lucky the eagle's talons didn't perforate his chest, which might have caused his lung to collapse."

The puppy stood up slowly on the examination table. He yawned, stretched, and shook his head, body, and tail.

"That's a good sign," Dr. Vogel smiled, as he cleaned the dog's back with water-soaked gauze pads and disinfectant.

"You might want to give him a bath when you get him home," he added. Opening his medicine chest, he removed some capsules from a large bottle and placed them into a smaller one. He pasted a label on the smaller bottle and wrote the instructions by hand. "OK, give him one pill twice a day. They might cause diarrhea. If they do, put some rice in his food…what are you feeding him?"

The doctor gave Al and Carrie a short lecture on appropriate diets for puppies, then commended them on bringing the dog to his office. Al asked Dr. Vogel about his fee, and the vet said he would send a bill to his parents. The couple thanked the doctor before returning to Al's car.

With towels on her lap, and the dog on top of them, Carrie sat comfortably next to Al, as he drove them home.

———— ✦ ————

CHAPTER 8

Wednesday morning, June 21, 2006

BRENDA AND HER family awoke to a dark, cool, rainy day. While she and her husband, Henry, dressed, Brenda's mother was in the kitchen making breakfast. Brenda went to her daughter's room to help find a suitable outfit, as Joy was going to accompany her father to work.

Joy was already up and pulling out tee shirts from a bureau drawer when Brenda entered her room. She held one up to her mother. Brenda smiled as she regarded her daughter. Joy was looking more and more like a teenager, yet her demeanor remained trusting and innocent.

"You're going to need something a little warmer, honey," suggested Brenda.

"It's raining out," Joy said pointing outside.

"Yes, it is," her mother replied

Holding up a sweatshirt, Joy asked, "Can I wear this?"

"Sure. That should work. You're going to the shop with Daddy today."

"I know."

"We need to make you a lunch, too."

"Can I have peanut butter and jelly?" Joy begged.

"Of course you can have a peanut butter and jelly sandwich."

"I got my period," Joy said.

"OK. Are you feeling all right?"

"Yes."

"Did you use the Kotex I bought you?"

Joy was embarrassed, "But I messed my underpants."

"It's OK, honey. Where did you put them?"

"In there," Joy admitted, pointing to the closet.

"Are you wearing a pad now?"

"Yes. I have a pad."

"OK, so what do we do when we soil our underpants, Joy?"

"Put them in the hamper."

"Right, we put them in the hamper. But what do we do first with soiled underpants?"

"Wash them?"

"Good girl. We wash them in the sink before we put them in the hamper. Now, remember to take some pads with you in case you need to change at Daddy's shop. OK? Now, please go into your closet, and give me your underpants. I'll wash them for you this time. Thank you. Now, go downstairs to Grandma and start your breakfast. Oh, tell her to make a sandwich for you. Also, your medicine, Joy. Make sure Grandma gives you your pill."

"I will."

"Good girl."

Brenda returned to her bedroom. She told Henry Joy had her period and asked him to remind her to change her pad at least once during the day. Then she asked her husband how Joy was doing at his shop.

Henry said Joy was extremely helpful. She loved organizing shelves and was compulsive about making sure the different screws, washers, and bolts were in their correct boxes. She dusted the toilets and sinks on display every morning without being asked. She was pleasant to customers, too. There were occasions when people couldn't understand what she said, and she became frustrated, sometimes stomping away to the back room. In addition, there were kids and a few adults who stared at Joy, making her feel uncomfortable.

"She's playing good tennis, too. I watched her last night," Brenda said. "She's coming to net better, because her approach shots have really improved since state. Tom has been working with her on that and her serve. He thinks her game is really impressive…are you ready for breakfast?"

The couple went downstairs where Grandma had French toast with bacon waiting for them and was making sandwiches near the sink. Henry sat down to eat. Brenda bent down to kiss her son on his head, then went over to her mother to give her a quick hug.

Rain began pelting the house siding; it sounded like a continuous spray of small pellets were being shot at the windows. "So, no tennis for you today," Brenda addressed her son, Ricky. "What are you going to do?"

His father wondered if he wanted to come to work with Joy and him. Ricky liked the idea and asked his Grandma to please make him a sandwich, too. Peanut butter and jelly would be fine.

After breakfast, Brenda left for Few Hours A Day Nursery. She was scheduled to meet with someone from the county to renew their daycare license. This process occurred annually. Some people who worked for the county were pleasant. Others took advantage of their positions and made visits extremely arduous. Brenda arranged for her assistants to take care of the children in Room One during her conference.

She went to her office and waited. Ten minutes after the appointment was scheduled, a woman Brenda instantly recognized came through her door. Brenda stood up, "Hello."

"Hello. My name is Helen Nystrom, Mrs. Bjorkman. How are you today?"

"Fine." Brenda knew Helen Nystrom. She wanted to pronounce it HELL-N, because the woman was officious and obnoxious. Brenda went to her filing cabinet and removed a couple of folders in preparation for the inevitable incursion. First on Mrs. Nystrom's list was the air conditioner. Helen wanted to know when it was last serviced. Brenda explained a work crew had just been there. A new part would be installed today.

HELL-N remarked, "You're lucky it's cooler today, aren't you!"

Mrs. Nystrom continued down her list of questions. Brenda was able to respond to most of them without difficulty. Concluding her inquiries, Helen wanted to tour the facility with Brenda. "It looks pretty muddy out there," HELL-N pointed out as they examined the yard where rain was showering playground equipment. Brenda assured her that children played outside only when it was dry. "You mentioned in your updated report that you have installed cameras. Is that right? So parents can keep an eye on you during the day I assume?" Brenda ignored the barb and disclosed that there were cameras in both classrooms plus two on the playground, allowing parents to see their children by computer whenever they wanted. "And you have had them sign releases?" inquired Mrs. Nystrom.

"Releases?" Brenda asked quizzically.

"Well, if you are videoing children, you know, capturing them on camera and recording them…their parents have to give their permission for that, Mrs. Bjorkman."

Brenda assured her inquisitor that she would be glad to comply and asked where she could find permission forms. "On our website, of course. You do have that URL don't you, Mrs. Bjorkman?"

"Of course," Brenda answered.

As their meeting drew to a close, Helen pointed out that both bathrooms needed cleaning. She said the smell of urine was strong. She also thought all trash barrels outside should be covered to prevent children and animals from rummaging around in them. Finally, she asked Brenda to send her a copy of the invoice she received from the air conditioner company to confirm the unit had been fixed. "Thank you for your time, Mrs. Bjorkman," HELL-N said, as she left with her back straight and her chin up. "Oh, one last thing…don't forget those forms."

"I won't."

"And I'd love to see the videos."

"Actually, they're not up and running yet," Brenda said deceitfully.

"Really? Well maybe next time I come," she said with a grin.

Brenda met with her partner, Marie, during rest period following lunch and told her about HELL-N's visit. Brenda was optimistic that their license would be renewed. She cited the flaws Mrs. Nystrom mentioned and explained about the forms they were required to download for video recordings.

Marie informed Brenda the air conditioner would be working by afternoon. Repairmen were replacing the damaged part now. As for the cameras, Billy Williams's crew was still adjusting them, but they began videotaping on Monday to find the best locations. He wanted to review the recordings with them after everyone else left this afternoon.

Brenda felt panicky. She continued to worry that a camera had caught her inappropriate episode with Ellie. If it had, she didn't know how she would explain it. Consequences of her actions could be devastating. She could even be sued.

"So, let me see if I understand this," Brenda inquired. "In addition to parents being able to see their kids in real time, there will be permanent recordings, too?"

"Exactly," replied Marie.

Brenda asked if each camera had its own recording device. Marie explained that videos were recorded centrally, and the recorder was located in their utility room. When Brenda asked her partner if she had seen any recordings, she said she had and thought the quality was excellent, but the scope was limited. Marie said that Billy discussed using wide angle lenses to improve areas of observation, especially in both classrooms.

C H A P T E R 9

Sunday evening, July 13, 1975

WHILE THE PUPPY slept on Carrie's lap, Al tuned his radio to WROX. The D.J., Jonathan Libby, was the most esteemed disc jockey in Jefferson County. His melodic voice coupled with an incredible knowledge of popular music, made him the disc jockey everyone in junior high and high school listened to. Al turned up the volume as Barbra Streisand sang *The Way We Were.*

Although it was becoming cooler out, both teens felt comfortable. There was a sense of relief after their visit to Dr. Vogel, because their furry friend was going to recover.

"Can you believe what we witnessed today?" Al asked.

"No. It seems surreal to me."

"I mean the size of that eagle. He was enormous…just humongous."

"I thought it was all over when he had the pup over the lake," Carrie admitted.

"Me, too…look at him now. You'd never know anything happened."

"He's sleeping like a baby," she mused.

"I think that's the most frightened I've ever been in my whole life."

"Me, too…Dr. Vogel sure is nice and thorough."

"He is," agreed Al. "I've never been to his office or house. I've only seen him in church, but everyone speaks very highly of him as a veterinarian."

"There's no place open to buy dog food, but I think we have some hamburger at home. I know he'll like that…if he's hungry," Carrie advised, readjusting her patient.

"One more meal without real dog food won't matter."

"I really don't know how long my folks are going to let me keep him, Al. Do you think one of our students would want him?"

"Good idea. If he's feeling better, maybe we could bring him to tennis with us tomorrow."

"It could work out," Carrie said hopefully.

"I got to tell you. I feel guilty placing his care on your shoulders again tonight. It really isn't fair. You were up all last night. I can tell how tired you are today. Another night like that, and you'll be like a deflated tennis ball…no bounce"

"I can manage."

"No, I mean it. Unfortunately, my folks just don't care for dogs. My mom was bitten when she was a little kid and never got over it. What if I stayed in your basement with him? You could stay in your room upstairs in your own bed and get some sleep. Do you think your folks would go for it?"

"I don't know, but you don't have to do that."

After discussing it further, the couple decided to ask Carrie's parents if Al could stay. When they arrived at the Archibalds, her parents were out front talking to a gathering of neighbors.

Carrie lived in a split-level clapboard dwelling with a full basement. White with dark green shutters, it was built in 1972 specifically for her family. Her parents discovered the property when the house was in its early stages of construction and altered its design to their liking. Carrie's folks were originally from the east coast. Her father was an archeology professor at the University. Mrs. Archibald was an artist, and her medium was clay. She worked at a pottery shop in downtown Oakbrook. Carrie's older sister was a student at a small college in Maine.

"So, this is our little warrior," said a neighbor. "He's not so little! How in hell did that eagle lift him up?" he wondered out loud, admiring and patting the dog in Carrie's arms.

The conversation continued with every detail reviewed. When the puppy began to wiggle, Carrie put him down. As soon as she released him, he squatted to urinate. "Good boy!" she praised him.

"Guess you won't have to water the lawn tonight," another neighbor joked with Carrie's father.

The puppy seemed comfortable and curious, so Carrie allowed him to circulate. He loved being the center of attention, wandering from shoe to shoe sniffing and licking. Everyone got to pat him.

Carrie's dad told Al he phoned the Andersens to tell them what had happened. Al thanked him for informing his parents and reached into his pocket for the money he had borrowed. "What, no interest?" Mr. Archibald teased.

"How about staying for supper, Al?" Mrs. Archibald proposed. "We already received permission from your mom and dad."

"Thank you," responded Al. "I'd love to."

Carrie was shocked by her mother's invitation. Although she was going to be a senior in high school, Carrie had never had dinner at her house with a boy. Her parents were cautious, making her suspicious of this breach in their routine. She smiled at her mother. "Um…do Al and I have enough time before dinner to give the puppy a bath? The vet thought it would be a good idea."

"Sure," answered Mrs. Archibald. "Where are you thinking of doing it?"

"In the upstairs tub in my bathroom? Is that all right?"

"I think so. You may want to use your baby shampoo. It's milder than soap."

As the teens entered the bathroom, Al inhaled a familiar scent. "Baby shampoo! That's what I smell when we're kissing. I'm learning all kinds of things about you, young lady," he teased, taking the dog from Carrie.

"Shh," she elbowed him. "My parents are downstairs!"

"Oops."

"And don't tell Sadie about the shampoo either," she demanded, turning on the bathtub water. Testing the temperature with her hand, she casually flicked some water at Al.

"Hey," he complained. "That's not fair."

Mrs. Archibald shouted up to her daughter, "Carrie, please use the old yellow towels in the bottom of the linen closet for the dog instead of the good ones."

"Thanks. Will do."

When the couple finished bathing and drying the puppy, they couldn't believe the transition. His previously matted fur was pure white and soft. He looked like a snowball. Carrie's parents were shocked, too. "Is that the same dog you took upstairs?" her mother asked.

"I think so. Where would you like us to put him while we eat?" Carrie asked, entering the kitchen with Al and the puppy.

Carrie's dad suggested tying him up outside during dinner, but Carrie didn't want to, fearful that something bad would happen to him again. She recommended placing the dog in the pantry instead. They would have to lift some boxes and other chewables off the floor, but the room had a door. At least he would be contained.

Dinner did not go well. The pup yelped, whined, and scratched at the door. He was not happy away from the action. Carrie attended to him several times, but his protests continued unabated.

During dessert, Al decided to air the proposition he discussed with Carrie. He asked the Archibalds if he could stay with the dog in their basement to allow Carrie and the rest of their family to sleep. He claimed he didn't mind caring for the puppy. In fact, he felt it was his responsibility. Mr. Archibald said Al had done enough by taking the dog to Raven. Mrs. Archibald concurred. Al pressed his case saying he felt guilty his family would not allow the puppy in their house. He wanted to do his part by caring for him at night, too. To Carrie's amazement, her parents finally agreed.

Al needed to return home for a change of clothes and his tennis gear for Monday morning's lesson. Driving her family car, Carrie followed Al back to his home, waited for him to gather his things, then drove him back to her house.

There was unexpected silence when the teens entered the Archibald residence. Carrie's mother was washing the few remaining dishes and pieces of flatware from dinner. They approached, asking where the puppy was. Mrs. Archibald said downstairs with her husband. The teens descended the cellar stairs. When they reached the bottom, there was Carrie's dad reclining on a cot with the puppy's head on his lap. All four eyes were closed. A stuffed lamb from a previous era shared the cot with them. Tranquility, however, was short-lived. The puppy's nose began to twitch. He opened his eyes and yawned. Seeing his two buddies, he rolled off the cot and whined as he landed on the floor.

Mr. Archibald awoke from his nap rubbing his neck. "Hmm, I must have dozed off."

"Thanks for sitting for him, Dad." What's he lying on?"

"Oh, that's your old stuffed animal."

"Uh huh…always the archeologist! Where did you dig him out from?" Carrie teased.

"Your closet."

"Really?" she continued. "That was supposed to become a family heirloom! I thought you were saving it for my kids."

The pup rolled over quickly, stood up, and accosted Carrie. Growling weakly, he jumped on her. "Easy, little guy," she warned. "You've had a difficult day."

Clearly uncomfortable, the dog whined before sitting down in front of her. Carrie took the stuffed animal, known as "Lammy" and tossed it to the pup. Instead of playing, he lay down with his head on Lammy. "I know someone who's still tired," Carrie smiled. "We should probably take him out one more time before he goes to bed," she advised Al. "I can carry him."

Everyone went upstairs, with Carrie holding the dog. Mr. Archibald excused himself, saying he had some reading to do. Carrie kissed him goodnight, and Al shook his hand. The young couple took the dog outside, placing him on the grass.

Instead of relieving himself, he lay down on his side. Al suggested that Carrie go back inside the house as it was becoming chilly, but she wanted to stay.

"So," Al began, "do I call your dad Mr. Archibald or Professor Archibald?"

Carrie said her father usually referred to himself as "mister" when in the community and "professor" when he was on campus or on a dig. She told Al that her father frequented the Orient where he performed some of his archeological work. "I should have him show you slides he has collected. They're very interesting."

Al asked Carrie if she was interested in archeology; she said she was more interested in biochemistry. She thought she might like research or medicine.

During their conversation, the puppy wandered away, pooped and peed, then ambled back to his friends. Al lifted and carried him into the house.

In the hall, giving him a kiss, Carrie told Al she should get ready for bed. They lingered for a short time lips together, eyes closed.

"You'll have to use the bathroom on this level," Carrie instructed Al. "We don't have one downstairs. Sorry," she smiled. "Goodnight little guy," she said kissing the pup's head. "See you both tomorrow morning."

Al brought the puppy to the basement, took out his overnight bag, and changed into pajamas. Before going upstairs, he sat down to pet the dog. When he looked up, Carrie was coming toward him. She wanted to give the puppy his medicine and said she would sit with him while Al went upstairs to use the bathroom.

Al used the toilet, washed up, brushed his teeth, and went downstairs. He sat next to Carrie on the cot. The dog was asleep beside her. Carrie was wearing a bathrobe over her nightshirt. She teased Al about his pajamas, which were covered with Wisconsin banners and pictures of Bucky Badger. Carrie looked very different to Al; her hair wasn't tied in a ponytail but hung over her back. He put an arm around her to draw her closer to him. Then he locked his mouth onto hers and they kissed more passionately than they ever had before. When their mouths parted, Al kissed Carrie's forehead and nose. Then he placed his mouth on hers and they kissed again, hard. Al moved his hand from Carrie's shoulder to the front of her bathrobe and held her gently with his fingers. She seemed comfortable. As he reached inside her bathrobe, through her top, she took his hand and held it.

"I'm a little afraid," she admitted, "because my folks are so close, but I also don't think I'm ready yet, Al."

"It's OK. I understand. Honest."

"I'm sorry. Are you mad at me?"

"Absolutely not. I want you to be comfortable. It takes time. We'll take it slow together."

Carrie kissed Al on his cheek. "I don't mean to make it awkward for you. This is all very new to me. I've never really had someone I could call a boyfriend before."

"I understand. There's no rush. I just want you to know how I feel about you."

"I do. Thank you. That means a lot to me."

"And you mean a lot to me, Carrie Archibald."

"I'm glad we can talk about it."

"Most important part of a relationship is being able to talk. Of course, kissing is a good thing, too."

"Yes, it is," she smiled.

They kissed a little longer before saying goodnight once again…their four-legged chaperone slumbering beside them.

———— ❧ ————

CHAPTER 10

Monday morning, July 14, 1975

"Good morning sleepyhead," Carrie said softly to Al, who was barely awake. He rolled over, squinted his eyes open, and smiled up at her. At the foot of the cot, a somnolent puppy stirred, too. He crawled over to Carrie and plopped down beside her.

Al described his night of intermittent sleep with multiple trips outdoors to prevent the puppy from fertilizing rugs and watering the tile. He complained the dog was already spoiled, refusing to sleep on the floor. Grudgingly, Al had agreed to share his cot with him and had endured multiple face licks, several foul-smelling belches, and numerous kicks to his abdomen. Carrie was sympathetic to Al's plight besides being grateful for his chivalry.

As Al dressed, Carrie brought the dog outside once more before breakfast. Al joined Carrie and her parents in their kitchen to retell his evening saga. Once breakfast was over, Al brushed his teeth, retrieved his gear from downstairs, and thanked Carrie's parents for housing him. Mr. Archibald encouraged Carrie and Al to find a home for the puppy. He unabashedly admitted his attachment to him but, at the same time, reiterated his older daughter's medical history.

Carrie tried to cajole her father into changing his mind, reminding him that Jessica was away for three months at Woods Hole. Mr. Archibald explained to Carrie that dog dander permeates a home and could exacerbate Jessica's allergies when she returned.

The teens left for Taylor Park, Carrie holding Al's tennis paraphernalia and overnight duffel bag, Al carrying the puppy. Mrs. Archibald had graciously allowed Carrie to use her new Ford Mustang. Al tuned the radio to WROX, and they listened to Paul Anka sing *I Don't Like to Sleep Alone.* It was another beautiful day in Oakbrook, making their short ride pleasant.

When they reached the parking lot, Al placed the pup on the gravel. He asked Carrie if she had the rope leash. Unfortunately, she had forgotten it. The dog seemed to enjoy his freedom but stayed very close to the teens' heels. Clearly, he had learned his lesson.

When students arrived for their clinic, the puppy instantly became the center of attention. Players surrounded him like hungry mosquitoes on a bare-backed Wisconsin camper. The dog loved the attention; his tail wagged incessantly. He made his rounds of kids squatting down to pat him, licking hands and faces, provoking smiles and laughter.

Brenda arrived a little late. Her mother had driven her to the park. When they saw the commotion under the oak trees, both went to discover what was happening. There was the puppy with his audience around him. Brenda and her mother watched intrigued, charmed like the others. Brenda asked to whom he belonged. One youngster replied that Al and Carrie brought him, but he didn't know if he was theirs.

When Al saw Brenda with her mother, he walked over to greet them.

"Mom, this is Al."

"It's nice to see you again, Al."

"You know him?" Brenda said surprised.

"Certainly. I've seen him at the library…how are you? For some reason I didn't put two and two together when Brenda told me who was teaching tennis this summer."

"We are really enjoying having Brenda in the group, Mrs. Nelson. She's quite a competitor."

"Yes, she's a good girl."

"She's going to be a good tennis player, too."

"She should be. She's always out banging balls against the high school walls."

"What do you two think about the puppy?" Al inquired.

"Whose dog is he? He's so cute!" exclaimed Brenda.

Al related the puppy's history, including his encounter with the eagle. Brenda and her mother were blown away. When Al told them he was looking for a home for the dog, Brenda began pleading with her mother to adopt him. Mrs. Nelson was skeptical. She was worried about costs and whether or not her family would be home enough to care for him properly.

As Brenda wandered over to play with the puppy, Al and Mrs. Nelson talked alone. Al said he didn't want to be presumptuous. After all, he had only known Brenda for a few weeks. He was concerned, however, about Brenda's self-image. She isolated herself from the group and didn't defend herself against verbal attacks. Mrs. Nelson agreed with Al and admitted that Brenda was withdrawn and her communication laconic. She also confided that Brenda had no close males in her life. Her father had left the family, both grandfathers were deceased, and no uncles were in proximity. She told Al that he had made a huge impact on her daughter. Brenda talked about him all the time.

As she unburdened herself to Al, Mrs. Nelson began to realize the positive impact a dog could have on Brenda's life. Dogs were nonjudgmental and unconditionally affectionate, exactly what Brenda needed, a good friend. There were so many loose ends, though. She would have to check with the police station and find out if anyone had called about the puppy. She'd have to make an appointment with a veterinarian for a checkup and shots. Where would he stay when they weren't home? The basement? Garage? At least she had access to a lot of books about raising puppies.

Al saw Brenda's mother deliberating and told her that if she decided to adopt the dog her decision was not irrevocable. Al felt confident that there were other families in town who would take him if he became a burden to her. He also offered to help. He told Mrs. Nelson he would be glad to take the puppy to the same vet who had seen him previously. Dr. Vogel could check his wounds plus give him his shots. He had already had a complete exam. Al offered to take Brenda with him, too, so she could meet the doctor and learn how to properly care for the dog. He was very encouraging.

"Thank you, Al. I'm just not sure what to do. I've never had a dog before. I'm sure my son would love him and help Brenda care for him. I go home every day for lunch, so I could let him out and feed him."

"It's a good time of year to housebreak him, too, because the kids are home from school."

"That's true. I didn't think of that…I would just hate to disappoint the children if things don't work out."

"I understand."

"But, I have a feeling he could really be good for Brenda."

"Well, I think you're right."

Brenda came back and stood beside her mother. Mrs. Nelson told her about the conversation she was having with Al. Brenda couldn't believe her mother was actually considering taking the dog in. Brenda promised she would be responsible for him; feed him, walk him, take him outside when he needed to go, and perform any other jobs related to his care. She was more animated than her mother had seen her in months. "Please, Mom," she begged.

"It's a lot of work, Brenda," her mother warned. "And there's a lot that needs to be done right away."

"I know, Mom."

"I want you to know that Al volunteered to help us get started. It was very gracious of him."

"Thank you so much," Brenda said to Al.

"You're welcome," he replied.

"Oh, Mom. Could we? Can we have him? Please!" Brenda pleaded.

"I tell you what…we'll give it a try, dear. We can see if it works. As I told Al, my biggest concern is disappointing you if we can't care for him properly."

"I know it will work. It just has to."

Mrs. Nelson looked at Al, "Well, young man, where do we begin?"

"If you could call Dr. Vogel's office from the library to see if he has an opening today—he's in Raven—that would really be helpful. Then I can drive Brenda and the dog to you after her lesson to find out the appointment time. It's still early in the day. I'll bet he has an opening for us. Oh, and one other thing…could you double check with the police to make sure no one has claimed him, please?"

"Oh, Mom. Thank you. Thank you so much."

"I'll make those calls as soon as I get to work."

"I can't believe it. I can't believe I have a puppy."

"I'm glad you're happy, dear. Now, have a good lesson, and I'll see you home after work."

"With the puppy."

"Yes, with the puppy."

Brenda's mother gave her daughter her usual perfunctory hug and left for work.

Brenda went back to the circle of children. She chose not to update them on the puppy's new status. Instead, she blended into the group as another admirer. Al took his cue from Brenda, corralling the dog as he ordered all players to Carrie. "Carrie will tell you what court you are on," he said.

Meanwhile, Carrie created the lineup and wheeled two shopping carts filled with tennis balls onto the courts. Her students followed, and Sadie and Dee Dee were right behind Brenda.

"So, Mommy drop you off today? She and Alsie seemed to have a nice cozy talk," Sadie scoffed.

"Isn't that sweet!" followed Dee Dee.

"Mommy sucking up to Al for you? Maybe Al can take you home with him, so he can have two puppies," Sadie added.

Dee Dee began to pat Brenda's head, "Nice doggie. Good doggie," she taunted.

"By the way, nice shorts you have on today. Did you buy them in the boys' department?" Sadie asked laughing...that same forced laugh Brenda heard in the park bathroom. It sounded like an antique car starting in the cold. "Ka-ka-ka-ka."

Brenda pulled away from Sadie and Dee Dee, edging towards Carrie, who was assigning players to their courts. "Before you go, let me tell you what we're going to work on today," Carrie instructed. "Today we're going to hit serves. Even though you have total control of the ball on your serve, it's still a difficult shot to master. A good serve not only has speed, more importantly it has accuracy. Placement is crucial. And believe it or not, the ball toss is the most important part of the serve. So, today, I want even experienced players to work on their ball tosses. I'm going to give each of you a penny. Place it on the court where you want your ball to land after you toss it."

Carrie explained where to place the pennies and demonstrated a few tosses. Almost all of her balls landed exactly on their mark. "OK, you guys, let's all try it on this court together. Remember, we're not swinging at the ball. We're just tossing it up and letting it land on the penny."

"This is so lame," Dee Dee complained to Sadie.

"Dumb," agreed her friend.

Brenda moved away to the opposite side of the baseline. She looked over at Al sitting on a bench with the puppy between his feet. She could barely concentrate on her ball toss. She couldn't believe her mother was allowing her to keep the dog. She was so focused on her new pet that she almost forgot about Sadie's and Dee Dee's recent jibes.

After she practiced her toss as instructed, Brenda moved to a different court with three other students. With two players on each side of the net, they practiced serving crosscourt to one another. Carrie came onto their court to show them how to keep their arms straight when they placed the ball in the air and taught them to hold the ball with their fingertips rather than concealing it with their palms at the beginning of the toss.

When the lesson ended, Brenda bounded off the court to the puppy. He was asleep under the oak trees. Gently, she stroked his tummy. A few other children joined her before leaving for home. The puppy stood up to stretch. He tripped on a twig as he wandered under a bench, then plunked down to nap again.

As Al drifted over to the oaks with Carrie, he told her about the plans for the puppy. He asked if she could drive to the library, so he could talk to Brenda's mother about her calls to the vet and police.

"Then if you drive me home," Al said, "I can get my car to take Brenda and the dog to Raven."

"What! And miss all the fun? No way. I'll take you guys home and see if Mom will let me drive you to Raven. Let's stop at the A&W for lunch. OK with you, Brenda?"

"Sure, thanks. But I don't have any money."

"My treat. It isn't every day I can have lunch with two beautiful girls."

"Oh, boy! He's slinging it now," Carrie smiled.

"Um, we forgot one thing," Al commented. "What are we going to do with him?" he said pointing to the puppy.

"Well, he's going to need a leash and a collar," Carrie pointed out. "How about stopping at the hardware store first. Then we can tie him up with the leash at an outside table when we eat."

"Excellent!" agreed Al.

Al picked up the dog and transported him to the car. After Brenda squeezed in back, Al placed the puppy on her lap and sat in the passenger seat. Carrie drove to Main Street, past both car dealerships, past a furniture showroom, and parked by the hardware store. They exited the Mustang and went inside with the puppy. They were wandering around examining the huge variety of merchandise, when they encountered the proprietor standing near a sign that read "Pet Supplies."

Mr. Christiansen explained that they needed more than just a leash and collar. Puppies required special chow, bowls for water and food, treats, chew toys, and, of course, a pooper-scooper.

"Ah, yes. Of course. A pooper-scooper. Brenda is going to become an expert using that thing," Al teased.

"That can be my brother's job," Brenda deferred.

"Fat chance of that, kiddo," retorted Al.

Mr. Christiansen smiled and patted the pup. "So, what's the little guy's name?"

Al replied, "He doesn't have one, yet."

"Where'd you buy him?"

"Actually we didn't. We found him," Carrie answered.

"Where was he?"

"In the park—near the oak trees."

"Wonder if he's from Dunham's farm. Look at those paws. He's going to be big. They've got a few Great Pyrenees and some St. Bernards there. Have you called the police?"

"We have," Al replied. "And Brenda's mom, Mrs. Nelson over at the library, was going to call again today."

"Where is his farm exactly?"

"It's Phil Dunham's dad's place, Carrie. He graduated a few years ago," Al reminded her.

Mr. Christiansen realigned a few boxes of dog treats on the shelf in front of him. "Yup. Lives right across the street from the park."

"I hate to say this guys," Al apologized, "but before we purchase all this stuff, we had better check with your mom, Brenda, to see if the police have received any calls about the puppy."

———— ⚜ ————

CHAPTER 11

Wednesday afternoon, June 21, 2006

WHEN BRENDA FINALLY returned to Room One after meeting with Helen Nystrom, it was no longer raining, and a few rays of sun glinted through the windows. The children had formed a ring in the play area with Brenda's assistants interspersed among them. Stuffed animals lay on their backs in the center of the circle along with a CD player that serenaded everyone with nursery rhymes.

Her assistants told Brenda the morning had gone smoothly. When she arrived, one mother had informed them that she might be a little late to pick up her daughter, as she had a doctor's appointment. The children had already received their snacks and should be ready for their naps soon. And, a couple of workers had removed a video camera above the cubbyholes, replacing it with a new one.

Brenda joined the group on the floor and began to sing along with the music. Her thoughts, however, fixated on video cameras. Maybe at lunchtime, she could examine the utility closet where recording devices were housed. Most staff members would be in their rooms then, and Billy's workers would be on break.

The farmer in the dell
The farmer in the dell
Heigh-ho, the derry-o
The farmer in the dell

Unfortunately, Brenda did not understand much about electronics. How difficult could it be to remove a disc, though?

The cow takes the dog
The cow takes the dog
Heigh-ho, the derry-o…
The cow takes the dog

She looked up at the new camera. Its lens didn't look much different than its predecessor's. A small red light on top of the apparatus turned on and off at indeterminate intervals.

The cheese stands alone
The cheese stands alone
Heigh-ho, the derry-o…
The cheese stands alone

Marie entered Room One and signaled Brenda to join her in the hall. She informed her that the video crew was ready to show them some of the data they collected. Brenda followed her partner past the utility closet, and into the conference room where she heard Billy Williams in mid-conversation, "…all cameras or just that one?"

One of Billy's workmen replied, "That's what I'm trying to figure out."

"I know both on the playground recorded," Billy stated. "I don't seem to have any from the classrooms, though."

A third workman asked, "Are those old ones or new ones using the wide-angle lenses?"

"These are from today. They're new ones," replied his co-worker.

"What's up guys?" questioned Marie.

Billy responded, "I dunno. We thought we had recordings from Monday and today. I was going to show you the difference in quality using wide-angle lenses. I know the cost is greater, but the pictures are fantastic."

"I can't seem to locate any classroom videos. Why don't we just show them stuff from outside for now. I'll work on the rest after lunch," a workman stated.

"OK. So here's the playground on Monday, or are these from Tuesday?" Billy asked.

"I don't know," one of his workers answered.

"It doesn't matter, really. Both days were shot with the smaller lenses," Billy indicated. "OK. So, look at these images. You can see the swing sets and area around them but not much more. Now, fast forward to today. Look at the playground now. See how much more you can see?"

Brenda was not listening and was not focused on the same issues as the others. She was praying that no videos from Room One were found.

Marie tried to reel her in. "So, what do you think, Brenda?"

"There is quite a difference between the lenses."

"Is it worth another five hundred dollars?" her partner asked.

"I don't know, Marie. I don't know."

"Well, shall we think about it, before we make a final decision?"

"That's fine with me."

"OK with us," Billy injected. "Why don't we meet again tomorrow to discuss it? Meanwhile, we'll try to find earlier clips from the classrooms to compare them to data we collected today."

During lunchtime, Brenda watched Billy Williams's crew take their usual break on the playground. She knew Marie and all the assistants were with the children. Cautiously, she entered the utility room. All recording apparatus was on the upper shelves humming with activity. Brenda could not determine which appliance recorded classrooms and which recorded the playground. She stood on her tiptoes to survey the equipment more carefully. A loud voice startled her, and she jumped. Her heart beat like the roll of a kettledrum. "Can I help you, Brenda? Sorry, I didn't mean to scare you," Billy Williams apologized.

Brenda was breathless. "Um, no. Marie told me the recording equipment was in here. I thought I would look at it myself."

"Sure. It's all up there," he said pointing to the top shelves. "All those wires are from cameras in the classrooms and playground. They go into that central hub—that black box with wire mesh on the outside— where they are assimilated. While parents can watch their kids for extended periods of time, the recorder only catches snippets of action, because it shifts its recordings from site to site at varying intervals."

"Oh, I see."

"Pretty neat, huh," Billy said proudly.

"Very."

"Well, I was just going to see if I could find data from the classrooms."

"You know," Brenda intervened, "I think we saw enough from the playground to make a decision. And, I think we should go with wide-angle lenses, even if there is an extra cost."

"That would be a smart move, Brenda. The difference between the two recordings is quite dramatic. I think the cost is worth it."

Brenda left the utility room hoping Billy would, too. He didn't. She could see him examining some equipment as she walked back to her room.

With the air conditioner working, Few Hours A Day Nursery was comfortable again. The children in Room One had finished their lunches and two assistants were placing them in their cribs for their second nap of the day. Brenda walked over to Ellie, who was on her back looking up hypnotically at a mobile with yellow ducks spinning around. She glanced at the back of Ellie's right hand as Ellie reached up. A slight discoloration was still present. Brenda bent down and talked to her in a soft voice. Ellie turned her head, looked up at Brenda and smiled. Was all forgiven, Brenda wondered?

Brenda offered to stay with the napping children to allow her assistants some free time. They thanked Brenda but declined, because they knew she had other duties to perform. So, Brenda went to her office and sat down at her desk. There were bills to pay, employee evaluations to update, even the payroll to complete. She needed to access the internet to download release forms for parents, too. These tasks were usually easy, but today they felt burdensome, almost overwhelming.

Brenda reached for her laptop and opened it. She clicked on her solitaire application and began playing. A ding resonated, indicating a new email. It was from her husband.

To: B.Bjorkman@minutes.com
From: henrytheplumber@minutes.com
Subject: Joy

Hi. Tom called. wants to work with Joy before dinner. Do you want me take her? Hope you are having a good day.

Love you, Henry.

Brenda responded.

> To: henrytheplumber@minutes.com
> From: B.Bjorkman@minutes.com
> Subject: Re: Joy
>
> Hi. I may be home a little late.
> Could you take her to the park?
> I'll meet her there and take her home.
> Thanks Love you, too. B.

Henry replied.

> To: B.Bjorkman@minutes.com
> From: henrytheplumber@minutes.com
> Subject: Re: Re: Joy
>   Sure. No problem.
>   L.H.

Brenda played a few more games of solitaire. Before returning to Room One, she found Marie to tell her about the conversation with Billy. Brenda explained that both of them felt five hundred dollars was a reasonable price to pay for enhanced video surveillance afforded by wide-angle lenses. She thought they ought to make the decision now and forego viewing a comparison of classroom videos.

Her partner disagreed. Marie felt five hundred dollars was a large sum and reminded Brenda that the projected cost without wide-angle lenses was going to be over two thousand dollars.

"But you said the quote Billy gave us was very good," Brenda recalled.

"I know," Marie said, "but two thousand dollars is still a lot of money. Let's just see what the difference looks like in the classrooms…that is if they ever find the right recordings. Then we can make a more knowledgeable decision."

Discouraged, Brenda returned to Room One to help remove the children from their cribs and change their diapers. The remainder of the afternoon passed slowly. Once the children went home, Brenda returned to her office to update each child's log. She also got on the internet to find the release forms HELL-N requested but decided to download them another time.

Her ride home was brief. Driving down Main Street, away from the golf course, she passed Winetraub's drugstore. She began thinking about all the changes that had occurred since she was a child. The bakery, which used to be next to the pharmacy, was gone, as was the hardware store. The furniture showroom had been converted into a coffee shop. Neither car dealership existed, either—one replaced by a pottery store, the other by a mall filled with eclectic gift shops.

At a little after five o'clock, Brenda entered her empty home. Henry had probably dropped Joy off at the tennis courts and returned to work. Her mother usually volunteered at the library on Wednesday afternoon. Ricky was at a friend's house for a sleepover. Brenda changed into a cotton top and tennis shorts, then drove to Taylor Park.

As she turned into the parking lot, she looked across the street at the dirt road leading to the Dunham farm, remembering her visit years ago with Al and Carrie.

She left her car to walk to the tennis complex. Tom and Joy were at the far end on Court Six. Brenda sat down and reached inside her purse for an article she kept about Joy that was published in *The Oakbrook Current*, a local weekly newspaper. She read it again.

Oakbrook Teen Goes to National Special Olympics in Tennis

OAKBROOK. Five years ago, Coach Tom Carrabas saw one of his former student-athletes, Brenda Nelson Bjorkman hitting with her daughter, Joy, at the Taylor Park courts. He had just returned from teaching Special Olympics tennis coaches how to train and work with their athletes and had served on a committee with psychologists, pediatricians, and other tennis aficionados to devise a program that met the standards of Special Olympics of North America (SONA).

SONA requires each athlete to have a coach in attendance at every event, and all coaches have to be certified. They are required to watch an online video on *General Orientation* and another on *Protecting Behaviors*. After watching the videos, coaches have to pass brief tests on both subjects. Finally, they are required to attend a three-hour clinic on teaching, cross-training, rules, and other topics specific to individuals with disabilities who play competitive sports. Once they qualify as Wisconsin SO coaches, they must be recertified every three years.

Like other coaches at the conference, Tom Carrabas became certified, and when he returned to Oakbrook he asked Mrs. Bjorkman if he could coach Joy. He said while SONA still honored every athlete who participated in Special Olympics, they had begun to recognize adults and children with disabilities who were bonafide competitors, too. He felt Joy could participate at a high level, and he wanted to help her.

When Coach Carrabas and Mrs. Bjorkman shared the idea with Joy, the ten-year-old was delighted. Now, five years later, the relationship continues to thrive, and Joy has exceeded her coach's and parents' expectations.

Wisconsin only has thirty to forty tennis players with disabilities who compete every year. Unlike other Special Olympics sports (softball, bocce, track and field, swimming, and volleyball, for example) there are no divisional tournaments for tennis. Participants in other sports usually play in one of seven regions, then go to state after placing in the top tier of their districts. With tennis, however, players bypass regionals and go directly to state, Coach Carrabas informed this paper.

Three years after the lessons began, Coach entered Joy in the Special Olympics state tennis tournament. Players competed based on their competency level rather than on their age. Joy entered her first state tournament when she was thirteen. She competed on a regulation court with special balls that helped slow the pace of the rallies, and Joy was hooked on the competition. A year later, in 2005, she entered state at a higher level. Again, she participated on a regulation court, but this time with standard tennis balls, and she won her division.

Along with three women from the Milwaukee area, Joy will represent the state of Wisconsin in tennis beginning July 1 at the inaugural quadrennial Special Olympics USA National Games in Ames, Iowa. All four athletes have been to camps twice at UW-Oshkosh in preparation for nationals, where they will compete in singles and doubles.

Tom Carrabas's extensive career playing and teaching tennis made him an easy choice to coach the Wisconsin team. "I feel all four athletes will be very competitive in their divisions," he told this reporter. "Joy is one of the youngest competitors, but she holds her own quite well on the court."

There were only nine days until nationals, and Brenda felt a lot more pressure than Joy. The tension associated with watching someone you love play exceeded the stress of actually competing yourself. And preparing properly for the trip demanded that she fill out multiple forms, make reservations for Tom and her entire family, obtain coverage at the nursery, help her kids pack, and more.

Brenda sighed, standing up as Joy approached with Tom.

"She did great again today, didn't you Joy?" Tom commended.

"I did, Mom."

"I saw you, honey. You were terrific."

"My serve is really hard now."

"It is, Joy," Tom agreed. "You were serving very well. Do you remember when you first started and served underhand?"

"Yup!"

"You don't need that any more do you?"

"Nope."

"I got us rooms in Ames, five minutes away from the university," Brenda informed Tom.

"Please let me know what I owe you, Brenda."

"You don't owe us anything. With all you've done for Joy and for our family…no way! I hope you'll travel with us. We're going to take the van, and there's more than enough room for six."

"Six?"

"Grandma Ellen absolutely insists on coming, too."

"Of course."

Joy jumped up and down. "Grandma's coming?"

"She sure is," her mother answered.

"You know, I think my wife wants to go, too," Tom said.

"How is Nancy?" Brenda asked.

"She's great. Loves being a grandmother. We just wish the kids and grandkids lived a little closer."

"There's certainly room for her, too. The van is pretty large."

"Wonderful," Tom agreed.

Brenda slipped the newspaper article back into her purse. "So, when would you like to get together with Joy next, Tom?"

"Let me look at my calendar. I'll email you when I get home."

"Thanks."

"Thanks, Coach," Joy said, waving goodbye.

"You're welcome, Joy. See you soon."

✧

CHAPTER 12

Monday afternoon and early evening, July 14, 1975

BEFORE GOING TO Mr. Dunham's farm, Carrie drove to the library. She stayed in the car with the puppy, while Al and Brenda found Mrs. Nelson looking through books about dogs.

Al asked her if she had any information from the police department, and she did; no one had called about a missing puppy. As Al requested, Mrs. Nelson made an appointment with Dr. Vogel for 3:15 that afternoon. Al updated Brenda's mother about their hardware store trip. They were going to the Dunham farm after they left the library. Al asked if he could use a phone to call his parents to explain what was happening.

When Al and Brenda returned to the car, Carrie shifted the pup from her lap onto Brenda's. Al told Carrie what Mrs. Nelson said, as they began a subdued ride to the farm. Carrie turned into the dirt road across from the park and was immediately greeted by three Great Pyrenees. Each polar bear-like dog weighed well over one hundred pounds. Pure white with occasional patches of gray, their heads were enormous. They loped alongside the Mustang, pink tongues protruding, barking loudly at their trespassers. The puppy stood up in Al's lap. "Does this baby belong to you?" Al asked the Pyrs.

The canine detail followed the car to the farmhouse, where two more massive dogs were waiting. Brown, black and white with sad eyes, the St. Bernards were more docile than the Great Pyrenees but just as big. Carrie stopped her car, and both St. Bernards wandered over to sniff the strangers. In the background, the Great Pyrenees continued their rant.

Mr. Dunham came out of his house waving. But, no one in the Mustang was anxious to leave its confines.

"Hi there. Welcome," Mr. Dunham greeted his guests.

"Hello, Mr. Dunham," Al replied.

"OK, guys. That's enough. Quiet down now," the farmer said to his Great Pyrenees. "Sorry about that. You're Al, right? You know my son, Phil."

"Yes, sir. Phil was a few years ahead of me. What is he doing now?"

"He's at UW in the Ag school. Really likes it. He's going into his junior year."

"Please say hi to him for me when you speak to him."

"I will. And who else do we have here?"

"This is Carrie Archibald and Brenda Nelson…and…"

"Yes," interrupted Mr. Dunham, "I see you have a familiar looking puppy, as well. I figured one of the coyotes got him. I should have known better with my three henchmen over there. Where did you find him?"

"At the park," Al said, "a few days ago. We went to the police station Sunday to see if anyone called in about him, then we called again a couple of more times, but no one phoned. Brenda, here, wanted to adopt him, so we went to the hardware store today for a leash and other supplies. That's when Mr. Christiansen told us about your dogs. He wondered if the puppy belonged to you."

"Yes, he does. His St. Bernard mommy went into heat, and before I could kennel her, one of the Pyr's hopped on board. She had a litter of two. Cute puppies, though. C'mere. I'll show you his sister…it's OK. It's safe. Great Pyrenees are all bark and no bite, unless you're a coyote or a wolf. Then you don't have a prayer in hell."

Mr. Dunham escorted his guests with the lost pup into his barn. There, in a pen strewn with hay, was a little female whining. The siblings clearly knew one another and struggled to reunite. When Al picked the male up to gently drop him next to his sister, the two dogs yipped and began nibbling at each other's ears and muzzles.

"He's a lot cleaner than she is," Mr. Dunham observed.

"That's because we gave him a bath," Carrie said launching into the story about the eagle.

The farmer was impressed. "That's an incredible tale. I'll bet he's glad to be back with his sister."

Brenda started to cry. Immediately, Mr. Dunham walked over and put an arm around her shoulder. He told Brenda he had not planned to sell the puppies, as they weren't purebreds. Since his farm already had too many dogs, as cute as they were, he didn't want to keep them either. He already promised the female to his paperboy who fell in love with her and came every day to visit. He wondered if Brenda would like to keep the male. Brenda cried harder and put her arms around Mr. Dunham's waist. Making the rounds, she hugged Al then Carrie, too. This was the best day of her life. She was going to have a puppy who would grow to be huge like those dogs outside. Perhaps she had better not let her mother know just how big the pup was going to be.

Back to the hardware store they went, Al, Carrie, Brenda and the puppy. They needed all the paraphernalia Mr. Christiansen recommended for…what was his name? What were they, or rather, what was Brenda going to call him? Gerry? For President Ford? No, that didn't work. How about a tennis term? Volley? Fault? Topspin? It was Brenda who finally came up with Rally, and Al and Carrie loved it. Rally was perfect. Rally dog. Brenda couldn't wait to tell her mother.

After picking up dog food, a leash, a collar, some chew toys, bowls for food and water, and, of course a pooper-scooper, the crew in the Mustang returned to Oakbrook library. Brenda, who was holding Rally in the back seat, shoveled him to Carrie and ran inside. She found her mother working with card catalogues. Briefly, Brenda relayed the events at the farm and told her mother the name she selected for the dog. Mrs. Nelson was pleased for her daughter. "You'll need some money," she said, "to pay for Dr. Vogel. Did you charge the things you bought at the hardware store to our account?" Brenda said she did. "Here is a little extra for lunch for you, Al and Carrie. We need to show them how appreciative we are."

Next, was a stop at the A&W. Al tethered Rally to an outside table with his new leash as Brenda gave him some dog food. Carrie took the water bowl to the Ladies' room to fill it. Brenda told Al and Carrie that her mom was buying lunch and waited outside with Rally while her friends ordered their meals. When Al and Carrie returned, Brenda went into the A&W, ordered her meal, paid, and took all three lunches outside on a cardboard tray.

After lunch, they left for Dr. Vogel's office. Only twenty minutes from Oakbrook, the ride to Raven through back roads was beautiful. A tractor pulling hay slowed them down but also allowed more time to enjoy the countryside. Undulating hills were on the right, flatter farmland on the left. Some fields lay fallow but most were saturated with robust crops. The woody sound of cranes occasionally eclipsed songs they were listening to on WROX.

Dr. Vogel examined Rally's wounds and reported they were healing well. He encouraged Brenda to continue the antibiotic he had prescribed. Then he called Mr. Dunham to find out how old Rally was (just under three months) and what shots he had received (one series). He returned with a syringe, and Brenda held him as the doctor injected a combination vaccine into his back. Brenda winced, but the pup was completely oblivious to his injection.

On the way home, Carrie stopped by the roadside. She was nauseated and had a pain in her belly. Opening the car door, she left the vehicle to vomit in a ditch adjacent to the shoulder. She was so embarrassed, she wanted to leave the Mustang and walk home.

Al sensed her discomfort, so he left her alone initially. After Carrie finished vomiting, however, he got out of the car to comfort her. She couldn't look at him, apologizing several times before walking back to the vehicle. Al felt awkward in his attempts to reassure her. He wondered if she had food poisoning, but Carrie was doubtful. She had the same lunch they ate, and they weren't sick. Al offered to drive home and Carrie accepted. "I'll be OK," Carrie insisted. "Take yourself home, then I'll take Brenda and Rally to their place."

By the time Al reached home, Carrie felt slightly better. She had less nausea, and her pain wasn't as severe. When Carrie reclaimed the driver's seat, Al reached in and squeezed her arm. "Don't worry about that," he empathized. "I'll give you a call later on…and Brenda and Rally, good luck with your first night…oh, Carrie, don't forget to give Brenda Rally's pills."

Brenda moved into the passenger seat with her puppy. "Good night, Al. Thanks again for everything."

Carrie drove to her own home to retrieve Rally's medicine. Alone, the girls talked about other players who took lessons at the park with Brenda.

"Sadie is so mean," Brenda opined. "I think Sadie is short for Sadistic. That should be her real name, Sadistic Winetraub."

Carrie laughed supportively.

"So, I need to ask you a personal question," said Brenda uneasily.

"Sure."

"My mom isn't really good at this. I've noticed…your complexion is so nice, Carrie. Do you have special medicines you use?"

"I do. Actually, I've seen a dermatologist—you know, a skin specialist. I'm sure you've noticed the birthmark on my temple. When I was young, there was a raised red mark there called a hemangioma. So, my folks took me to this dermatologist. With treatment, or maybe on its own, it shrunk. All that's left now is this red mark, and I think even that is fading. Anyhow, when I was your age, I had acne, too. So, I went back to my dermatologist. He gave me some lotions to rub on my face and back and an antibiotic, too. And they worked. I also use non-perfumed soap a couple of times a day. I could give you my dermatologist's name. His clinic is in Madison."

"Wow. That would be great. Mom got me some cream from the drugstore, but it isn't working."

"This doctor is kind of nerdy, if you know what I mean. But, he seems to know what he's doing."

"Thanks."

After stopping at her house to pick up Rally's pills, Carrie drove to Brenda's home. Brenda attached a leash to Rally's collar and led him inside, as Carrie followed with bags from the hardware store. Carrie greeted Brenda's mother and met her brother, who jumped up and down when he saw the dog. "Oh, I love him," he said. "Hi, Rally, I'm John. Can I take him for a walk? I'll be careful. I promise. What's in there?" he asked, pointing to the bags. Excited and not watching the terrain around him, John tripped on Rally's leash and fell down next to him.

"For god's sake, John. Be careful," his sister scolded.

"He's OK," Mrs. Nelson said to Brenda. "John is just a little excited, aren't you, son."

Carrie said goodnight to Brenda's family and returned to the Mustang. She felt ill again. The intense pain in her belly, which had lessened briefly, was back—so was the nausea. She placed a hand over her abdomen for a few moments before driving herself home.

CHAPTER 13

※

Monday night, July 14, 1975, at the Nelsons

AFTER CARRIE LEFT for home, Mrs. Nelson bent down to pat the puppy's ears and neck. His fur was soft and warm. Rally rolled onto his back so she would rub his belly. As she tickled him, his right rear leg began to scratch the air vigorously. Brenda and John laughed. Rally raised his head staring at Mrs. Nelson. "You are a cute little guy," she admitted. "So, Brenda, what were his mom and dad like?"

Brenda described the farm scene in more detail, beginning with the greeting from the three Great Pyrenees. She explained that Rally's mother was a St. Bernard and his father a Pyr. Both were "good-sized" animals. The Pyrs seemed very protective; the St. Bernards were more laid back. Brenda told her mom and brother about Rally's reunion with his sister. She thought it would be fun to bring him back to the farm to see his sibling, but Mr. Dunham's paperboy was adopting his sister, and she didn't know where he lived.

John knelt down with his mother and hugged the dog tightly. Rally squirmed and whined a little.

"Easy, John," Brenda said. "Don't squeeze him to death! He's just a puppy!"

"I know!" John retorted.

Mrs. Nelson suggested they purchase a wire cage for the puppy to stay in when no one was home and at night. She referred to a book she read at the library that encouraged crating puppies. The hardware store was closed, and she doubted they had any in stock, but tomorrow she would order one. She thought Brenda could sleep with Rally in the TV room for the night, because there were no carpets for him to soil or wet. John was upset.

"Why does she get to stay with him? He's my dog, too."

"Yes, he is," his mother confirmed.

"He's not his dog," insisted Brenda.

Mrs. Nelson stood up. "He's our family's dog, Brenda. He's going to be part of our family. We're all going to be responsible for taking care of him."

"But, I'm the one that found him."

John placed his hands on his hips. "Uh, uh. You said Al and Karen found him. They just offered him to you."

"It's Al and Carrie, dummy, not Karen," Brenda corrected.

"No name-calling, Brenda," her mother admonished.

"I want to sleep downstairs with him. Why does she get to do it?"

"Right now, your sister knows more about the dog than you or I do. She's been with him all day. She talked to the vet about him and has already had to care for him. You'll get your chance, too, John."

"That's not fair. She gets to do everything with him, and I don't get to do anything."

"You will. Be patient," his mother promised.

Brenda mocked her, "Patient! Are you kidding?"

"Why don't you two take him out again and see if he has to go to the bathroom, while I make supper. John, I want you to let Brenda show you how to walk him, because I'm sure he's not very good on a leash yet."

"No, he's not. Sometimes he digs his paws into the ground and won't move," Brenda confirmed.

"I read that's very typical. OK. Go ahead out, and I'll see you soon. Oh, don't forget that contraption to pick up his poo," Mrs. Nelson reminded.

"That's called a pooper-scooper, Mom," instructed Brenda.

"Whatever. Don't forget it. And please don't throw his poo in the barrels. For now, let's use a plastic bag. I'll buy a small bucket tomorrow and we can throw it in there until trash day."

"I'll get the leash," John directed.

"Give it to me, and I'll put it on," demanded Brenda.

"I know how to do it."

Brenda waited as John struggled with a clasp that connected the leash to the collar. After fidgeting with it for a while, John successfully attached the leash and began pulling it. Rally rose, chomped on the leash with his teeth, and shook his head from side-to-side playfully.

"What's wrong with him. Why is he biting his leash?" John asked.

"He's just playing," Brenda observed.

John screamed at him, "Stop it, Rally!"

"John, please don't yell. There are a lot of things he has to learn," Mrs. Nelson directed.

"Well, he doesn't have to bite it."

"It's OK, John," his mother reaffirmed.

John started to cry, "No it's not. He shouldn't do that. He doesn't do anything right for me. Here, you take him!" John dropped the leash on the floor, ran up to his bedroom, and slammed the door. Brenda looked at her mother and sighed.

Mrs. Nelson motioned for Brenda to join her in the kitchen, where they could talk privately. She urged Brenda not to berate her brother. She explained that he was hyperactive and had difficulty controlling his emotions. His hyperactivity also interfered with his schoolwork, because his span of concentration was short. His difficulty in school made him very self-conscious, and calling him names like "dummy" lowered his self-esteem even more. Mrs. Nelson confided that Brenda's father had the same condition. And, because he did not have a good support system when he was John's age, he struggled into adulthood with hyperactivity.

In the past, Brenda's mother refused to discuss anything about her former husband with the children. Brenda had no inkling where he was, what he did, or whether there was communication between her mother and him. She really wasn't sure why they divorced. Since she was six years old when her father left home, Brenda recalled little

about him. Without pictures in the house, she had difficulty remembering what he even looked like.

"So, do you still talk to him?" Brenda inquired.

"Ralph? Yes, occasionally."

"Does he live around here?"

"He lives up north."

"In Wisconsin?"

"Yes."

"What does he do?"

"Oh, a bunch of different things. He's kind of like a
handyman."

"When did you talk with him last?"

"Actually, just a week ago."

"Why doesn't he come to see us?"

"I haven't let him."

"Why?"

"I felt he would not be a good influence on you and
John. He has trouble controlling himself. He just shoots his
mouth off. And he has a wicked temper. I felt you would be
better off if he stayed away," her mother confessed.

"Did he want to see us?"

"Yes, but we made an agreement. So, he stayed away."

"Oh."

"And, there is another reason. Your father was in prison.
He didn't kill or hurt anyone, but he did steal some items
a few years ago."

"Oh, my god. Do people in Oakbrook know about
him?"

"I'm sure some do. Not many."

Brenda immediately thought about the repercussions of her father's incarceration. She could envision Sadie and her friends telling other tennis players during a lesson. If that secret emerged, she would never be able to face anyone in Oakbrook again.

"So, why didn't you tell me this before?"

"I thought you should be older, and I think you are old enough now."

"What if I want to see him?"

"You're old enough to make that decision, too."

"How about John?"

"I don't think we should keep it from him. That's part of the conversation I had with your father the last time we spoke."

"I don't get it. Why can we see him now if we want to and yet you wouldn't even talk about him before?"

"This last year or so when we've talked, he seems more stable. He has a drinking problem, and he claims he's gotten help for it. He told me he was self-medicating with liquor for his hyperactivity. When we've been on the phone lately, he talks like he's sober. He used to call me when he was drunk, and he'd get nasty on the phone. He hasn't done that lately. Plus, he asks more about you and John—and me. He never used to do that."

"So, what am I supposed to say if someone teases me about him—especially if they mention the prison thing?"

"Same thing I do, Brenda. I just acknowledge that he served his time and now he's out and on his own."

"Easy for you to say."

"You know what? Every family has skeletons in the closet. Secrets they don't share with other people."

"This is a pretty big skeleton. Don't you think?"

"It is. I agree."

Rally, who had been waiting patiently, began to stir. He grabbed his leash between his teeth, shaking his head back and forth again. Then he stopped, looked up at Brenda and barked for no apparent reason. She bent down to scratch him, and he rewarded her with a quick chin lick.

Brenda called upstairs to John, asking him to walk the dog with her. He came bounding down and grabbed the leash. Rally cooperated, so John took him outside without a problem. Brenda followed closely behind.

Mrs. Nelson made dinner while her children walked Rally. After supper, she helped Brenda make up the couch with a couple of sheets and a blanket. Anticipating a long night, Brenda brought down her bathrobe and slippers, placing them by the door for easy access.

—— ⚜ ——

CHAPTER 14

Monday night, July 14, 1975, at the Archibalds

BY THE TIME Carrie reached home after leaving Brenda's house, her belly pain had eased some again. She parked the Mustang and greeted her parents in the kitchen. There was a lot to tell, as she recounted the day's events during dinner. She had no appetite and ate very little even though her favorite meal, lamb chops, was the entree. She described feeling sick in late afternoon and told her folks how embarrassed she was throwing up in front of Al. As she chronicled the day, Carrie's nausea and pain increased again. Abruptly, she ran to the bathroom to vomit. Her mother accompanied her.

Vomiting relieved her nausea, but Carrie still had significant tenderness in her belly. She decided she would go upstairs and rest. She took her tennis shoes off and laid down on her bed. The most comfortable position was lying on her side with her knees tucked up to her chest. A half hour later, her mother came upstairs to check on her. Carrie's eyes were closed, but she was awake. Her mother asked how she was feeling, and Carrie said her stomach pain was pretty bad—worse than any pain she had ever had. When her mother put on the bedroom light, she noted how pale Carrie looked and called for her husband.

Mr. Archibald was alarmed when he saw his daughter. He thought she should go to the emergency room immediately. Carrie said she didn't think it was that serious and suggested waiting another hour or so to see what happened. Twenty minutes later, as the pain was intensifying, she changed her mind. Mrs. Archibald helped tie her shoes, as it hurt Carrie to bend over to put them on.

Her father suggested going to University Hospitals in case the problem was surgical, because they had pediatric surgeons there.

The drive to Madison was difficult. Carrie's nausea was constant, and she felt a surge of pain with every bump in the road. Thankfully, her mother remembered a bowl in case she needed to throw up. Carrie tried to vomit, but she no longer brought anything up; she had the dry heaves. Periodically, she tried to lie down in the back seat, but the urgency to vomit stifled her attempts to rest.

Fortunately, the emergency room was not crowded. Carrie sat with her mother in the waiting room as Mr. Archibald provided the receptionist with insurance details and other required information. He returned to his wife and daughter promising Carrie would be taken to an examination room soon. Carrie leaned over to rest her head on her mother's lap.

Shortly, a woman in her thirties wearing a white uniform introduced herself and ushered the family into a cubicle. Her name was Roxie. She was a nursing assistant. With pen and clipboard in hand, she asked Carrie to explain why she was in the emergency room. Carrie told her about her nausea, vomiting, and the pain in her belly.

"Well, I'm sorry you're not feeling well, Carrie. We've got a good staff here. I'm sure they'll find out what's wrong and fix you up," Roxie encouraged.

"Thanks."

"So, where do you go to school?" asked the nursing assistant.

"Oakbrook High."

"What year are you in?"

"I'm going into my senior year."

"Good for you. Do you plan on going to college?"

"Yes, I do."

"Is there anything you're especially interested in?"

"I love the sciences, so I'm actually thinking of studying biochemistry or medicine. I really like being around kids, too. I volunteer at a nursery in Oakbrook during the school year—the same nursery I attended when I was little. Then during the summer, I teach kids to play tennis."

"Great."

"My dad teaches archeology here at the U."

"I'm afraid that's one course I didn't study… I've got to take your vital signs now. OK?"

"Sure."

After taking Carrie's temperature, pulse, and blood pressure, Roxie recorded them on her clipboard, then said goodbye to the family.

A few minutes later, a twenty-something-year-old woman in a short white lab coat with pleated skirt entered the cubicle. The badge on her left lapel read "Susan Stabler, M.D., Pediatrics." She smiled at Carrie extending her hand. "Carrie, I'm Susan Stabler, the pediatric intern on duty tonight. Hello." She walked over to the Archibalds to shake their hands, too. Then she went to the sink and washed before sitting on a stool in front of Carrie. "So, I understand you are interested in medicine," the doctor noted. Carrie nodded, as Dr. Stabler continued, "Perhaps when you're feeling better we can talk about that. It's a great profession. I love it. But, let's get back to your belly pain and see if we can help you. I am going to ask you a number of questions with your folks in the room. After that I'm going to ask mom and dad to excuse themselves, so we can talk privately and do an examination. OK?"

Carrie said she didn't mind if her mother stayed the entire time, but Dr. Stabler said Carrie was entitled to some privacy and if she wanted to share the confidential conversation they had, she certainly could.

With prompting from Dr. Stabler, Carrie retold her story, wincing intermittently with pain. No, she did not eat anything unusual. No, she had never had pains similar to the ones she experienced today. The "vomitus" was yellow not green, and there was no blood in it. Where was the pain? It began in the middle, over her bellybutton. Recently the pain moved to her right side. No, no cough, no headache, no rashes. She did have a birthmark on her temple, which was a hemangioma at birth.

Dr. Stabler questioned Mrs. Archibald about her pregnancy with Carrie, Carrie's birth weight, her immunizations and a few developmental landmarks—including when she walked and talked. Childhood illnesses? She didn't have measles or mumps or German measles, because she had the vaccinations, but she had chicken pox when she was in second grade. Other illnesses, in particular urinary tract infections? No, none. Previous surgeries? No. Finally, she asked both parents about illnesses in their families, including appendicitis. The only family member to have an appendectomy was Carrie's aunt, Mr. Archibald's sister.

Tactfully, Dr. Stabler asked Carrie's parents to return to the waiting room. She handed Carrie a gown and asked her to remove all her clothing except her underpants and change into it. "The ties go in back," she instructed. "I'll be right outside the room. Let me know when you're finished."

Carrie stood up cautiously to put on the gown. Her pain was still severe. After tying the strings, she told Dr. Stabler she was ready.

"So, Carrie, I asked Mom and Dad to step out because I have more questions I need to ask you. Some of them are very personal, and, as I told you before, I wanted you to have some privacy," Dr. Stabler began.

"Mom knows pretty much everything about me. We don't have many secrets."

"It sounds like you have a good relationship."

"We do."

"You are entitled to tell your mom and dad anything we talk about in this room, but I will not, unless you tell me it's OK. If you give me information that leads me to believe you are in danger, then I would also be obliged to share that with your parents. Do you understand?"

"Yes."

"OK. Have you had any diarrhea?" Dr. Stabler asked.

"No."

"When did you have your last bowel movement?"

"This morning."

"Was there any blood in it?"

"Um, I didn't look."

"Was there any on the toilet paper?"

"No, I don't think so."

"When you urinate, does it burn? Have you ever had burning when you pee?"

"Not that I remember."

"How old were you when you had your first period?"

"Let's see, I was in eighth grade…I was thirteen."

"Are your periods regular, roughly once a month?"

"Pretty regular."

"And, do you have any discomfort with them?"

"Not really."

"When was your last one?"

"Oh, about three weeks ago."

"Was it normal? Was it longer than usual? Did you bleed longer?"

"No, it was normal."

"OK. Now, even more personal questions…Do you have a boyfriend?"

"Yes."

"And, how long have you two been going out?"

"Well, we were just friends before we became boyfriend and girlfriend. So, we've known each other for quite a while, but we've been going together for a little over a month."

"Do you have a good relationship with him? That probably sounds like a dumb question, Carrie, but sometimes kids that are going together don't get along that well. You would think they'd split, but sometimes one of the partners is afraid to let go or just can't seem to get out of the relationship."

"No, we're not like that at all. We get along really well."

"Good. That's important. Have you ever had sex with him?"

"No, I haven't."

"Do you see it happening in the next few months?"

Carrie started to wince again with pain and lay down on her side, "I don't think so."

"You look pretty uncomfortable to me, Carrie. Let's see if we can move this along. Just to explain—the questions I asked you are to help clarify where your pain is coming from. You have a lot of organs down in your belly like your bladder, ovaries, uterus, intestines, and appendix. Any one of them could cause the pain you are having. So, I have to make sure you don't have a twisted ovary, or a bladder infection, a kidney stone, or pain from your period and even make sure you aren't pregnant. OK?"

"Yes, I understand."

"So, we're done with the questions," Dr. Stabler said. "Well, I'm done with my questions. There will be other doctors who will be in to talk to you. Next, I am going to examine you. I'll be right back. I'm just going to ask a nurse to assist me. I wish I could give you something for pain, but it might mask what's going on and make the diagnosis more difficult. Do you have any questions for me?"

"Not really."

"See you in a minute," she said.

Dr. Stabler returned to the bedside accompanied by a young woman in a light blue and white finely striped uniform. Her badge read "Mary, Student Nurse." Mary introduced herself and held Carrie's hand as Dr. Stabler examined her.

Towards the end of the exam, Dr. Stabler felt Carrie's abdomen. She asked Carrie to show her precisely where she felt the pain, and Carrie pointed to the lower right side of her belly. Gently, the doctor pushed down over the targeted area, and Carrie grimaced. "I'm so sorry," Dr. Stabler apologized. "I know that hurts. I have to listen there, too," she explained, placing her stethoscope on Carrie's abdomen. "So, one last thing," she instructed, "I need you to remove your underpants so I can make sure everything they cover is OK, too. Then I will be done."

At the conclusion of the examination, Carrie asked Dr. Stabler what she thought. "I think you have appendicitis, Carrie. Your pain is over the appendix, the history of nausea fits, and you have a slight fever. I'm going to order some blood and urine tests." Carrie asked what the test were for. Dr. Stabler said the blood test would evaluate her white blood cell count and see what types of white cells were present. With appendicitis, she explained, the white cell count is higher than normal, and pus cells predominate. The urine test is to look for a urinary tract infection. "Even though I know you told me you weren't sexually active; I always do a pregnancy test on females in the reproductive age group. It's not that I don't believe you."

A laboratory technician entered Carrie's room, introduced herself, and took some blood from Carrie's arm. She also gave Carrie a small plastic bottle and asked for a urine specimen. She told Carrie there were instructions on how to collect the sample taped to the mirror in the bathroom.

When Carrie returned to her bed, she was hunched over. A second physician was waiting with her parents. Bob Chow was a third-year pediatric resident who supervised Susan Stabler. Dr. Chow introduced himself and took an abbreviated history from Carrie and her parents. After excusing the Archibalds and summoning a nurse, he performed his examination.

Completing his assessment, Dr. Chow asked the Archibalds to return to Carrie's cubicle. He told the family he agreed with Dr. Stabler's diagnosis and wanted to obtain a surgical consult. Mr. Archibald asked if a pediatric surgeon was available and if he could see Carrie soon. It was obvious Carrie was extremely uncomfortable. He was anxious to have the diagnosis confirmed and surgery performed if it was necessary. Dr. Chow promised to page the pediatric surgeon on-call.

Fifteen minutes later, Dr. Syd Sewall entered the room. He recognized his colleague immediately. "Professor Archibald, how nice to see you." Then looking towards the bed, he said, "And you must be Carrie. I'm Dr. Sewall. Your dad and I are on a campus committee together. It's nice to meet you, although I wish the circumstances were different." Dr. Sewall said hello to Carrie's mother before sitting down on the bed next to his patient. "Are you sick and tired of all the questions and probing?"

"Kinda," Carrie admitted.

"I certainly understand why. It's laborious and time-consuming, but multiple interviews and exams provide multiple opinions with less chance for error. That's lesson number one for FPAs."

"FPAs?" Carrie inquired.

"Sure, Future Physicians of America. I heard all about you."

"I'm sure learning a lot today."

"I'll bet you are. And, this experience will make you a better physician, because you'll know what it's like to be a patient. Think how much more empathetic you will be now...so, Carrie, I am a pediatric surgeon. The pediatricians asked me to visit with you, because they suspect you have appendicitis. I've reviewed your history with them, so I will try to be brief. I know you've done this before, but can you point to the spot where you hurt the most, please."

Carrie complied. Dr. Sewall pushed down with his fingers then released the pressure quickly everywhere on her abdomen, except the right lower region. Gently, he palpated there, too, eliciting an "ouch" from his patient. Dr. Sewall arose from the bed and told the Archibalds he wanted to find out the results of the laboratory tests, but he was quite certain Carrie had appendicitis and doubted the appendix had ruptured.

When he returned a few minutes later, Drs. Stabler and Chow were beside him. Dr. Sewall said that the blood test was compatible with the diagnosis of appendicitis and explained that the safest course of action was surgical removal of the appendix. He elaborated for Carrie, explaining that the appendix was attached to a portion of the large intestine and was a "vestigial organ," which meant the organ's function became less useful as our species evolved. The appendix still probably played some role with humans, working to keep the best type of bacteria in the intestine and enhancing the immune system. Dr. Sewall followed his brief lecture with an explanation of the surgery and post-operative period. He encouraged the Archibalds to stay with Carrie until she was wheeled to the OR (operating room).

Dr. Sewall turned to Dr. Chow, "I'm going to call the OR and anesthesia." Could you call admitting and secure a bed for Carrie? Also, could you see if an orderly is available to prep Carrie for surgery." Turning to Carrie, he said, "I'm going to have them start an IV and give you some pain medication to help relieve your discomfort. Do any of you have any questions?"

Carrie asked if she could have her appendix.

"Are you kidding?" her father intervened.

Dr. Sewall smiled and replied that he had to send it to pathology first, but he was sure she could have it.

Carrie's next visitor was an orderly named Maggie. She was fortyish and cheerful with a wide smile and Southern accent. "How y'all doing? I'm Maggie, and when I'm done with my job, Carrie, you'll never forget me. I am in charge of your pre-op, my dear, and pre-op is what educated people call a euphemism. You know what that is? Well, pre-op stands for preoperative, but what it really means is a shave and a enema."

"What?" Carrie asked.

"Well, honey, I've got to shave you so's none of those hairs sneak in to contaminate your operation site."

Carrie was exasperated, "What? It took me eighteen years to grow them and you're going to shave them all off? Really?"

"Yes, Ma'am. Then I got to give you a enema. Do you know what that is? It puts water in your bottom and makes you go number two; so's you don't have to worry about your bowels after surgery. It doesn't really hurt, but it can be uncomfortable."

Carrie's eyes filled with tears. She had had to answer all kinds of sensitive questions, change into a gown, which was like wearing no clothes at all; then she had three doctors examine her, had her blood drawn, had to pee in a cup, and now this. She felt denigrated and embarrassed. Maggie understood. Going about her business after the Archibalds left the room, she entertained Carrie with funny tales related to her job. When the procedures were finished, Carrie admitted they weren't as bad as she had anticipated.

Dr. Stabler started Carrie's IV and hung a bag of fluid. A nurse added Demerol, a pain killer, to the solution, and Carrie became drowsy. The Archibalds stayed with their daughter until two orderlies arrived to wheel her up to surgery.

A little over an hour later, Dr. Sewall sat down with Professor and Mrs. Archibald to tell them Carrie was fine. She did have appendicitis, and the surgery went well. Presently, she was in the recovery room, where she would stay for a few hours. He expected her to be hospitalized for two to three days and encouraged the tired couple to go home and rest. "There are no restrictions on visiting hours at Children's Hospital. You can come whenever you want."

Professor and Mrs. Archibald expressed their gratitude and left the hospital reassured.

———— ✣ ————

CHAPTER 15

Thursday, June 22, 2006

THE BJORKMANS AROSE to prepare for another day. All bedroom windows were open, as the previous night had been cool and comfortable. When they looked outside, they saw sunshine and leaves undulating slowly in the quiet breeze. Chickadees argued, robins sang, and a muffled siren moaned in the distance.

Brenda walked to the bathroom and saw Ricky dressed in his tennis clothes.

"Hey, Ricky," his mom said, "today's Thursday. You don't have tennis."

"Coach said a lot of big kids are going to be gone today, so he invited some of us low-lifes to play in his group."

"I remember playing in his group when I was a kid," Brenda recalled.

"I know, Mom. You've told me a hundred times."

"Sorry. I am just very fond of him. That's all. I can drive you there on my way to work if you like."

"That would be great. Maybe one of the older kids can drop me off after we hit."

"Joy?" her mother called. "How are you doing?"

"I'm in the bathroom."

"I know where you are. Let's get a move on. There are still a few people who need to use the bathroom."

"No! No!" Joy yelled. "I don't like it!"

"Joy?" Brenda called. "Do you have a problem?"

"I don't want it! I want the other one!"

Brenda knocked on the bathroom door. "Joy, what is going on? Please let me in."

Joy opened the door holding her toothbrush and cried, "I don't want this—mine."

"Joy, that *is* yours," her mother explained. "That's your new toothbrush. Your old one needed replacing. That's your new one."

"No! I want mine."

"What's wrong with the new one?"

"I don't like it."

"I know you don't like it, but why don't you like it?"

"I want my red one."

"OK. OK," Brenda answered. "I'll buy you a red one today. Can you use that one for now?"

"No! I don't like it."

"It's my fault, Joy. I'm sorry I changed it and didn't ask you what color you wanted. Rinse your mouth out with water for now, and you'll have a new red one tonight."

Joy huffed and threw the toothbrush she was holding into a wastebasket. Taking the plastic cup from its holder near the medicine cabinet, she filled it and swished water around in her mouth before forcefully spitting it into the sink and exiting the bathroom.

As usual, Grandma had breakfast ready. Brenda told her Henry wasn't home. He had received an early morning call about an emergency at the Torkelsons. Something about a water leak. She asked her mother if she could keep Joy company until he returned. Ellen had nothing on her agenda and said she would be glad to.

After breakfast, Brenda drove her son to Taylor Park. When Brenda entered the parking lot, she saw Tom Carrabas near the courts. He waved and motioned for her to join him. She parked her vehicle and walked over with Ricky.

"Hi, son," Coach said to Ricky, "so glad you can join us today." Turning towards Brenda, he continued, "It would be nice to get Joy a few matches with some local kids before she goes to nationals. I wanted to ask you if there was anyone in particular you thought she might like to play."

Previously, Brenda refrained from asking any Oakbrook children to compete against Joy. No player she knew, no matter how young, would know how to handle a loss to a child with disabilities. And none had experience playing against one either. Over the years, Joy had occasion to hit with other children on the park courts, but she never had real matches. The only sets she played in Oakbrook were against Ricky and her mother. This past year she practiced singles and doubles with three women who lived in and around Milwaukee. The same foursome was preparing to represent Wisconsin at the Special Olympics USA National Games.

It was curious Tom never invited Joy to play with his summer group or encouraged her to join the younger kids who still took lessons from high school players. As compassionate as he was, he had drawn a line. Perhaps he was concerned about parents who paid for his time and would be upset if he treated one player preferentially. Or, he might be waiting until she was older, so he could supervise her interactions with others on the court like he did during Special Olympics.

Brenda told Tom she would think about an opponent for Joy and kissed Ricky goodbye. "Have fun," she said to him. She pondered Tom's suggestion as she drove to work and almost missed the left turn onto Lawn Street where Few Hours A Day Nursery was located. What confused her were flashing red lights emanating from the parking lot. Is that why they heard sirens before breakfast?

Brenda knew immediately why police cars and a Sheriff's vehicle were there. But Henry's truck, too? Brenda contemplated driving away, but what good would that do? She envisioned the next scenes playing out; her trial, dissolution of her partnership with Marie, her inability to find another job, maybe prison; the shame…it was overwhelming. The kids! Oh, my god, the kids! How would they be able to grow up in Oakbrook bearing the same shame she bore because of her father. It was history repeating itself, wasn't it.

Immobile, she sat in her car contemplating what she would say when questioned. Perhaps she shouldn't say anything until she consulted a lawyer. She wondered if the Femrites, the only attorneys in Oakbrook, would even handle her case. Brenda sank deeper in her seat and placed her head on the steering wheel.

She thought about Henry. Could there be a better husband? He stood by her when Joy was born and didn't breathe right away. Joy, who was so tiny they had to transfer her to the newborn intensive care unit where she stayed for several months. Geneticists were consulted but could not identify a syndrome. Cardiologists were brought in because of a heart murmur, which eventually disappeared. When she had her first seizure, a neurologist saw her. And, during that time, Henry brought Brenda to Madison every night after work and never complained. So many men leave their families after learning a child will have disabilities, but not Henry. He became a participant. He learned to change diapers, to feed Joy, and to allow Brenda the respite she needed. It was no wonder she loved him so much.

A tap on the window scared Brenda. She looked up and saw a young police officer she did not recognize. She pressed a button to lower her window.

"Are you Mrs. Bjorkman?" he asked. "Can you come with me, please?"

As she opened the car door, Henry ran over. "I'm so sorry, Brenda. I can't believe that happened in good old Oakbrook." Brenda was limp, and Henry supported her while explaining the daycare had been robbed. "The police think someone broke in early this morning and stole the new video equipment, cameras and all. Marie noticed the front door had been jimmied. When she went inside, she saw the utility room open and hardware gone. She called the police immediately."

Henry said he was on his way home from the Torkelsons when he noticed flashing lights and stopped. "Are you OK?" he asked with a concerned look.

No, Brenda was not OK. She was relieved the videos were stolen, but what about the people who burglarized Few Hours A Day Nursery? Would they discover video segments showing she abused Ellie? Was this nightmare ever going to end? She looked up at Henry and kissed him. "I'm so glad you're here. This whole thing is terrible. I don't know what to think any more."

Henry comforted Brenda. He hugged her, telling her not to worry. Of course, he didn't know what she was worried about. And she couldn't tell him, because she was guilty and felt acutely remorseful for what she had done. Although Brenda knew he loved her, Henry would never understand the extent of her animosity towards Sadie, probably because it was totally irrational.

"May we talk with you, Mrs. Bjorkman?" the young police officer inquired again.

Brenda thanked Henry for stopping and kissed him before following the officer into the conference room. Marie was already seated and talking to a sheriff's deputy

Brenda recognized. Marie stood up to hug Brenda; she was tearful and tremulous. She told her partner she found nothing else missing but the video cameras and recording equipment. Marie said she had not called their insurance company yet.

When her interview with law enforcement officials ended, Brenda went to her office. Some drawers were open, but the contents seemed intact. Her computer was not on her desk, however; she looked around the room for it, but it was gone. She thought about information it contained and could not recall anything damaging except personnel data and the Quicken application, which contained the daycare checking account. All notes about children were still written in longhand. Usually, she shut down her computer at day's end, but she couldn't recall whether she had on Wednesday afternoon.

Brenda listened to the turmoil of arriving children. She wasn't ready for another day at the nursery because of uncertainties in her personal life. It was extremely unlikely whoever stole the video equipment would plod through the recordings. Other than parents, who wanted to see a bunch of children eating, playing, crapping, and napping? Even if someone found the scandalous footage, Brenda felt confident they wouldn't try to extort her; if they did, she would identify them as the daycare burglars.

She left her office for the chaos of the entryway and began informing inquisitive parents about their recent robbery.

———— ⚜ ————

CHAPTER 16

Monday, July 28, 1975

Two weeks after surgery, Carrie returned to Taylor Park and received a standing ovation from Al and their students. As she approached the oak trees, her gait was almost normal. Even Sadie was cordial and asked how she was feeling. Carrie explained it would be a couple of weeks before she was able to play tennis, but she was doing better every day. She thanked the group for their cards and flowers.

Nibbling at her left foot was Rally tethered to Brenda's leash. "Welcome back," Brenda greeted Carrie.

"Brenda. Rally," Carrie responded, as she admired the pup. His transformation since the last time Carrie had seen him was amazing. He obviously weighed more, but his head was bigger—everything was bigger. "He's beautiful," she smiled. "And his coat looks so soft. Do you brush him every day?"

"Almost every day," Brenda answered. "He really likes to be brushed. At first he would bite the brush. Now he just lays down and stretches out… it's good to see you. Al told us you were coming to the park today, so I brought Rally. Would you like to hold onto him during our lesson?"

Carrie was glad to watch Rally. She took the leash from Brenda and began patting and talking to him. He was definitely calmer and wasn't biting or pulling on his leash any more. "You're a good boy," she said to Rally. "I bet you like your new home, don't you." He gazed at her with big black eyes, then licked her knee.

After Al assigned courts to the students, he blew Carrie a kiss and told her he would see her after the lesson.

Carrie thought about Al. That night she went to the hospital, he called and left a message on the answering machine. Her mom returned Al's call the following morning and explained the previous evening's events. On Thursday, four days after her appendectomy, Al visited her at home. She was in bed and drowsy from her pain pills, but she was glad to see him. He brought flowers with cards from their summer students, which he left on her bureau. He also presented her with his own bouquet of roses in a vase. She thanked him and told him to place them close to her on the nightstand, then watched expectantly as Al searched for a suitable spot. He moved the book she was reading, *Arrowsmith* by Sinclair Lewis, and discovered exactly what she hoped he would find, a fluid-filled bottle. Al stared at the immobile worm-like remnant floating inside. Without a clue, he asked what it was. When she casually told him it was her appendix, Al turned pale, almost dropping the vase on her floor. "That's what?" he asked.

"My appendix," she said proudly.

Al gasped, "I don't believe you!"

"You know, it's a pretty personal body part. I'm not going to show it to everyone," she teased. "Cool, huh?"

Al looked at her shaking his head in disbelief, "Whatever you say."

Rally ended Carrie's reverie by pulling on his leash. She stood up and walked him closer to the courts. As he squatted to relieve himself, Carrie heard Sadie talking to her partner.

"He pisses like a girl dog," she said. "I wonder if he's gay like Brenda."

Carrie restrained herself. Did her responsibilities include reprimanding students for inappropriate language and bullying? Should she fight Brenda's battles for her?

She decided not to say anything. Instead, she wandered around the courts with Rally. When she came to Brenda's court, she stopped and watched her foursome play a set. Brenda's forehand and backhand were strong as usual, and Carrie was impressed with her movement on the court, too. She was paired with one of the boys, and their opponents were another mixed doubles team. Brenda communicated well with her partner, calling "mine" or "yours" during some of the rallies. Teamwork paid off, and they won the set 6-4.

When tennis clinic ended and all the students went home, including Brenda, Al sat down on a bench beside Carrie. He asked how she was doing, and Carrie said well. She had very little discomfort. She told Al she couldn't believe how much Rally had grown and what a sweet pup he was. She was pleased Brenda was taking such good care of him.

She also related Sadie's comment to Al asking him what he thought. Like Carrie, he had witnessed girls' relationships, often wondering why there was such a disparity in the way boys and girls handled themselves. When boys were playing and became angry with one another, they might yell or swear or even fight. But fifteen minutes later, they were playing together again. It wasn't the same with girls. If they argued and were angry or just didn't like each other, it could be months or years before they resolved their differences. Sometimes the rift was permanent. Modifying his comments, Al added, "I don't mean to be sexist, but that's what I've seen. There's a difference. Don't you agree?"

Carrie did. She felt girls were much harder on themselves and on each other than boys were. She spoke about her own childhood, when companions made fun of her birthmark, making her cry by calling her "Spot" or "Dottie." She was so easily offended she started wearing long bangs to cover up her birthmark. "There are some girls I still don't talk to," she admitted. "They were nasty, but I was too sensitive. I think that's why I want to stick up for Brenda. I feel her pain, because I haven't gotten over mine." Carrie discussed her ambiguity in dealing with the problem—wanting to interfere and tell Sadie off herself versus encouraging or letting Brenda censure Sadie.

Al was sympathetic to Carrie's comments and shared his eagerness to help Brenda, too. "From the first day," he admitted, "her low self-esteem drew me in—I wanted to support her. And that day I drove her home after Sadie spilled water on her…I just felt terrible." Al added he had witnessed lots of conflicts between girls over the years, but this one seemed more vengeful. He wondered if Brenda would ever be able to stand up to Sadie.

Carrie saw some changes in Brenda; she seemed more conversant and more comfortable around the other kids. Carrie wondered if Rally was the catalyst for her transition. She certainly couldn't have a more loyal or less judgmental friend.

Al thought another explanation for Brenda's transformation was the confidence she was gaining on the tennis court. Her game had improved in the past month. When she first arrived at summer clinic, she had strong ground-strokes, but they often sailed long. Now she had much more control. Her serve was weak, but Al thought she still could win the end-of-the-year novice tournament.

Carrie mentioned Brenda's match that afternoon. "You're right," she said, "she's a lot more consistent. And you should have seen her direct her partner today. She has good court sense, better than some of the advanced players."

Carrie inquired about the other kids they were teaching, and Al told her about his recommendations to Coach Carrabas regarding Sadie and Dee Dee. "I haven't discussed their personalities with him," Al admitted. "That could be a problem. I just told him both freshmen were good candidates for the JV team."

While in the hospital, Carrie said she started to think about where to apply to college. Her parents were graduates of Eastern schools, and, like her sister, she was thinking about small colleges in New England. Her adventure as a patient had piqued her interest in medicine more, so she wanted a place with strong science departments and a good pre-med program.

Al had already applied to the U and a few smaller state schools. He was undecided about a career but was leaning toward teaching. Eau Claire had a particularly good program in education, and he was planning to visit their campus before school started. Carrie suggested he wait until fall semester began, so he could meet students and monitor some classes.

"Good idea, as usual. It's great to have you back," he said, "I know it was a short time, but I really missed you." Carrie smiled and held his hand. "It's hard to believe we're going into our senior year, isn't it? I hope they let us teach tennis together again next summer. Wouldn't that be fun?"

Carrie wondered if graduating seniors could still teach at the park and pondered how long ago the summer program had been organized and how old the tennis courts were.

Al thought tradition dated back to the late 1960s, guessing the courts were built around 1952. A city forester estimated the surrounding oaks were planted in the early 1700s...before we even became a nation. "Two hundred and fifty years of conversations here," Al said imaginatively. "And the oaks heard them all."

He explained there were more varieties of oaks in North America than anywhere else in the world. Some species were evergreens. Many didn't drop their leaves until Spring, and an oak tree in Louisiana had been alive for over fifteen hundred years. Acorns were actually fruit. Each contained one to three seeds.

"You're sounding like a teacher already, Al…so, if I go east to college, will you come out for homecoming when I invite you?" Carrie asked.

"I'd love to. That would be fun."

"Do you promise?"

"Yes, I do. I promise"

"I have six witnesses," smiled Carrie, pointing to one of the oak trees.

———— ✤ ————

CHAPTER 17

Saturday, June 24, 2006

For almost fifty years, Oakbrook tradition dictated that Saturday mornings in summer begin with matches at the Taylor Park tennis courts. Tom Carrabas had monitored those contests since 1971. Brenda remembered back to the first time she watched, when Al and Carrie played. Now, as an adult, here she was, standing in the same setting with her children.

The game of tennis had endured numerous changes over those years. Manufacturers made racquets larger and strings more versatile. Players created more velocity on their serves and groundstrokes and used different grips on their forehands and backhands. Some even ran around their backhands to hit forehands; you rarely saw anyone play that way years ago.

As Brenda and her family approached the courts, Tom, charming as usual, spotted them and jogged over. "Looks like we have almost all the Bjorkmans here today," he said. "How are you? The matches should end shortly, then we're going to practice some, Joy. OK? I take it you're here to watch your sister hit, Ricky?"

"I am," Ricky answered.

"You sure are a good brother."

"Sometimes," injected his mom.

"Mom!"

"No, you are, honey. You're a wonderful brother."

"Thank you."

"And you're a good tennis player," Tom addressed Ricky. "I'm looking forward to your playing for the high school team. You played really well when you filled in for the older kids the other day."

"Thanks, Coach."

"Tom, I should have called or emailed you," Brenda said apologetically. "I found someone to play with Joy this morning, like you suggested, and I'm sorry I didn't let you know ahead of time."

"Don't worry. That's perfect. I'm so glad you set that up. Playing a match at this point is more important than just hitting."

"Who am I playing, Mom?" Joy asked.

"Allison. You remember. I told you last night? She's the little girl I saw you hit with a couple of weeks ago."

"Both of us hit with her, Joy," Ricky reminded his sister.

"Allison?" Joy repeated.

"Right. I called her mom, and she was very gracious."

"Gracious?" Tom questioned. "She should be honored. Her daughter will be playing against a state champion. Is that the Allison who takes lessons from the high school kids?"

"Yes. Same one. Nice kid," responded Brenda.

"I've seen her play, and she has a good game. I think she is going to be a freshman at the high school," Tom recalled.

"I think that's right."

Tom inquired, "What time are they meeting you?"

"I told them to come at eleven. I thought that would give you a little time to yourself."

"Actually, that gives Joy and me a half hour to discuss strategy and maybe warm up some."

"So, we'll talk about the match?" Joy asked Tom.

"Right…and maybe hit a little bit…you and me. OK?"

"Sure."

"OK. I'll wait for my students to conclude their matches and be back for you shortly."

Tom returned to the courts. When finished, his players filed out and sat under the oak trees. Coach Carrabas joined them and relayed a few of his observations. "It's very important to talk to your partner in doubles. He or she needs to know where you are and what your expectations are. Don't be afraid to call out 'yours' or 'mine,' especially before hitting overheads. Another thing…when hitting your overheads, remember to turn to the side. I see too many of you facing the net when you hit that shot.

"Now before you leave, how does communication on the court relate to communication in life?"

"It's an important part of relationships," a girl pointed out.

"Good point. Why do you think that's the case, Elise?" encouraged Coach.

"Because, if you can't communicate with someone well, you probably don't have a good relationship with them. Right?" she asked.

"I think that's true," one of the boys agreed. "Whether it's your doubles partner or your girlfriend, you gotta be able to talk to them," he explained as the group chuckled.

"Interesting point, Barry…OK. Overall, good job today, gang. Have a nice weekend. See you Tuesday. Oh, remember, I won't be here next Saturday, because I'll be at Special Olympics in Iowa. I'll return to Oakbrook two weeks from today."

Tom's students stood up and headed for the parking lot. As a small contingent passed the Bjorkmans, one of them said something to her peers and pointed towards Joy. The others looked over, too, and one waved to her.

"They recognize you, Joy," Brenda said. "Wave back."

Tom watched the interaction as he returned to the benches, "It's nice to be noticed for your accomplishments, isn't it Joy? Pretty special…OK, so let's figure out what you're going to do this morning." Sitting down with the family, he strategized with Joy, encouraging her to draw ideas from previous matches.

Joy recalled her coach's lessons. "Hit it high to her backhand when I really need a point. Right?"

Tom nodded and complimented Joy for remembering his advice, then asked how she would make the ball go high. Joy answered she would lob it, and Tom smiled, pleased with her response. He told Joy to think about what they were working on—the approach shot. He wanted her to approach the net after hitting a lob, because most players at her level could not return a high shot to the backhand with much depth. After their discussion, Tom took Joy to Court One, where Joy practiced their game plan.

Allison arrived at the park with her mother and sat next to Brenda and Ricky just as Tom and Joy were leaving the courts. Ricky said hello to Allison shyly. Brenda thanked Mrs. Randall (please call me Cheryl) and Allison for coming.

Brenda asked Allison a few questions about herself, and Allison responded. She said she was going into her freshman year at Oakbrook and was taking advanced math, French, biology, and English. She loved school and loved to play tennis. Her father introduced her to the sport a few years ago. She hadn't played any tournaments but wanted to try out for the high school team this fall.

"Hi, I'm Tom Carrabas," Coach said to Mrs. Randall as he approached the oak trees. "Hello, Allison. I've seen you play, and you have a very nice game. I hope you're going out for our team this fall; we could use a player like you. Why don't you two head out and warm up. Then just go ahead and play a set. OK?"

When the girls left, Tom sat down with Cheryl, Brenda and Ricky to watch the girls rally. "She hits consistently," Tom said to Cheryl, referring to Allison. "Very nice. As I said, I've watched her before and also talked to the high school kids teaching her this summer. I honestly think she could play varsity tennis for us, even as a freshman."

After practicing serves, Joy and Allison began a set. Allison served first, winning the opening game. They changed sides for the second game, which went to deuce several times, before Allison won again. While Joy's ability paralleled her opponent's, she was tentative and allowed Allison too many opportunities to win points. After the set, which Allison won 6-4, both players joined the spectators. Tom complimented the pair on a nice set of tennis and asked if they wanted to play another. After drinking some water, both were eager to resume their match.

When Allison and Joy started back to play, a voice called out, "Hi Joy." Joy turned around and waved to the boy who greeted her. He waved back and sat down cross-legged close to the chain-link fence.

"Who is that?" Brenda asked Ricky.

"That's Michael."

"Who's Michael?"

"That's Joy's boyfriend."

"Her what?"

"Her boyfriend."

"Joy doesn't have a boyfriend."

"Yes, she does."

"Well, I've never seen him before, and Joy's never said anything to me about a boyfriend. Where does he go to school?"

"He's at the high school with Joy. He's in her class."

"Well, I know everyone in her class, and I don't know him."

"He's a nice kid. He moved here towards the end of school."

"Where does he live?"

"I don't know."

"Well, how did he get here?"

"Gee, Mom, I really don't know. Relax. He just wants to see her play."

"Has he been to the park with her before?"

"I've seen him a few times when Joy and I were hitting. Sometimes he comes over and talks to us."

"How come you never told me?"

"I don't know."

Michael watched the girls play, clapping after a long point.

Watching, Cheryl commented, "Looks like she has her own cheering section."

"I'm sorry, Cheryl."

"Don't apologize, Brenda. I think it's cute."

"It's good for her to have an audience," Tom noted. "She's going to face one in Iowa."

Brenda stood up, "I'm not worried about an audience. I'm worried about a boyfriend."

"She'll be fine. It happens at this age," Cheryl assured her.

"Heaven help me. I'm not ready for this."

"How old is she now?"

"Fifteen."

"Oh, a year older than Allison."

Joy played a better second set. She lobbed a few shots to Allison's backhand and followed them up with the approach shots Tom taught her. The game plan was effective, and she won 6-4. By the time Joy and Allison returned to the benches, Michael had disappeared.

Tom commended the girls, "Nice match. I thought you both played well. Allison, your strokes are very smooth, and I like the way you change from defense to offense. I really want you to come out for the tennis team this fall. And, Joy. I liked the way you lobbed and approached in the second set." Turning to Allison, Tom asked if she could play with Joy again before her tournament. Allison checked with her mother and they agreed to meet on Tuesday after work. The date and time worked for Brenda and Joy, too. Tom said he would return to the park after his high school session to supervise their match.

As everyone left for the parking lot, Cheryl pulled Brenda aside to tell her how impressed she was with Joy's game. "She is amazing; especially given the barriers she faces. You should be very proud of her."

Brenda said she was proud of Joy, but she was very impressed with Allison, too, for offering to play with her daughter.

"Why shouldn't she play with Joy," Cheryl continued. "She's great competition and good for her game."

Brenda really wasn't focused on Joy's tennis, however. She was concerned about Joy's relationship with Michael.

Upon entering the car, and before leaving the parking lot, she began to cross-examine Joy about her "boyfriend."

"He's just a boy in my class."

"Ricky said he was your boyfriend."

"I guess he is. But Ricky likes Allison."

"I do not."

Brenda looked at her daughter intently. "Never mind Ricky and Allison. What do you mean he's your boyfriend?"

"He's nice to me."

"Nice?"

"He talks to me."

"And I've seen you two holding hands during lunch," Ricky teased.

"Oh, god," Brenda choked.

"Lots of kids hold hands at lunch."

"But you…I…how did he know you were going to be here today?"

"I don't know." Joy pointed across the street. "He lives there. Sometimes he comes to the park."

"At the old Dunham farm?" her mother inquired.

"What farm?" Joy questioned.

"The old Dunham farm."

"I don't know."

"What's Michael's last name?"

"I don't know…are you mad at me?"

"No, I'm mad at me. I haven't talked to you enough about boys."

"Now you're in for it, Joy," Ricky admonished. "You're going to get the famous S-E-X talk."

"For goodness sake, Ricky," his mother retorted.

"Joy knows more than you think she does, Mom."

"I'm sure she does, and who's been teaching her?"

"Not me," Ricky denied. "She learns that stuff at school, and I don't mean in the classroom."

"You're mad at me," Joy stated.

"No, sweetheart, honest I'm not. We just need to sit down and talk. Let's go home now."

"But I didn't do anything bad. We didn't have sex."

"I'm sure you didn't, Joy, but you know what? All kids and their parents should have conversations about boys and girls."

"And sex," Ricky insisted.

"Yes, Ricky, and sex. You're right. And, by the way, I'm not entirely sure you came to watch your sister play today, wise guy."

"What do you mean?"

"I think you were watching someone else, too."

"I was not."

As they drove out of the parking lot, they saw a familiar figure plodding along the dirt road toward the old Dunham farmhouse. Joy looked away, but Ricky noticed, "There's Michael!" he announced.

Joy poked him in the ribs with her finger.

"What?" he questioned. "I just didn't want you to miss him."

"Are you teasing me?"

"Yes. That's what little brothers do. They're supposed to tease their older sisters."

"Oh, no."

"Oh, yes!"

"Do you like Michael?" Joy asked Ricky as the siblings continued their banter.

"I do. He makes jokes. He's funny."

"He's nice," Joy added.

"Yes, he is. Does he play tennis?"

"No. He doesn't know how."

"Does he play any sport?"

"He likes to bowl, but he doesn't bowl in Special Olympics."

"Does he have any brothers or sisters?"

"A sister."

"Older or younger than him?"

"Older, I think."

"Does she live at home with him?"

"I'm not sure. I think she lives with her father somewhere."

"Are her parents divorced?" Brenda interjected.

"Yes," Joy replied. "He has a stepfather that lives with him."

"I'm sure we'll see him at the park again," Ricky speculated.

"Yes, he'll come back," his sister agreed.

CHAPTER 18

＊

Monday, August 4, 1975

A SUMMER LESSON in 1975 rarely passed without Sadie making a derogatory comment to or about another player. Brenda received many of Sadie's barbs, and while she seemingly deflected them, down deep she seethed. Sadie the sadist berated her tennis, her clothing, her relationship with Al and Carrie, and even her dog. Brenda tried to avoid her, but Sadie went out of her way to stand near Brenda during every session. Accompanied by her sidekicks Rachel and Dee Dee, Sadie made life miserable for her.

"Nice zits. They're bigger than your tits, Brenda!" Sadie laughed "Ka-ka-ka-ka."

Brenda walked away dispassionately and took a drink from her water bottle. As she drank, she imagined throwing the bottle at Sadie's face and watching her cringe as it broke her perfect little nose. Boy, would that feel good! Lots of people would thank Brenda if she paid Sadie back for all the misery she caused.

What Brenda didn't understand was that Sadie was envious of her. She felt jealous of Brenda's relationship with Al and Carrie, of her improving tennis skills, of her dog, and maybe of her independence. She didn't need two sidekicks to buoy her up. Even though Brenda bore the brunt of Sadie's pejorative comments, she was still her own person.

"OK," Carrie began, "today we are going to play some doubles. Court One, Sadie and James against Brenda and Derek. Here are the balls. Good luck, guys. Court Two…."

Brenda couldn't listen to the other assignments. She was paralyzed. She had to play against her harasser, her intimidator. Why had Al and Carrie set up a match with Sadie? Surely they understood the difficulty Brenda had facing her. Did they have an ulterior motive? Were they making her confront her tormenter for a reason? Did they think she could compete with Sadie and James, too?

Derek walked towards Brenda, "Hey, partner," he said, "we can beat them. I've played against Sadie before. Her backhand is weak, and if you nail a few returns on her serve, she fades faster than a fart in a windstorm."

Brenda laughed at the metaphor and started to relax. Derek continued, "When you warm up with her, don't hit any shots to her backhand. Once we start playing, we'll pound everything there and blow her off the court."

As instructed, Brenda hit every shot to Sadie's forehand during warm-ups. Instead of keeping the ball in play, as custom dictated, Sadie tried to intimidate Brenda by belting balls at her. Brenda was unfazed and returned the shots skillfully. But Brenda did have one glaring weakness—her serve. After the foursome practiced serving, Derek told

Brenda not to worry about it. "Just get the ball in, and I'll try to distract them at the net."

The boys served the first two games; each won his service. Sadie served the third game, and both Derek and Brenda hit solid returns to her backhand, obviously shattering her confidence. After breaking Sadie's serve, it was Brenda's turn. As she started towards the baseline, she noticed Al standing by the fence smiling. He gave her a fist pump, which was all she needed.

Brenda kept her serve in play, and Derek, who was incredibly adroit at the net, picked off several returns volleying them for winners. By game four, Derek and Brenda were up 3-1. In the fifth game, with James serving, Brenda called one of Sadie's shots out. Distraught over the call, Sadie sprinted to the net to complain. Derek interrupted her and agreed with Brenda. "Sorry, Sadie, but I saw it out, too."

Sadie tried to stand her ground, but her partner interfered. "They called it out," James said. "It's their call." Sadie stomped back to her service line, clearly perturbed by Brenda's call and James's reprimand. The set ended 6-3 in favor of Derek and Brenda.

Sadie fumed and avoided shaking hands at the conclusion of the set. Derek gave Brenda a high five while praising her for her play, "You are a great partner. Nice set."

Al watched the foursome finish and gave Brenda a thumbs up. She mouthed a "thanks" back to him.

Brenda couldn't wait for her mother to come home from work to tell her she beat Sadie Winetraub and her partner in a doubles match. She told her about the line call and Sadie's tantrum, too. Brenda wanted to continue to work hard on her game. Being a better player would make her part of a team and provide her with a new circle of friends. Best of all, it would piss Sadie off.

Since she had her mother's attention, she asked about seeing a dermatologist for her acne. Kids made fun of her. Well, Sadie and her clique made fun of her. When Mrs. Nelson suggested consulting Mr. Winetraub at the pharmacy, Brenda had a fit. "What? Ask Sadie's father? No, I'm not doing that. We've tried the nonprescription junk and it doesn't work, Mom. I want to see a dermatologist. Please."

Just as Mrs. Nelson agreed to Brenda's request, a large puppy came bounding into the house pulling John behind him. It was difficult to discern who was breathing harder. Rally ran up to Brenda with his plume-tail waving and gave her a big lick. She leaned over and kissed him back.

"Did you miss me?" she asked. When he started to jump up on her, she made him get down and complimented him, "Good boy, Rally. You're a good boy." Turning to John, she asked, "Where did you take him?"

John said they went as far as the post office. They met a few people walking dogs along the way, and Rally was great with most of them. One dog, the Kiley's German Shepard, wanted to wrestle with Rally, John recounted. The dog repeatedly wrapped his paws around the pup and hugged his backside. John couldn't understand why Rally didn't appreciate the overture and wiggled with difficulty to get away. Raising both eyebrows, Mrs. Nelson looked at Brenda, who covered her mouth but said nothing.

As the conversation ended, Rally growled, woofed, then ran to the front of the house. A knock interrupted his barking momentarily, but it soon resumed with a vengeance. Mrs. Nelson tried to quiet him as she opened the front door.

"Hi, Ellen," a man said. Rally sniffed him and stopped barking. "Wow," he called out looking at the puppy.

Mrs. Nelson told the visitor to wait outside, as she closed the door to talk to her children. John wanted to know who was there. His mother said she would explain shortly, but she needed a few minutes alone with the caller first. When Brenda questioned her, she answered cryptically, then returned to her guest.

"Hi, Ralph. Um…"

"I know. You're going to ask what I'm doing here. Right?"

"Well?"

"When we spoke last, you said I could see you and the kids, so I decided to take you up on your offer."

"Do you think you should have called first?"

"Yes, I should have, but I was afraid you would change your mind and not allow me to see all of you."

"I think you still should have called."

"You're right. I don't know if I could have taken the rejection if you refused, though."

"If you had asked, I would have told you it was OK."

"Sorry. I know you may not understand, but I was so nervous about coming. What if they don't like me, especially with everything I've done? What did you tell them about me?"

"You know what, Ralph, I just told Brenda the truth. I said you were in prison, that you had a drinking problem. But I also told her that you had changed and wanted to see them. So, tell me, how come you're here on a Monday? Don't you have to work?"

"I'm on my own. I do odd jobs, like fix things or do some painting. I didn't have any work today or tomorrow, so I decided I would come down to Oakbrook."

"How long are you here for?"

"I planned on going back home tomorrow. I thought I'd stay at the Inn tonight."

"OK."

"What do you want to tell the kids?" he asked.

"The truth."

"And you've already told Brenda?"

"Yes, but I haven't really talked to John about you."

"Oh."

"Do you think you're ready?"

Ralph paused. "I think so," he finally said.

"Let's go in, then."

When Ellen and Ralph entered the house, they found their children on the floor of the living room playing with the puppy. As soon as Rally saw Ellen, he jumped up and stood by her in guard dog mode. John, without waiting for an introduction, blurted out, "You're our father, aren't you!"

Their mother sat the children down to repeat the story she had already told Brenda. Ellen discussed Ralph's drinking, anger, the divorce, and his time in prison. Over the years, she explained, their dad had received help, and while he would always be an alcoholic, he hadn't drunk any liquor for over a year. He lived up north and worked as a handyman, helping repair people's homes and businesses. Now that he was feeling better, he wanted to see his children.

Brenda and John looked at their father, and Ralph confirmed everything their mother said. Next, he apologized, especially to Ellen, for drinking and for all the problems his drunkenness had caused.

Both children had questions, and their father fielded them as best he could. He served eighteen months in a penitentiary in Waupun. He lived in a cell with one other inmate who robbed a store. The experience was extremely unpleasant. No, he did not use a gun during the robbery and has never owned one. What did he do? He broke into a house, stole property—jewelry, a couple of TVs and some money. He began drinking when he was a teenager—about Brenda's age. Alcoholism runs in the family; both his father and grandfather were addicted to alcohol. Yes, occasionally he tried other drugs—mostly pot, but he hasn't used anything for thirteen months. He's been going to Alcoholics Anonymous meetings weekly for over one year. He lives in Eagle River in a cabin. He thinks about his children all the time and wishes he had spent more time with them. He speaks to Ellen a couple of times a month, and she tells him what's going on at home.

Brenda leveled her concerns at him; who in Oakbrook knows about his problems? Her father wasn't sure, but certainly some people in the community were aware of what he had done. Brenda hung her head, and her father apologized again.

Ellen came to Ralph's defense, telling Brenda and John, too, that every family had secrets—situations they tried to hide from the rest of society. Brenda was angry and said that no one had worse secrets than her family, and they weren't even secrets. Some people in Oakbrook actually knew what her father had done.

Ralph said when he was at Waupun, he met a lot of inmates who had done far worse things. There were rapists and murderers and child molesters. Some inmates were serving sentences greater than twenty years.

"I don't give a damn about them, and I don't give a damn about you either," Brenda said to her father. "All you've done is make my life more complicated than it already is. I'm sorry you came back. I wish you had stayed up in Eagle Glen or Eagle River or wherever you live and let us alone." Tears streaming down her face, Brenda ran upstairs to her room.

Ralph was glum and asked Ellen if she thought he should leave. She encouraged him to stay. "It may take Brenda awhile to build a relationship with you. She's almost a teenager and can be really emotional, but she's a good kid. Let's give her a chance."

Ralph replied, "I sure hope she gives me a chance, too."

CHAPTER 19

Saturday, August 9, 1975, with the Nelsons

"WHERE ARE YOU and Rally going, Brenda?" her mother asked.

Brenda said she wanted to walk Rally to the park. A few older kids had matches, and she hoped to watch Al and Carrie play. She also wanted to give Rally a good run. Mrs. Nelson offered to drive them to and from Taylor Park. Brenda accepted. During the ride, Brenda's mother reminded her that Ralph was coming to town and wanted to take them out to dinner that evening. When Brenda didn't respond, Mrs. Nelson encouraged her to reestablish a relationship with her father.

Arriving at the park, Brenda thanked her mother for driving and hopped out of their car with Rally. Without a leash to restrain him, he bounded around the parking lot before taking off for Pierce Lake. Brenda was unconcerned; no eagle could carry him off now. Rally waded into the water to chase minnows. His big furry paws slapped and splashed the surface, but he could not catch them. Eventually, tired, he retreated to Brenda, showering her with water as he shook vigorously to dry off. "Rally," she chided him, "cut it out! You're soaking me." The big pup shuddered again, then rolled on the grassy shore. Brenda put on his leash and led him towards the tennis courts.

Coach Carrabas had divided his players into male and female foursomes. Brenda brought Rally under the oak trees, close to Court One, where Carrie and three other varsity players were competing. Although only four weeks had passed since Carrie's surgery, she was playing like nothing had happened. Effortlessly, she hit shot upon shot deep and hard. Brenda was mesmerized.

Al was playing with his partner on Court Three. Brenda compared the two courts and marveled at how much better girls' returns of serve were compared to boys'; maybe because boys served harder. But, even in mixed doubles, Brenda thought girls' returns were more effective and more reliable. Brenda caught Al's eye and he waved to her as he changed sides of the court.

"Who is that big moose beside you?" he yelled. "Has he ever grown. He's going to be huge!"

"He eats us out of house and home," Brenda replied.

Coach Carrabas wandered over to introduce himself to Brenda and to admire the puppy. "Hi, I'm Coach Carrabas."

"Hi. Yes. It's nice to really meet you. I'm Brenda Nelson."

"Yes, I know. It's nice to meet you, too…and this is the famous Rally, I take it."

"Ya."

"I've certainly heard a lot about him. He's beautiful!"

"He's a good boy."

"So, Al and Carrie said you are an up-and-coming player. They think you will do very well in the season-ending novice tournament. You're going into eighth grade, right?"

"No, seventh."

"Ah. Well, you keep up the good work. By the time you reach high school, you should be playing some pretty darn good tennis."

"Thank you. Carrie and Al have really been great teachers."

"Yes, they are excellent instructors. Super kids, too."

"Are they going to be able to teach next summer?"

"We haven't decided that yet. I'm not sure they know what they're going to do next summer. We'll have to see. Good luck in the tournament. I'm looking forward to watching you play, Brenda."

"Thank you. Bye."

Rally had seen enough tennis. He wanted to run to the lake again and pulled Brenda in that direction. She unhinged his leash to let him go. Bounding playfully, he ran into the water to resume his fishing expedition. Brenda sat close by watching him wade up to his neck, then duck his head to nip at minnows. Eventually, he sprung out of the lake and lay down beside her.

After an hour or so, her mother came back to Taylor Park to retrieve them. Returning to the car, Brenda opened the rear door and entered with her dog. Ellen announced that Ralph had come early. She hoped they would have a better visit than their last one. Brenda acknowledged her mother's comment with a brief nod, and they drove home silently.

Ralph greeted his daughter when she arrived home and petted Rally somewhat cautiously. He had never had dogs and was uncertain how to show them affection. He really didn't know how to show affection to his daughter or son either. A general uneasiness permeated the house as the adults discussed plans for the evening. Ralph wanted to take his family out to dinner and intended to stay at the Inn again before returning to Eagle River the following morning. He asked Brenda and John where they wanted to eat, and John suggested the A&W. Ellen recommended the Pub, which, under new management, had an excellent reputation. Ralph liked Ellen's proposal but wondered if they needed reservations; Ellen said she didn't think so.

As noon approached, Ellen wondered if Ralph and the kids wanted a picnic lunch. They could go to the other side of the lake, eat, and rent a boat for a couple of hours before returning home. While neither child was especially enthusiastic, Ellen launched her plan and began preparing sandwiches. Ralph sat uncomfortably on the couch in the living room watching Brenda and John playing with Rally.

"I could use a little help in here," Ellen called.

Brenda joined her in the kitchen. "Do I have to go, Mom? I really don't want to."

"I think you should… could you wrap these sand-wiches for me, please?"

"Sure, should I use Saran Wrap?"

"You can use Baggies."

"He doesn't really talk to us."

"He feels uncomfortable. He's not used to being around kids, plus he knows you aren't really excited to see him… let's bring some Coke from the fridge."

"I'm not excited to see him."

"Maybe if you tried to start a conversation with him, he would be more responsive," her mother suggested.

"I wouldn't know what to talk about. I don't really know him or know what he's interested in…should I get pickles, too?"

"Thanks, that would be great… well, I know he likes sports. Why don't you tell him about your tennis?"

"Does he even know how to play?"

"I don't think he's ever played a match, but we used to hit a little when we first met. I bet he reads about tennis. He's actually a very smart man, Brenda. He reads a lot… what would you like for dessert?"

"Fruit is fine. Are there apples in the fridge?"

"Yes."

"He's obviously had lots of time to read," Brenda said sarcastically.

"That's not fair. He read a lot before he went to prison. I was always bringing him home books from the library. Good books, too. Steinbeck and Hemingway and other famous authors. He always read a lot of sports, too. He used to have a subscription to *Sports Illustrated*…it's tough for him to try and join a family of three that has lived together for a lot of years without him."

"Well, it's tough growing up without a father, too."

"Yes, it is."

"Can Rally come with us?"

"Why don't we leave him home. He's never been in a boat, and I don't know how he would react. Besides, he had a good romp this morning, didn't he?"

The family, such as it was, enjoyed lunch by the lake, but John could barely sit still long enough to finish his apple before roaming the shoreline impatiently. Brenda asked her father if he followed professional tennis. He said he did. He threw out names like Borg, Vilas, and Nastase, then talked about the Wimbledon final and how Connors never should have lost to Ashe.

"What do you mean?" Brenda asked.

"Connors should have whipped him. He's a better player."

"Not that day, he wasn't."

"Those two aren't even in the same league. Ashe isn't good enough to polish Connors's shoes."

"Why is that?"

"They're just not the same."

"Not the same? What do you mean?"

"Connors learned the classical way. Ashe—I don't know. He was from a ghetto."

"So what?"

"There's just a difference."

"You're prejudiced."

"Maybe."

"That's really sad."

"Just wait until you go out in the real world. You'll see—there's a difference."

"Wow! You're something else."

"Way I was brought up."

"Well, it's never too late to change."

"Perhaps."

"What about women players? Do you follow them?"

"Not really. Most don't hit the ball hard enough. I don't like watching them on TV. I like to see the ball hit, not tapped."

"Some of the all-time greats are competing now, and they can really hit—like Billie Jean King."

"You mean Billie Jean Queen, don't you?"

"OK. I think that's enough," Ellen intervened. "Why don't we see if we can rent a boat…John…John! Come on! We're going down to the dock," she called.

They leased a small motor boat and cruised around the periphery of Pierce Lake looking at beautiful homes facing the best vistas in Oakbrook. They also passed the cemetery on the hill. Ralph steered as Ellen named past and present owners of every residence they surveyed. "That's where the Christiansens live," she pointed, "in the old Marchant house." Then turning to Ralph she continued, "They own the hardware store on Main Street."

John asked if he could drive and lurched toward the stern. "Be careful, John," Brenda warned, as her brother tripped over her foot, nearly falling into the water. "Take it easy."

Ralph showed John how to operate the throttle and how to steer. "No, John, you turn the handle left if you want to go right," he admonished. "That's better. Don't lean on the motor, otherwise the propeller comes out of the water— here, let me have it. You've driven it enough for now." John returned to his original seat and began to cry. "Come on," his father barked, "you're a man, and men don't cry."

Dinner at the Pub really didn't go much better than lunch by Pierce Lake. Instead of tennis, politics was the main course for the evening meal. Ralph was still upset over Nixon's resignation and worried that President Ford wasn't strong enough to run the country. He despised the North Vietnamese for overrunning Saigon in April and felt the United States had pulled out of Vietnam too early because of those radical peaceniks in Madison. "They're too young and stupid to understand the real world. And all of those professors just put more and more liberal ideas into their empty heads."

Ellen, Brenda, and John ate their meals quietly, listening half-heartedly to Ralph's ranting.

❦

CHAPTER 20

Saturday, August 9, 1975, with Al and Carrie

Saturday morning was perfect for summer tennis at Taylor Park. Coach Carrabas had scheduled two doubles matches, placing Al and Carrie on separate courts. Once their contests ended, Coach counseled his eight students. "Let's talk about serves," he began. "What do you think is the most important feature of a serve in doubles?"

Someone answered, "placement."

Another player said, "velocity."

"Interesting thoughts," Tom replied. "I think consistency is critical, too. More than anything, you want to get your first serve in. You should average between seventy-five to eighty percent of first serves in during every doubles match. Once you miss that first serve, you allow your opponents to move into the court to receive your weaker second serve. I agree placement is very important, too. If I had to choose between velocity and accuracy, I would choose the latter. Most players have a weaker side, usually it's the backhand, and that's where you want to serve them. However, if your partner is a mobile net player and good at poaching, you want to consider hitting serves into your opponent's body or down the "T," decreasing the chance of a wide angle return. Body serves also increase your partner's chances of being involved in the point...any other thoughts or questions?"

Carrie asked, "What do you do when you or your partner has a weak serve?"

Coach responded, "Excellent question. I have several suggestions. Again, get that first serve in—no matter what—especially if your first serve is weak, because your second serve will be even weaker. Second, net players should vary their positions, sometimes playing at net and sometimes playing back at the baseline. Third, think about playing the "I" formation, where the net player stands near the middle of the net and gives the server a signal telling her what side of the court she is going to cover. The "I" formation often confuses returners, because they don't know where the net person is going to be...is that helpful?"

Carrie nodded, "Thank you."

"Any suggestions on second serves, Coach?" a boy asked.

"I almost always try to serve into the body on a second serve—again, to decrease angles on the return. Having the net person throw in an occasional head fake—even a poach, doesn't hurt either...other questions or thoughts?" Nobody seemed to have anything else to add. "OK," Coach continued, "anyone want to throw out an aphorism related to our discussion about serves?"

One player questioned, "An aphorism?"

"Yes, an adage—a saying."

"Oh, like 'variety is the spice of life?'" suggested Al.

"Perfect," Coach replied. "Very good."

"How about 'there's more than one way to skin a cat?'" proposed another student.

"That fits, too. It's very important to examine different approaches to problems. When serving in tennis, that means trying to vary speeds and locations of the ball and positioning of the net player. In life it may mean studying a situation from different vantage points. Exploring different options…OK? Well, have a great weekend. I'll see you on Tuesday."

After Coach Carrabas finished, Al and Carrie sat down on the benches to talk. When Carrie asked Al how he played, Al said he won 6-1, 6-4 and felt like he was hitting the ball well. Carrie split sets with her opponents, but considering her recent appendectomy, she was happy with her game, too. She could feel some tugging where they performed the surgery and thought perhaps her belly muscles were still healing. Both mentioned seeing Brenda with the pup and marveled at Rally's size and Brenda's deportment. She seemed so much more relaxed, especially when Sadie wasn't around.

The teens had made plans a few nights before to go to Madison that evening and hang out at the union by Lake Mendota. A band was supposed to perform, and they asked another couple from school to join them. Al told Carrie that Dave was driving and they would pick her up around 5:30. They kissed goodbye and left the park in separate vehicles.

Al returned home with the family truck in time for lunch. Living out in the country was peaceful, but Al felt isolated from his friends until he got his driver's license two years ago. His parents were very accommodating with their two vehicles, and Al reciprocated by chauffeuring his seven-year-old brother Sharky whenever he could.

Al's mother worked in the front office of the Chevrolet showroom and was in charge of all the paperwork associated with purchasing cars. Darlene grew up in Oakbrook and graduated from the high school. She spent two semesters at Whitewater before leaving college for her present job. In 1952, she met her husband when he purchased a used car from the dealership. They dated for a couple of years and married in 1954.

Al's father worked as a sales clerk for a jewelry shop in Oakbrook. He grew up in northern Wisconsin and left after graduating from high school. During the Korean War, Karl was in the army, but he never talked about his experiences in Southeast Asia. He returned to the states after his tour of duty and had several different jobs before meeting Darlene and securing a position at Kuehn Jewelry.

Al was born in Madison two years after his parents married. A few hours after Al's birth, Darlene hemorrhaged and required emergency surgery. Her doctors told her she would never be able to bear children again. The couple considered adoption but never pursued the idea seriously until Karl's sister in Kenosha had a son she was unable to care for. Karl and Darlene gladly accepted three-month-old Sam into their household, and despite the ten-year age gap, Al welcomed him with open arms, too.

When Sam was a toddler, he discovered a deck of cards and confiscated them. He sat for hours piling then spilling them all over the floor of the living room. Sam's fascination with playing cards led to his nickname "Sharky."

A happy and affectionate child, Sharky adored his older sibling and followed Al wherever he went. As Al parked the truck, Sharky burst out the front door of the house to greet him.

"Hey, big guy, what's up?" Al asked.

"Can I help you mow the lawn after lunch?"

"Did you ask Mom and Dad?"

"Not yet."

As Karl came out of the house to greet Al, he asked, "How did it go today?"

"Pretty good, Dad. I felt like I played well. We won both our sets."

"That's great. Your little brother has been waiting patiently for you to come home."

"He's my best bud," Al said walking over to Sharky and giving him a hug.

"Can I help Al cut the grass, Dad?"

"Do you think you're big enough to handle a riding mower?"

"I can do it."

"How about you and Al sit together and do it?"

"OK."

"Fine with me," Al agreed.

"Do you two want to get a head start? Mom's gone to town for a few things. She should be back soon. We'll have lunch after she returns."

"That works. C'mon with me, Sharky. We'll start the lawn."

As Al and Sharky walked to the shed that housed the lawn mower, Al began to think ahead to next year. He was going to miss the little boy holding his hand. Al promised himself he would call Sharky regularly when he went off to college.

Al sat down on the riding mower, and Sharky hopped up in his lap. Before letting his little brother take the wheel, Al steered the machine out of the shed. Together they began to cut the grass behind the shed, and as they moved closer to the house, they noticed their mother driving up in her car. "Mom's home," Al said. "Let's finish this later. I'll race you back to the house!" Al stopped the mower and the two boys jumped down and ran to the front steps to greet their mother.

After the family completed lunch, Al and Sharky went back outside to continue mowing. It was almost 4:30 when they finished, so Al ran upstairs quickly to shower. When he undressed and turned on the water, Al felt a pang of anxiety and wondered if Carrie was looking forward to

their date as much as he was. He shampooed his hair trying to imagine her showering, too. Was she thinking about
him the same way he was thinking about her? Al turned
the water off, dried himself, and dressed casually.

Dave arrived at the Andersen house a little after five.

"Have fun, but be careful down there," Mr. Andersen
admonished his son, as he got into Dave's car. "See you later."

The sky was partially cloudy as the boys headed into
downtown Oakbrook. A pleasant breeze blew through
their open windows, and Al and Dave were looking forward to a fun evening. Carrie and Sherri lived only a couple
of streets apart, so by 5:30 all four teenagers were on their
way to Madison.

They passed the Triangle Inn, its parking lot already
crowded with cars and trucks and continued on routes 12
and 18 west, past pristine cornfields with fluttering tassels.
On the left, farmers in straw hats topped their tobacco plants.

"I worked in those fields a few years ago," Sherri admitted. "It's the hardest job I ever had. Everything is done by
hand. You plant tobacco, top it, and harvest it all by hand.
I barely lasted two weeks there."

"I've heard other people say the same thing," replied
Dave.

Al leaned forward in his seat, "You'd think with all the
farm machinery developed that someone would come up
with an easier way of doing things."

Sherri said, "As far as I know, nothing has changed in
tobacco farming since it began."

"So, what do they make from the crop? Cigarettes, cigars?" asked Carrie.

Al replied, "No, the tobacco grown in Wisconsin is used for cigar wrappers only."

Dave slowed the car down a little, "Really? I didn't know that."

"The finer tobaccos, which are used in cigarettes and cigars, are grown in the South. North Carolina is one of the biggest tobacco states," Al added.

Entering Madison, they drove by Copps Department Store on the right and passed Stoughton Road then Monona Drive by the Yahara River. They took the John Nolan exit near the coliseum to the University and parked in the Lake Street ramp. Wandering up State Street, they entered Ella's Deli for hot pastrami sandwiches and pop.

After supper, they ambled down State Street to Memorial Union, by The Tobacco Bar and several clothing shops and restaurants. The boys wore T-shirts, Al's emblazoned with the University of Wisconsin and Dave's with Oakbrook Football. All four wore shorts. The girls had pastel-colored sleeveless blouses with matching ribbons around their pony tails. Hand-in-hand, the couples intermingled with college students, enjoying their independence.

They reached the union just after seven, bought four Cokes, and found a table on the terrace. The sun had not set, and Lake Mendota was relatively calm with sailboats and motorboats crisscrossing it effortlessly. Music penetrated speakers by the building, but a band wasn't present.

"So, you've been kinda quiet, Carrie. What's up?" Al asked his girlfriend.

"Oh, just thinking—my dad got a job offer from a small college in Iowa and he may take it. They want him to be chairman of the Archeology Department."

"Wow! That's great!" Sherri said.

"Yes and no. It's great he got the offer, but it means that instead of returning here for vacations from college, I'll have to go to Iowa."

"You can still come here, too," Al suggested. "You can always stay at my house."

Dave smirked, "Now, that sounds like a plan."

"Why don't you go to school here?" Sherri asked.

"I don't know. I always thought it would be fun to study in a different part of the country. My grandparents are on the East Coast, so I'm looking at schools out there."

Sherri pushed her chair back to stretch her legs, "I received some brochures from a few schools in New England, and they all seemed pretty awesome. I don't know if I have the courage to go away to school, though, or money, for that matter."

"I'm going to look at some state schools. I thought I wanted to play football, but I'm not so sure any more. I'd like something smaller than the U. It's beautiful here, but it's so big," Dave said.

"Ya, I'm looking at some state schools, too. I'd love to do what Coach Carrabas does—teach and coach high school kids," confessed Al as he sipped his drink.

"You'd be good at that, Al," Sherri complimented.

"Thanks."

"He would," Carrie agreed, looking over at Al. "He gives me lectures all the time about things I don't know about."

"Oh, really. Tell us more," Dave responded.

"I don't mean that kind of lecture, Dave. He's really amazingly knowledgeable about lots of different subjects—like trees for example. Who else but Al would research the variety and longevity of oaks?"

"I bet whatshisname—you know, that kid with one eye that turns out? He would know stuff like that," Dave suggested.

"Barry?"

"Brian. That's his name. Brian," Dave finally remembered.

Sherri laughed, "You mean the one who used to go out with Twinkle Toes."

Al asked, "Twinkle Toes? Who's that?"

"You know. She's a sophomore. Always stands up on her toes when she talks to you," Sherri explained.

Dave added, "That's because she's so short."

Sherri pushed her chair back in, "I heard she used a cushion during driver's ed."

"Twinkle Toes. I never heard that before," Carrie laughed looking out at the lake.

"Well, they make a perfect couple. When they dance, her nose gets stuck in his belt buckle," Sherri joked.

"I'd like to see that," said Dave.

Sherri smiled, "I'd rather not."

Dave rubbed the side of his glass, "So, Al, do you ever hear from Jeff?"

"Landis?"

"Ya."

"He called me when he returned home from college. Loves Minnesota. You went out with him a few times, didn't you Sherri?" Al asked.

"Yup. He's a nice guy. Smart."

"He is. Wants to be a lawyer like his father."

Carrie stirred the ice cubes in her glass, "I didn't know his father was a lawyer."

"His parents are divorced. His dad lives in Chicago and is a big-time attorney there," Al told her.

Sherri asked, "Is he still seeing Stacy?"

"Last I heard he was, but I think they're both dating other people, too. Guess that happens sometimes when you go off to college," Al said, gazing down at the boats.

Carrie gripped Al's hand reassuringly, and he squeezed hers back. College, their relationship and separation was on both their minds. Despite the short time they had been dating, their bond had become tight. They thought about each other a lot, and no day was complete without a kiss or at least a phone call.

As darkness settled over the lake, a band came out to entertain the crowd. They were loud, and the music wasn't exactly what the teens expected. Dave suggested they take a drive; he had a way to make the evening perfect. "None of you guys are eighteen, yet, are you?"

They all shook their heads. As they squeezed into his car, Dave pulled out his wallet and showed them the driver's license he acquired from a senior several years ago.

"That's Phil Dunham's license. How did you get that?" Al questioned.

"He gave it to me when he had to renew his. It's worked in the past."

Sherri turned her head, "There's a liquor store on University Ave. Let's grab some beers and go up on the hill near that dorm on the lake."

"That's funny! Al and I were just at the Dunham farm," Carrie stated. "We found a puppy who belonged to Mr. Dunham, and he let one of our tennis players keep him."

Dave made his purchase and brought a six pack back to the car. He drove close to the observatory that overlooked Lake Mendota, parked, and passed a couple of open cans back to Al. Carrie was inexperienced; she had had wine at home before, but she had never partied with friends who drank alcohol. Al neither encouraged nor discouraged her. She took a can from him and sipped it slowly. Thinking about next year, with all the hurdles she and Al would face, provided her with an excuse to experiment. While she didn't particularly like the taste, lightheadedness was pleasant.

Dave and Sherri moved closer together in the front seat and kissed. They wrapped their arms around each other, but the embrace seemed awkward.

"Uh, uh," Sherri warned.

"It's OK," Dave insisted, kissing her.

After a few minutes, Sherri admonished him again, "No, Dave. I don't want to."

"OK. OK. Let's listen to some music," he said, turning on the radio. When he tried to put his arm around her once more, Sherri pulled away.

"All righty. Jeez. I give up.," he said, picking up his beer and taking a long swig.

Half an hour later, Dave suggested going back to State Street. It was still early and would be fun to be where all the action was.

Dave drove back to the Lake Street ramp, where they left the car, and walked up State Street again. They stopped where a group of students had formed a circle around a bearded man playing a guitar. He sang vintage Joan Baez, *The Night They Drove Old Dixie Down*, *Love Is Just a Four-Letter Word*, and *We Shall Overcome*.

Dave was a little tipsy, and moving backward to regain his balance, he stepped on a student's foot. Her boyfriend let him have it.

"What in hell's the matter with you?"

"Sorry, man. I stumbled."

"You stumbled, did you?"

"Ya. Sorry," Dave repeated.

"Well don't apologize to me assface, apologize to her."

"I'm sorry," Dave said to the girl.

"How old are you anyway? Twelve?" her boyfriend asked.

"No."

"What's on your shirt? Oakbrook? What are you a high schooler? Isn't it past your bedtime?"

"Look…I was just…"

"I don't give a damn. You stepped on her foot, you jerk."

"It's OK, Brad. I'm OK," his girlfriend maintained.

Pushing Dave in the chest, Brad insisted, "It's not OK. This punk needs to learn a lesson."

"And I suppose you're the one that's going to teach me, huh tough guy?" Dave taunted.

"Do you want to see what it feels like high school boy?"

Before Dave could react, Brad stomped hard on his left foot, which was unprotected in an open sandal. Dave grunted, fell to the ground, and grabbed his toes. He writhed in pain on the sidewalk. When he tried to stand up, he was unable to bear weight on his injured foot. Al caught him by the arm and escorted him away from the crowd.

"Hey, let's call it a night, Dave. C'mon, time to go," Al insisted.

Dave was furious and yelled at Brad, "I'm going to beat the crap out of you!"

"Not tonight, buddy. Let's go home," Al directed.

Al supported Dave as he limped down State Street. When they arrived at the car, Al made Dave give him his keys and get in the back seat with Sherri. Not much was said as they rode back to Oakbrook. After he dropped the girls off at their homes, Al made Dave stay at his house for the rest of the night.

Sunday morning, after breakfast with the Andersens, Dave drove home. When he hopped out of the car, his father asked him what happened. Dave said he tripped on a curb on State Street, but his father didn't believe him. Later that morning, when Dave's father entered the car, he smelled alcohol. On the floor of the backseat were a few crumpled beer cans. After he confronted his son and learned the real story, he felt compelled to tell Al's, Carrie's, and Sherri's parents, too.

CHAPTER 21

— ✣ —

Tuesday, June 27, 2006

FEW HOURS A Day Nursery continued its usual schedule after the burglary. Brenda purchased a new computer and updated their checking account. Billy Williams, along with his crew positioned new cameras where old ones had been. All doors and windows had new locks. The video company also installed a surveillance system for better security. A claims adjuster promised to reimburse Few Hours A Day for damages to the door and replacement of the computer. Since the nursery had not finalized purchases of video equipment, Williams's insurance company was still responsible for that.

When families arrived Tuesday morning, parents were given packets with information on how to access their youngsters' rooms and playground by using appropriate URLs on their computers. Release forms, allowing children to be videoed were included in the handouts. Test runs of new equipment (complete with wide-angle lenses) had provided excellent images, and all the parents were excited about seeing their children at the nursery whenever they wished.

When Sadie dropped Ellie off, she complimented Brenda for initiating the video system and asked how Joy's training was progressing. "Everyone in town is talking about her," Sadie said, "and wishing her good luck in Iowa." Sadie asked if the draws were out yet, and Brenda explained that there are multiple draw sheets for players at different levels. Besides, all tennis players are rerated prior to every tournament, so draw sheets are composed after athletes are on-site. Since the *Oakbrook Current* ran its story on Joy the previous week, other mothers also asked Brenda about her daughter.

"Let's put it this way," Brenda said to them, "I'm a lot more nervous than Joy is. Tom Carrabas is coaching her, and he is as cool as a cucumber. I think Ricky and I are having the most difficulty sleeping at night. Henry and grandma seem to be doing just fine."

During the first rest period, an assistant informed Brenda the police station called wanting to speak with her. They said it was not urgent. Brenda's heart began to pound, and she felt sweat under her arms. She asked her assistant to monitor her room while she returned the call. First, however, she needed to go to the bathroom.

Brenda knew the police chief, Charlie Wasson—well, everyone in Oakbrook knew Charlie. When she called the station, she asked to speak directly with him. Fully informed about the theft at her nursery, Chief Wasson explained that a series of similar burglaries had occurred in the county during the past month. Thanks to an anonymous tip, the sheriff had recovered a number of electronic devices similar to those reported stolen. Chief Wasson wondered if any belonged to Few Hours A Day Nursery. Brenda hoped to examine the recovered property before Charlie discovered the video equipment still belonged to Billy Williams. Chief Wasson explained where the confiscated items were, and Brenda offered to look at them later that day.

After the nursery emptied, Brenda drove fifteen minutes north of town to a warehouse Jefferson county rented. Inside were scores of electronic devices including computers, video cameras, TVs, camcorders, and DVDs. She was overwhelmed by the assortment and uncertain which appliances belonged to their nursery until she saw the computers. She recognized her laptop immediately because of the dent on top. She opened it, turned it on, and entered her password, which confirmed it was hers. Concerned, she went back to the video equipment and looked again. When a clerk asked her what brand she was trying to find, she didn't know. Maybe the installer could help, the clerk suggested. Maybe.

Brenda took her computer and left the warehouse for home. She needed to pick up Joy, because they were supposed to meet Tom and Allison at the park. Brenda was concerned about the video equipment. If her computer was there, stolen surveillance equipment was probably at the warehouse, too. She continued to worry that her episode with Ellie had been recorded and agonized again over possible repercussions.

She picked Joy up and drove her to Taylor Park. Tom, Allison, and Allison's mother, Cheryl were already there.

"Am I late?" Brenda asked

Cheryl stood up, "Right on time."

"Sorry, busy day at the nursery."

"No problem," Tom said. Then turning to Joy and Allison, he suggested, "Why don't you two go out and warm up. I'll be right over."

"You look tired," Cheryl told Brenda.

"I am."

"Hang in there," Tom advised. "The torches were lit today in multiple cities in Iowa. They will all be carried to Ames for the ceremony on Sunday night. We're almost there, Brenda."

"Yes, we are."

"I'm going to go closer to the courts and watch the kids warm up. Maybe give them some advice," Tom announced.

"He's a great guy, isn't he?" Cheryl commented after Tom left.

"Yes, he is."

"And so good with kids."

"I agree."

"Is he from here?"

"Yes, he grew up in Oakbrook—played high school tennis here. He's an accomplished athlete in his own right and still plays tournaments."

"So, Brenda, as I said last time, I am so impressed with Joy."

"Thank you. She is pretty amazing."

"Would you take offense if I asked you to tell me more about her?"

"Not at all. I take it you mean why she has her disabilities?"

"Yes, but I don't mean to pry."

"Well, Joy was born prematurely, but her birth weight was quite a bit less than doctors expected for a thirty-week preemie. They told me her placenta was small and didn't provide all the nourishment she needed to grow properly when she was inside me. From her appearance at birth, they thought maybe she had some sort of syndrome, but geneticists really couldn't label her with anything specific. She didn't breathe spontaneously at birth, either, decreasing the oxygen supply to her brain, and probably resulting in a seizure disorder."

"Boy, that's a lot to deal with."

"Yes, it was. It is. She was in the neonatal intensive care unit for a long time before we were able to take her home. She also had a heart murmur, but that went away. Unfortunately, she still has a seizure disorder—epilepsy— but her medicines really help, and she hasn't had a seizure for over a year now."

"Was there anyone around to help you and Henry?"

"My mom was very helpful. Both Henry's parents were gone. My father lived up north, and we didn't see him much. Besides, he couldn't get over the fact that Joy had disabilities."

"He should be proud of her. She's a good kid and plays a great game of tennis…but, I'm curious. How come you didn't let her take lessons with the high school kids during the summer?"

"You know, that was Tom's call. We never really discussed it. I felt he was doing us this incredible favor by coaching her one-on-one without any compensation, so I didn't want to push things. It's my sense Tom was worried about how the other kids would react to Joy—how they would treat her. I think he wanted to be present during her lessons to help ease her into tennis with her Oakbrook peers. I also think he might have been concerned about how other parents would feel, spending money for lessons for their kids and knowing Joy might need special attention. But, I don't really know. As I said, I've let Tom make the decisions there. But, I will say this—he's talked about taking her into his group next year."

"That's exciting," Cheryl said enthusiastically.

"Very. But one step at a time. First, we have to concentrate on Special Olympics."

"I can't help wondering how great a tennis player Joy would have been if she hadn't had such a difficult start in life."

"Over the years, many people have said the same thing to me, Cheryl. My reply is simple. If that hypothetical child did not have to experience everything Joy endured she wouldn't be Joy."

"You're amazing, Brenda. You really are."

The girls returned from the court to their mothers, and Tom joined the foursome under the oaks. He complimented Allison and Joy for keeping the ball in play warming up rather than trying to hit winners like some players did.

When Allison returned with Joy to the courts to play a set, Cheryl turned to Brenda, "I went on the internet yesterday to look up Special Olympics. I had no idea it dated back to the sixties."

"Yes," Brenda added. "And did you see who started it? Eunice Shriver. Jack Kennedy's sister. At her own home in Maryland. She ran a camp there for kids with disabilities and expanded it into Special Olympics."

"With Kennedy money?"

"Money from the Kennedy Foundation."

"And now there are national and international events?"

"Right," Brenda confirmed.

"So how did Joy qualify for nationals? I assume she had to play other tournaments first, didn't she?"

"Tom, you explain it. You know that story better than I do."

"Did you see the article in the local paper, by any chance?" Tom asked.

Cheryl replied, "Sorry, I didn't."

"I'll show it to you later. I have a copy," Brenda said.

"There are not a lot of tennis players with disabilities who compete in Wisconsin. Since draws are so small, the only tournament they play to qualify for nationals is state. Protocols differ from state to state. The more players available, the more venues they play in."

"So, is it like the Summer and Winter Games we watch on TV every four years?" Cheryl asked.

"Very similar," Tom agreed. "This is the summer portion of Special Olympics."

"So, will Joy play kids her own age?"

"Not necessarily," Tom responded. "At every tournament, certified coaches rate each player according to her ability to hit shots and on her mobility. Believe it or not, Joy could actually play someone in her thirties, but her opponent's level will be similar to Joy's."

"I see."

The women sat for a while watching their daughters. Brenda thought about the times she was in high school and played on those courts, and the pressure she felt. She remembered Rally, too, and how he sat under the oak trees waiting for her matches to end. Just looking over at him helped to calm her. When she walked off the court, he would happily greet her regardless of whether she won or lost. Her anxiety level was even higher now when Joy had a tournament, and, of course, Rally was no longer around. She wasn't sure how she was going to cope with the tension in Iowa.

A young spectator casually walked by shuffling toward the courts. He waved to Joy and sat cross-legged in his previous spot to watch the tennis.

"Michael," Brenda pointed, whispering to Cheryl.

"Yes, I saw him."

"Oh boy. What am I supposed to do now?"

"You sound like Allison's father. Every time he sees a boy anywhere near her, he wants to bring out a baseball bat. He is so protective. I keep telling him he remembers too well what it was like being a teenage boy."

"Henry is better with this than I am. I think he's happy she has some male attention," Brenda admitted. "My problem is I don't know how much she knows, and I don't know how much to tell her...has Allison shown any interest in boys yet? She's so cute, I can't believe they haven't discovered her."

"She hasn't had any dates. Her dad won't permit that. She hangs around with a group of girls and sometimes a group of boys, too. But I haven't seen any one-on-one relationships. I think tennis helps keep her occupied and out of trouble."

"I'm sure that's true. Have you talked to Allison about sex?"

"I have. My husband won't even spell the word in front of her. But Allison and I have had several conversations. Right now she thinks sex is gross, and of course, her father wants to keep it that way...I'm sure with your mom being a librarian, you know some good books for kids that age to read, too."

"Yes, there are some in the library, and I know Mom would be glad to take you to them. Unfortunately, there are none that deal with special needs kids. You wouldn't believe all the controversy out there. Do you know that there are some doctors who advise sterilization? So they won't get pregnant? I feel like I'm trying to protect her all the time, and Henry wants her to live as normal a life as possible. Don't get me wrong…he's a wonderful father and husband."

"Joy's lucky to have two parents who care so much about her. It's probably good that you and Henry come at the boy-thing from two different sides. I'm sure you'll figure it out together."

"Excuse me," said a fortyish-looking woman in red shorts and a sleeveless top, "I'm looking for…oh, there he is…sorry. Um, are one of you Joy's mother by any chance?"

"Yes, I am. Brenda Bjorkman. This is my friend Cheryl Randall."

"Oh, it's so nice to meet you both. We just moved in across the street a few months ago. I'm Sally Morehead, and that's my Michael over by the fence. I hope he isn't causing you any problems."

"Not at all," Brenda smiled.

"He sure is fond of your daughter, Joy. He talks about her all the time."

"He seems very sweet," Cheryl joined.

"He is," Sally assured her. "And, I read in the paper about your prodigy. Sounds like she is pretty famous. Which one is she?"

"She's wearing the yellow top. Allison is in the light blue."

"Boy, they both play well, don't they?" Sally admired. "Michael said he's in Joy's class at the high school. I'm so pleased with Oakbrook. They seem to take great care of all their students. Michael has adjusted really well already.

It was nothing like this in Arkansas. I recently remarried, and my husband and I moved up here with Michael. He farmed down South and wants to try his luck up here...I'm sorry for gabbing so much...I haven't had a lot of adults to talk to, I'm afraid."

"Not at all," Brenda assured Sally. "Why don't you sit down and join us?"

They watched Tom Carrabas walk onto the court where the girls were talking near the net. "The set must be over," Brenda opined. All three mothers watched as Tom took Allison's racquet from her and gestured some instructions. He left them on the court to continue playing and said hello to Michael as he returned to the oaks.

"Another good set," he announced. "Both played well again. Allison is the perfect opponent for Joy, because she is so consistent. She is forcing Joy to be patient."

"What were you showing them?" Cheryl asked.

"Both girls were dropping the heads of their racquets on their forehands. It's a very common mistake. I was telling them to keep their racquet heads up through the entire shot."

"Tom," Brenda introduced, "this is Sally. That's her son, Michael over there near the fence."

"Hello, nice to meet you. I've seen your son at school. You just moved here didn't you?"

"Yes, we did. We live across the street."

"Ah, at the old Dunham farm?"

"Yes."

"Welcome to Oakbrook."

"Thank you."

"Shall we let the girls play one more evening?" Tom asked.

"Fine with us," Cheryl responded. "Does Thursday work for everybody?"

"Sure," Brenda replied. "Is that OK for you, Tom?"

"Should be fine. By the way, Allison played great today. And so did Joy. Allison won the set 6-4 with her usual steady play, but I was pleased with Joy's game, too."

Before everyone left for the evening, Cheryl told Brenda, "I play tennis, too and learned that some ladies in town have a team. They're practicing early tomorrow morning, and the captain asked me to attend. I can't remember her name… she's kind of heavy set..."

"Do you mean Sadie?"

"Yes. That's it. Sadie."

"Sure, I know her. We played on some of the same high school teams. I wanted to play adult tennis, but with my work schedule, I can't. But, by all means, give it a shot, Cheryl."

"I think I will."

"Do you have a moment to meet Michael?" Sally asked Brenda.

"Of course," replied Brenda. "I'd love to."

Michael was still in his reserved seat by the fence. Cross-legged as always, he had his elbows on his knees and was watching the girls play.

"Hi, honey," Sally said to her son. "This is Joy's mom."

"Hi Joy's mom," Michael said grinning as he stood up. "Nice meeting you."

"Nice to meet you, too. Joy has told me lots about you."

"Oof."

"Oh, no. None of it's bad. She likes your jokes."

"I make her laugh."

"Yes, you do."

"She's sweet. Sometimes she makes me laugh, too."

"Yes, she is sweet, and she can be goofy, too, especially with her brother."

"He's nice, too."

"Thank you, Michael. Do you play tennis?"

"No, I bowl. I'm a good bowler."

"That's a fun sport. You should teach Joy how to bowl. I don't think she knows how."

"Could I?"

"Sure. Let her get through this tournament, and your mom and I will arrange a time. OK?"

"Yes. I would like that."

"I'm glad I met you Michael," Brenda said.

"Me, too," he replied.

"Sally, let's arrange a bowling outing when we return from Iowa."

"I'll give you a call."

"Bye, Joy's mom," Michael beamed.

"Bye, Michael. See you soon."

CHAPTER 22

Monday, August 11, 1975

THERE WAS A lot of whispering under the oak trees when Mrs. Nelson dropped Brenda and Rally off at the park Monday morning. Al and Carrie weren't there, but everyone else was. "Did you hear what happened, Brenda?" a girl asked running up to her. "Al and Carrie got in trouble for drinking. I think they're going to be kicked off the tennis team. I don't know if the cops caught them or what. We don't even know if they're going to show up this morning…can I pat him?" she asked walking over to the dog.

"Of course… but what happened?"

"I'm not sure. I didn't know anything until just now. I heard they went to Madison and got caught for drinking beer. One of the football players was with them."

"Who told you?"

"Sadie. She seems to know what went on."

"Figures."

Al and Carrie drove into the parking lot together and immediately noticed heads turning in unison to watch them. Obviously, their students had learned about Saturday evening's debacle. The teens looked at each other apprehensively. "Let me talk to them," Al suggested, as they walked from the parking lot to meet the silent gathering.

"As I'm sure you've heard by now," Al began, "Carrie and I did some stupid stuff this weekend and now we have to pay the consequences. Fortunately, no one was hurt—well, at least not seriously hurt. But there are rules, and we broke them. Both of us apologize for letting all of you down. Since this involves other students, I don't think it's fair to go into detail about what happened. We hope our offenses won't affect you and your lessons here, but we'll know more after we talk with Coach Carrabas."

"Did the police catch you?" someone asked.

"As I said, other people were with us, and they are entitled to their privacy. That's why I'm not explaining more. But, no, the police were not involved."

The group was pensive and quiet. "OK," Carrie said. "Let's get going. Here are your court assignments for the first hour." As Carrie started to read off names, Rally ambled over and nuzzled her hand. "Hi, big boy," she admired. "Thank you. I'm sorry, but I don't have an assignment for you." As if he understood, Rally plopped to the ground with a groan and lay beside her. After reading her list, Carrie reminded players about the end-of-the-year tournament. "Singles is this weekend. Please find some practice matches to play before then so you are ready. Novices will play their tournament Friday. The winner will be included in the main draw, which begins on Saturday morning."

"This format is exactly like professional tournaments. They have qualifying events prior to the main draws," Al added. "But please be sure to practice. If there are specific things you want us to work on with you, tell us, and we'll try to incorporate your requests into our daily plans."

As the lesson was winding down, Coach Carrabas drove up, approached the courts, and sat down on a bench. Everyone noticed him and understood why he was there. No one stayed around very long after the session was over, except Al and Carrie.

"I'd like to talk with you," Coach said, as the teens drew near. "Needless to say, I am deeply disappointed in both of you. As leaders in the high school and role models for younger kids, you have let everyone down." Tears welled in Carrie's eyes, and Al hung his head. "You are the last two athletes I would have expected to disgrace this program."

As if preplanned, both teens uttered, "I'm sorry," together.

"Fortunately, both of you have clean records. I met with your principal, Mr. Harris, this morning to decide what punishment should be meted out. Following Wisconsin high school guidelines, you are both going to be banned from interscholastic competition for two weeks at the onset of your respective athletic seasons. It's a shame this has to occur during your last year of high school competition. Another thing—even though you may be angry with Dave's father for telling your parents and notifying us, he did the right thing, and I commend him for it."

"What about the rest of the summer program?" Al asked timidly.

"You have both done an excellent job with the kids—this summer and last summer. We see no need to curtail your teaching. Besides, there are only a few weeks left until school starts. Do you have any other questions?"

Both shook their heads.

"Remember, you get two serves in tennis—you've already used one up. I don't want any double faults from either of you. Am I making myself clear?" Coach asked, as he rose to leave.

"Yes, sir."

The teens sat together for a while. Al reached for Carrie's hand and she looked at him with reddened eyes, then leaned her face into his shoulder and sniffled. "So, what did your parents say?" she asked with a muffled voice.

"They wanted to know where we got the beer. I just told them that I didn't buy it." I explained that you and I had very little to drink—that I drove home, which they already knew."

"Are you grounded?" Carrie asked.

"No. My folks felt missing two weeks of athletics was a reasonable punishment. They're pretty realistic and weren't surprised that we had something to drink before we graduated. But I had to promise them that I will never drink and drive and that I will not be a passenger in a car with a driver who's been drinking. How about you?"

"Girls' tennis starts in two weeks, and since I can't play, Dad is going to take me out east to see some colleges. I must admit my folks were pretty understanding, too."

"Where are you going?"

"New England, mostly. My sister goes to Androscoggin College. She loves it, and I've already visited her. I'd like to look at a few other schools out there, too."

"And how about your dad? Is he going to accept the job in Iowa?"

"Yes."

"Wow, that's great."

"They're going to allow him to stay here for a couple of semesters, so I can finish my senior year at Oakbrook, which is really nice of them."

"Why don't you look at your dad's college in Iowa?" Al inquired.

"Colonial? I would, but I don't want to be on the same campus where he's teaching. I want my own experience, and I want to live on my own. Don't get me wrong, I love my dad. I think he understands that I need my independence, too."

"You're lucky you can go to a college out East."

"I am. You're right, and I don't take it for granted. Even though some schools have reciprocity with Colonial, which means my tuition could be less than some of my class-mates', it's still expensive."

"You've worked hard, Carrie. You deserve to go where you want to. I don't know any member of the class who puts more time and effort into her assignments than you. We all admire you for it."

"You're sweet. Thanks. That means a lot to me, but I know students just as qualified as I am, who can't attend private colleges unless they get loans or scholarships—you are every bit the student I am, Al and more. I still wouldn't know squat about oak trees, or tobacco, or a few other things if it wasn't for you!"

"What other things?"

"Never you mind! Have you heard from the U yet?"

"No, but I took your advice. I'm waiting for school to start before interviewing at Whitewater and Eau Claire.... talking about colleges...you know what? I forgot to tell you...that guy on State Street broke Dave's foot when he stomped on it. He had to have a cast."

"Are you serious?"

"I am."

"Is he going to be able to play football?"

"They think he may be out four to six weeks."

"What a bummer. Part of that time he was suspended anyway, but now he's going to miss more than half the season."

"Tough way to learn a lesson," Al said.

"It sure is. I suspect he learned a *few* tough lessons that night."

"Yes, he did. I think we all did...well, I suppose we ought to get going. Are we still on for Wednesday night? That Nicholson movie, *One Flew Over the Cuckoo's Nest* is playing at the Deer Point Drive-In."

"Sounds good to me...come on, I'll drive you back to my house and you can pick up your car," Carrie said.

CHAPTER 23

———— ✢ ————

Wednesday, August 13, 1975

By THE TIME Brenda and John dressed, their mother had breakfast on the table. Fresh-squeezed orange juice, cold cereal, fresh cut strawberries sprinkled with sugar, and toast. Rally had already eaten his meal and was lying on a mat in the corner of the breakfast nook, head up, on alert.

"Rally slept with me last night," John bragged.

"That's because I kicked him out of my room," Brenda said.

"Why did you do that?"

"Because he was farting. He really stunk. He cuts the worst ones in the world."

"I wonder why that is," Mrs. Nelson interjected. "Is someone feeding him from the table by any chance?"

"I didn't smell anything," John declared.

His sister reminded him, "Probably because your nose is stuffed from your allergies."

"How come I don't get medicine like Brenda?"

"We tried allergy pills for you. They just make you more hyper. Besides, Brenda's pills are for her skin. They aren't allergy pills, John. And by the way, Brenda, your face looks much better. I'm so glad the medicine is working. Please remember to put on sun screen. The doctor said you can get a rash from those capsules."

"I have been."

"Guess I can't call you pimple puss anymore," her brother teased.

"John!" his mother reprimanded, then looking at Brenda, she added, "I need some help from you today."

"Me?" asked Brenda.

"Yes. I don't have anyone to sit for John. So, I'm going to drop him off at the park with you and Rally. After tennis, your father is going to pick both of you up and take you home."

"When did you speak to him?"

"Last night. He wants to see you play."

"Great," Brenda said sarcastically. Just what she needed, she thought, Ralph at the park for everyone to see. Ralph, the alcoholic, the criminal, the absentee father.

"I'll take Rally for a walk when you have your lesson, Brenda," John suggested.

After breakfast, Mrs. Nelson drove her kids and Rally to the park and dropped them off. John removed Rally's leash, and immediately he ran to the lake. Into the water he bounded, snapping at minnows with his teeth and clawing at them eagerly.

Brenda headed to the courts with her tennis gear. She sat on the sidelines with the novices, while more advanced students were assigned to their courts. Carrie sat down with the foursome. "You four are going to play singles shortly and a different group will sit out when you play. So, let's talk a little bit about singles. We've mostly played doubles this summer. What's the biggest difference between singles and doubles besides the number of players on the court?" No one answered. "Come on, guys. Think."

Astutely, Brenda suggested, "Without doubles alleys you don't have all those angles in singles, and you also play more from the center of the court. You even serve more in the center."

"Right you are, Brenda. You also need more patience in singles and more endurance. I think it's more competitive than doubles. You don't have a partner to blame if things don't go well," she teased. "It's all on your shoulders."

"You mean it's all on your racquet, not your shoulders, don't you?" one of the boys, Philip, blurted.

"Very funny," Carrie responded.

"Do you play singles and doubles in high school?" a second boy, Jamie, asked.

"You are eligible to play both and many players do. But some specialize in either singles or doubles."

"What do you play?" Philip, asked.

"I play both."

"I bet you like mixed doubles best, because you get to play with Al," Jamie smiled.

"Unfortunately, they don't have mixed doubles teams in high school. Maybe someday they will…Court Four is finished. Looks like it's your turn to play. Let's start with

Jamie and Brenda. Why don't you warm up for a few minutes and then play a set. The balls should be on the court. When you finish, leave the balls by the net and return to me, please. Have fun."

As Brenda and Jamie walked toward Court Four, Sadie and her opponent passed them heading for the oak trees. "Isn't that cute?" Sadie smiled. "Young love. Ka-ka-ka-ka."

Brenda lowered her head and Jamie snickered. They continued to the court without a word to begin warming up. After a few minutes, Carrie yelled over to them to begin their set. Brenda's serve was steadily improving. She placed it accurately to Jamie's backhand, and he had no answer. The pace on her forehand was too much for her classmate, too. She won the set 6-1. Jamie was gracious and complimented Brenda on her play, "You hit it harder than most boys do."

"Well, you get to everything. It's the only way I can beat you. Nice set."

They walked back to Carrie and were about to sit down when Carrie told Brenda she was sending her back onto a court right away to play Kelly, another novice.

"What court?" Kelly asked.

"Six. Why don't you start your set right away, since you already warmed up."

A short time later, the girls returned. With little effort, Brenda won 6-0. Carrie complimented both players. As they sat down, a furry wet canine ran over and jumped on Brenda's lap. "Oof. Hi, Rally. You're soaked. Come on, you're getting dirt all over me you big lug." He licked her face gently. Kelly petted him, too, and he leaned his head over to nuzzle her, making her giggle.

John wasn't far behind. "I can't even get him out of the water sometimes," he complained. "All he wants to do is chase minnows. He never catches them. Then he comes out of the water and rolls around on the sand and gets all dirty."

"It's OK, John," Brenda comforted. "That's what dogs do."

"Are you done? Can we go home now?" he asked.

"In a bit, John," Brenda said, grateful Ralph hadn't showed up to watch her play. She didn't want to remind John, either, that they had to wait for their father to pick them up.

"I'm bored."

"Why don't you take my tennis bag. Here, I'll take all my junk out of it. See how many acorns you can find under the trees?"

"Can I?"

"Sure. Here you go."

With John occupied, Brenda went closer to the courts to watch other singles matches. Rally stayed under the oaks, tired from chasing minnows. Derek, Brenda's doubles partner when she played against Sadie, was on Court One. He had beautiful strokes and was clearly the best player in the group. Al noticed Brenda and wandered over to talk with her.

"He has a nice game doesn't he?"

"Yes."

"He'll be playing for the high school this Spring."

"Wow."

"I know another student who is going to be playing for the high school."

"You think so?"

"I do, Brenda. I saw some of your points in that first set today. You played very well."

"Thank you…what's going to happen to you and Carrie?"

"You mean because of what we did?"

"Ya."

"We are both suspended for the first two weeks of the season."

"I'm sorry. That's too bad."

"We deserved it. We did a stupid thing."

Brenda didn't know how to respond, so she sat uncomfortably watching Derek play.

Al broke the silence, "Are you ready for the weekend?"

"I think so."

"If you get through the novice tournament, and I think you will, you will be in the main draw with the more advanced kids."

"I know, and that makes me a little nervous."

"You'll do fine. Is your mother going to come and watch you play?"

"I'm not sure."

"You should invite her."

"I hate to bother her, because she has to work."

"I understand…well, I better see how some of the other kids are doing. See you later."

During a changeover, Derek waved to Brenda. "How did you do?" he mouthed.

"I won them both," Brenda answered. "How are you doing?"

"OK. I'm up 4-1," he whispered holding fingers up on both hands to reflect the score.

"Good," she said, as he gathered the balls preparing to serve.

"Dad's here," John announced running up to his sister. "He just drove in."

"Did you get a lot of acorns?" Brenda asked standing up.

"Yup. Look in the bag."

Before she could gather her racquets and Rally, Ralph appeared. He was dressed in a stained white tee shirt and jeans. He hadn't shaved for a couple of days, and he was covering his forehead with his hand to shade his eyes from the sun. "Hi Brenda, did I miss your matches?"

Brenda nodded.

"Are those your racquets?"

Rally rose and ambled over to stand beside the children.

"Yes, they are," was Brenda's response.

"Lemme see one of those."

"Here," she said handing him one.

"Let's go on the court and see what you got," he commanded.

"I can't. They're playing matches out there. We shouldn't disturb them."

"C'mon. That court on the end is free."

"I think we should wait until they're all done playing," Brenda insisted.

"What's up, boy?" Ralph said to John. "What you got in that bag?"

"Acorns."

"Lemme see 'em," Ralph growled, taking the tennis bag and removing some acorns. "Perfect," he said. Tossing one in the air, he belted it with Brenda's racquet; then he did it again. "Pretty good, huh?"

"May I please have my racquet back. That's not good for the strings. And shouldn't we get going?" Brenda asked.

Ralph smiled, "Not before we hit some."

"Hello," Al said as he joined the threesome. "I'm Al, Brenda's instructor."

"This is Ralph," Brenda said softly to Al.

"Yes, I'm her father," added Ralph.

"Mr. Nelson. So nice to meet you."

"Just call me Ralph."

"Yes, sir. Your daughter is a fine tennis player."

"So I've heard. I wanted to see her play, but I guess I'm late. I had a few errands to run," he apologized, rubbing the end of his nose briskly with an index finger.

"Maybe you can watch her play in the tournament this weekend," Al suggested, looking over at Brenda.

She did not meet his eyes. Looking down at the ground, she asked again, "Shouldn't we get going?"

"Don't you want to play some tennis with me?" Ralph inquired.

"I played all morning. I'd really like to go home now."

"What do you think, John?" Ralph tapped his son on the shoulder.

"Ya, I think we should go. Come on, boy," he said to Rally.

"See you later, Al," Brenda called, heading towards the parking lot.

As Brenda moved into the back seat with Rally, she waved to Derek, who was walking toward the bike rack behind their car. He gave her a thumbs-up; he had won his match. Brenda clapped silently.

Ralph put the car in gear and accelerated. Instead of moving forward, the vehicle lurched backward, abruptly smashing into something behind them. Ralph slammed on his brakes.

Brenda hoped it was only the bike rack he hit, but when she looked out the rear window she realized the car struck Derek and his bicycle, too. She opened her door quickly and ran to the rear of the car. Derek was lying on the ground, his legs still wrapped around his bike. The front wheel was severely bent. Derek had blood on his legs and was writhing in pain.

"Oh, my god," Brenda cried, "are you all right?"

"My leg!" he cried out. "Ohh, my leg!"

Hearing the collision, Carrie ran to the parking lot. "Let's not move him yet," she suggested. "Can someone run to the shelter and call EMS…Derek, does anything hurt besides your leg?"

"He'll be fine," Ralph said stumbling out of his car. "Just let him rest for a second."

Ignoring Ralph, Carrie asked Derek again if anything hurt.

"No, just my leg! I think I broke it!" he cried out, attempting to sit up.

"Derek, try to lie down. I'll get something to put under your head. OK? How about your head and your neck? Do you have any pain there?"

"No, those are fine."

"Does it hurt you to move your arms?"

"No, not really."

"How about your back?

"No."

"Now tell me about your legs?"

"I can move my right one—my left is stuck under the bike. That's the one that's really killing me," he grunted trying to hold back tears.

"OK. Let's move your right one a little and see if we can lift the bike off your left leg. Can someone help me with the bike?"

"I'm right beside you, Carrie," Al said. "What do you want me to do?"

"I'll help Derek lift his right leg. See if you can slide the bike away from him, so we can make him more comfortable. Did someone call EMS from the shelter payphone?"

"Yes, Philip did," someone informed her.

"Can a couple of you help Al to gently lift the bike off Derek's leg. Slowly, please. Wait until I get his right leg up a little more...does anyone have a towel I can put under his head?"

Someone answered, "I'll get one."

"Do you think you should do that?" Ralph asked.

"I do," Carrie replied curtly.

Carefully they lifted the bike off Derek's leg. He moaned as they finally removed it. His left leg, which was partially hidden by the bicycle lay at an abnormal angle. As Derek tried to raise his head to see it, Carrie helped him lower it again. "You're going to be fine, Derek. EMS is on the way...Al, can you grab the blanket from the back of your car for him, please."

"Ohh...oww," Derek howled. "It's really hurting!"

"I'm sure it does." Carrie said sensitively. "Let's cover you up, even though it's warm out. Thank goodness you're in the shade. Did anyone find a towel?"

"Here you go," Al said helping her place it under Derek's head.

"It's broken, isn't it?" Derek asked peering up at Carrie.

"I think it is, but I'm sure the doctors can fix it. Are your folks around?" Carrie inquired.

"Mom should be home."

"Good."

It wasn't long until they heard sirens. Ralph paced nervously a few yards away from the scene. John had Rally tethered to his leash and was trying to stay as far away from Ralph as he could.

"How are you doing, Derek?" Carrie asked.

"I'm feeling a little woozy."

"Do you want something to drink? Some water?"

"A little, please."

"Here," Brenda offered, "take some of mine."

The red EMS truck arrived with their volunteer medics. One took notes as Derek and Carrie told their story. Another took Derek's blood pressure and pulse before examining his leg, which was clearly broken. After splinting it, they moved him onto a stretcher and lifted him into the vehicle. Some static came over the truck radio. "Transport to Madison. Please call ahead," a medic responded. "Ten-four."

A patrol car appeared a few minutes after the EMS truck. When Ralph saw it, he started to walk away quickly from the parking lot. A young policeman stepped out and asked who was in charge. Al said he guessed he and Carrie were. He asked Al to describe what had occurred, and Al explained what he had witnessed. "Can you identify the driver?" he inquired taking notes. Al pointed to Ralph, who continued to scurry away. "Hey," the officer yelled. "You, there. Hold it right where you are." Ralph ran awkwardly toward the trees and tripped on a protruding root.

Panting, he looked over his shoulder, stood up quickly, and raced toward the woods again. The officer pulled his gun from its holster and aimed it. "Stop!" he yelled again. "Stop!" When Ralph continued to escape, the policeman fired his weapon. Ralph hit the ground hard and laid perfectly still. Everyone in the parking lot was stunned. Rally began to bark as the officer ran to Ralph, stood him up, and escorted him back to the squad car. There was no visible blood on Ralph; the policeman had fired a blank which scared his escapee but did not wound him. Opening the rear door of his vehicle, the officer placed Ralph in the back seat. Brenda glared at her father through the window with as much hatred as she could muster.

After talking with her father, the policeman asked, "Can I speak to Brenda Nelson, please?"

"I'm Brenda,"

"Do you and your brother have another way home?"

Al interjected, "I'll take them home. I can take their dog, too."

"I would really appreciate it. I'll call your mom at the library and let her know you have transportation home," the officer said to Brenda.

"Thank you," Al answered for her.

As Al and Brenda walked over to John and Rally, Brenda broke down, "I should never have gotten in the car with that jerk. I could tell by how he was talking at the park that he'd been drinking. I could smell the alcohol on his breath. It's all my fault that Derek got hurt."

"No it isn't," Al reassured her. "Don't blame yourself… come on, I'll take you all home."

While Al drove off, Brenda looked out at the kids standing around and gossiping. Thanks, Daddy, she thought, for putting me in another shitty situation.

"Brenda," Al said after they had driven without talking a few minutes. "It's OK. And Derek is going to be OK. Honest."

"I hope he's going to be OK. And, I'm going to take a lot of crap from the other kids because of this."

"Anyone who gives you crap is just plain ignorant."

"Unfortunately, there are a lot of ignorant people around."

"There are some, but most of the kids are smart and understand situations like this."

"I hope so."

"John, are you doing OK?" Al asked.

"What's going to happen to Ralph?" inquired John.

Al continued driving, "I don't know."

"Who cares," Brenda responded.

When Al reached the Nelson home, Brenda thanked him for the ride. Rally jumped out with her, and John followed closely behind. Before they even reached the steps, the front door opened, and their mother met them with more emotion than she usually displayed. She hugged them both as they entered the house, and it was obvious she had been crying. In an unfamiliar voice, she confessed, "I was a damn fool for letting your father pick you up, and I'm so sorry."

"It's wasn't your fault, Mom," John comforted.

Rally slithered over to his mat in the breakfast nook and laid down.

"It was Ralph's fault," Brenda shrieked. "When he came to the park, I knew he was drunk. I could see it. I could smell it—I was afraid if I said something, the other kids would know, too, so I just let it go. I should never have let him drive, but what could I do? Take the keys away from him? With everyone standing around, I didn't want to create a scene…I hate him…I hate him…He's such a jerk. I hope I never see him again."

"He broke that kid's leg, Mom," John said, taken aback by Brenda's tirade.

"So, I heard."

"And he's the nicest boy. He played doubles with me against Sadie. He was so nice to me…I hope Ralph goes to prison again. I really do, and I hope that he rots in there this time."

CHAPTER 24

※

Wednesday night, August 13, 1975

"GOOD EVENING, MR. and Mrs. Archibald," Al said nervously as he entered Carrie's home. "I want to apologize for the other night. I am so sorry that I…I…provided…gave Carrie beer."

"Apology accepted," Mr. Archibald said succinctly. "You are both good kids. You just didn't use good judgment. Where are you two headed this evening?"

"To see a movie, *One Flew Over the Cuckoo's Nest*," Al replied.

"Wonderful story. I hope the movie does justice to the book."

Al said, "I didn't read the book, but the movie reviews were very favorable."

"They also made it into a Broadway play, dear," added Mrs. Archibald.

Mr. Archibald walked over to Al, "Have you heard anything about the youngster who was hit by the car?"

"Coach Carrabas called me after he spoke to Derek's parents this afternoon…sorry, Carrie, I should have called you, but I knew I was going to see you tonight…Derek was admitted to University Hospitals and had to have surgery. He fractured both bones in his lower left leg. He's going to be there for a while, but they said he has a very favorable… um… what do you call it?"

"Prognosis," Carrie assisted.

"Right," continued Al. "He will have a cast on for several weeks. They're going to give him physical therapy during his hospital stay. The good news is he should be back in plenty of time to play tennis in the Spring, and there's no doubt he'll make varsity."

"And what about that fellow who hit him?" Mrs. Archibald questioned.

"The last thing I saw was the police driving him away. I don't know any more than that. Unfortunately, he's the father of one of our students. She's fragile to begin with, and this situation is going to make things a lot tougher for her."

Mrs. Archibald clarified, "She's the one with the dog, right?"

"Right, Mom. Her name is Brenda."

"Poor kid."

"By the way, Sir," Al faced Mr. Archibald, "Carrie told me about your position at Colonial. Congratulations on being department chairman. I hear it's a great college."

"Thank you, Al. Yes, a fine institution. I am very much looking forward to teaching there…and by the way, Carrie told me you're interested in teaching as well."

"I am but probably not at the college level."

"Don't be too sure. Don't count it out."

"I won't, but I'd like to coach, too. So, I'm thinking more of teaching high school."

"Wonderful profession, Al...well, you two probably ought to be on your way. Good night, dear," Mr. Archibald said, giving his daughter a kiss on the cheek. "Good night, Al," he said, shaking Al's hand.

"Good night Mr. and Mrs. Archibald."

The teens headed for the car, and Mr. Archibald was pleased to see Al open the passenger door for Carrie. "Nice boy," he remarked to his wife.

The teens decided to stop at the Family Diner outside of Deer Point for a quick dinner before heading to the Drive-In. Still furnished in 1950s décor, the restaurant had a counter with stools for ice cream and sodas and juke boxes at each table. The couple sat down across from one another in a booth, and Al reached into his pocket, "I got a couple of quarters. What would you like to hear?"

Carrie flipped through the listings a couple of times. "Here's one, she said. "A22, *Please Mr. Postman*."

"I love the Carpenters," Al said. "What else?"

"You pick one."

"How about *Feel Like Makin' Love*? C16."

"You would pick that one," she teased.

"OK, you get another one."

"*Cat's in the Cradle*," Carrie chose. "Last one is yours."

"Um, um. Let's see. Oh, how about D4, *Fallin' in Love*?"

"I can tell what kind of mood you're in tonight. Do you think we'll watch *some* of the movie so I can tell my folks what it's about?"

"A little—maybe. So, what do you want to eat?"

"Just a salad with some chicken on it, and I'd love a milkshake. Strawberry."

"I feel like something different. I always have hamburgers, Al said."

"Get a salad. They're good for you."

"Too healthy for me. Maybe I'll get the meatloaf."

"That's just like hamburger."

"I suppose, but it sounds good to me."

As previous requests ended and *Mr. Postman* began to play, Al moved to Carrie's side of the table putting his arm around her shoulder. Soon, a waitress arrived to give them water and take their orders. She apologized for running out of meatloaf and suggested chicken pot pie instead. Al accepted her recommendation and ordered a strawberry milkshake for himself, too.

While they waited for their food and listened to their selections, they began to work on the draw sheet for the end-of-the-year tournament at Taylor Park. With Derek sidelined, they needed to select a new number one seed.

"You know; it could be Dee Dee," Carrie opined.

"I think Tyler is a lot stronger. I agree Dee Dee is really good, but I don't think she could stay on the court with Tyler."

"You're probably right," Carrie agreed. "I think she's better than any of the other players, though. I just wish she'd stay away from Sadie. Sadie is such a bad influence on her. I've been alone with Dee Dee, and she is a totally different kid when she's alone."

"What's Sadie's problem, anyhow?"

"Well, for one thing, I think she's anorexic. Have you noticed how skinny she's become?"

"Actually, I have."

They stopped talking to listen to *Feel Like Makin' Love*.

"Awesome song," Al raved.

"It is…but getting back to Sadie, she must not eat at all. Her arms and legs are so thin."

"So, what is anorexia?"

Carrie explained, "It's an eating disorder. There's bulimia, where kids binge and then throw up what they eat and anorexia, where they limit food they take in, but often throw up, too. From what I've read, they don't see themselves like we see them. When they look in a mirror, despite how thin they are, they look fat to themselves."

"That's crazy."

"There's an epidemic at Madison Central. I read about it in the paper. It's not as common in boys. It's almost always girls who have it. Smart girls, too. Many from upper class families."

"Why?"

"No one really knows. There are all kinds of theories. Most anorexics are compulsive about other things besides food. I think they opened or are opening a ward in one of the Madison hospitals for kids with anorexia."

"You can't die from it, can you?"

"Oh yes you can. I don't think it's just malnutrition that kills them. There are some other chemical things that affect their hearts, and they die from that. I don't really understand all that goes on."

Dinner was served, and the conversation slowed as the couple ate and listened to other juke box selections— *Rhinestone Cowboy*, *My Eyes Adored You*, and *The Hustle*.

"Aren't these metal tumblers they give you great?" Carrie enthused, slurping down the last of her milkshake. "Yum."

"So, we still haven't set up the rankings for the draw. Do you have a pen or a pencil in your purse?"

"I have a ballpoint pen."

"Perfect. Let's grab a napkin to write on and start ranking the kids while we wait for the check."

After they settled on an order, Al counted the players and said, "We forgot someone. There are only eleven names."

"That's because we left Derek and the four novices out, Dummy."

"Wait a second. A few days ago you told me you thought I was smart. Make up your mind."

"I think your mind is on something else," she smiled.

"Could be...so, someone gets a bye in the tournament, right?"

"No, it's more complicated than that. We have twelve players, right?"

"Ya."

"But you need eight players in the quarter-finals and four in the semi-finals."

"OK."

"To do that, you need to have four players with byes."

"Really?"

"Really. If you have no byes, you will be left with six players after the first round and three after the second round."

"Did you figure all that out in your head?" Al asked Carrie as the waitress approached with their check. "Thank you, I'll take that. Do we pay you or pay up at the cash register?"

"I can take it," their waitress answered.

"Could you also bring me some singles for this five?" he asked.

After Al left a tip, the teens returned to the car and headed for the drive-in. The night was chillier than previous evenings, so Carrie closed her window and put on her sweater. They listened to Jonathan Libby playing the top fifty songs on WROX. When they arrived at the drive-in, they found a line of cars waiting to enter, but it was still dusk once they paid, and it would be another half hour or so before previews came on.

Some search lights played tag on the screen as patrons waited, others stood outside their vehicles chatting with neighbors. A few went into the concession building for soda, candy and popcorn.

Al lowered his window, retrieved the speaker, and positioned it on top of the glass. "Mmm that looks good," he said gazing at the car next to them. "Want some popcorn?"

"Sure. I'll go with you. I need to go to the bathroom."

"What do you want me to get besides that?"

"Do you want to get a Coke, too, and we can share it?"

"Sure."

As they walked to the building, they were interrupted, "Hi, Al. Hi, Carrie." The teens turned around and recognized one of their students. "These are my two tennis instructors," Kelly said excitedly to her parents. "And these are my parents," she smiled.

Al and Carrie shook hands with Kelly's parents and asked if they were going to attend the end-of-the-year tournament. They said they didn't know about it, because Kelly hadn't said anything to them. Carrie suggested it would be a good opportunity to see how much Kelly had improved since the beginning of the summer. As they were talking, Kelly pointed to the screen. "Look. That silly time clock that eats all the food is counting down minutes until the show starts. Shouldn't we get back to our car?" she asked her parents.

Al bought popcorn and soda and waited outside for Carrie to return from the Ladies' room.

"So, where is their car parked?" she asked Al. "Right next to ours?"

"I don't think so. I saw them go to the other side of the lot."

"That would have been just what we needed, one of our little darlings spying on us at a drive-in," Carrie laughed.

"We are supposed to be teachers, you know."

"Ya, right."

They returned to the car and began snacking when the previews came on. "Oh, my god. I'd be so scared to see that!" Carrie remarked as a snippet from *Jaws* played. "That would frighten the crap out of me."

"Hey, you got me to protect you, you know."

"Ah, yes, I forgot," Carrie replied, as she leaned in and gave Al a kiss.

The main feature started, and the teens watched Mac and Nurse Ratched argue, as Chief sat around unperturbed. When Carrie said she was still chilly, even with a sweater on, Al went to the trunk for his blanket. He opened the passenger door and suggested they get into the back seat. Huddled together, Al placed the blanket over both of them. "Is that better?" he asked.

"Yes, much," and she kissed him again, this time more firmly. "Thank you, Sweetie."

Al melted. Leaning back, he wrapped his arms around her and drew her toward him. She fell on top of him as he laid down on the back seat, and they kissed some more. "Boy, isn't it nice to have some time alone together?" he said, rubbing her back with his hand.

"Yes, it is. I'm glad we decided to come here."

"This is what drive-ins were invented for," Al smiled.

"Really? I didn't know that. That's not what my mommy told me," Carrie said as she tickled Al in the ribs.

He tickled her back. "Hey, you aren't playing fair. You're bigger than I am."

They both sat up, and Al asked, "Are you warm enough now?"

"Yup. I'm actually too warm."

"Here, let me help you take off your sweater."

"Sure."

After Al removed her sweater, the couple continued kissing and touching. They could hear the movie in the background and see flashes of light from the screen. Despite the occasional opening and closing of car doors, they had the privacy they wanted.

"Are you comfortable?" Al asked.

"Absolutely," she said looking at him. "I'm OK," she added as she laid back down. Al laid beside her, and they began cuddling again. When they looked up, the windows in the car were steamy.

"I think people are going to know that we're not really watching the movie," Al laughed. "Want to take a break?" he asked sitting up and taking her hand.

"Sure," she said getting up, too. "Can I ask you a question? I get the feeling you're holding back?" she sensed. "Are you? Did I do something wrong?"

Al looked at her. "Absolutely not. This is great. I love being with you like this."

"But, you're holding back," she repeated.

"A little…"

"Because…why?"

"I don't know. I've thought a hundred times about being alone together, getting to know each other better," he said, looking at her. "It will probably sound stupid, but if you and I get married, I really don't want to go all the way until our wedding night. I want it to be a really special thing for both of us."

"I agree with that. I would like my wedding night to be special, too. But what if I want more now?"

"I'm not sure. I feel protective of you. It's almost like I'm protecting you from me—and maybe you from you! Isn't that crazy? But, I'm the guy…I can do anything and it's considered OK, but I would feel terrible if we went further and you regretted it. I guess I want to keep you safe and feeling good about yourself and me. This isn't a high school tennis court where boys and girls are on equal footing. When it comes to this stuff, people look differently at boys and girls. If a guy wants to go to second base or third base or all the way, that's cool. But it may not be cool for the girl, Carrie. I don't want to drag you down. I certainly don't want to be like Dave was with Sherri the other night."

"I don't feel like you're dragging me down, Al, and you're nothing like Dave. I'm kinda blown away at how sensitive you are."

"Is that a good thing—being sensitive?" he inquired.

"Yes, a very good thing. That's one of the reasons I like you so much."

"You mean there are other reasons, too?"

"Sure. You're a great tennis partner."

"And…"

"Yes, you are a great kisser, too."

"Thanks. That's what I needed to hear."

"I thought so," she agreed.

Al put his arm around Carrie and kissed her again. When they finished, he drew his head back to see her better and brushed the hair out of her eyes. She smiled at him, and he smiled back. "Want to see the rest of the movie?" he asked.

"Sure, if you do," she said.

They watched as the orderlies wheeled Mac back to the ward, where he remained subdued. "What did they do to him?" Al asked.

"They gave him a lobotomy. They actually carved a piece of his brain away."

"Do they really do things like that?"

"In severe cases of mental illness, they do. Sometimes."

"That's awful."

— ⚜ —

CHAPTER 25

Thursday, June 29, 2006

THURSDAY WAS COOL and cloudy with a northerly wind. Joy, Allison, and their mothers sat beneath the oaks, waiting for Coach to finish his lesson with the high school students. A few white caps surfaced on the lake. Leaves fluttered steadily above the tables and benches. No boats were riding on Pierce Lake, but an eagle glided overhead silently, catching currents from the wind. The girls stood up and wandered over to the beach.

"Are you nervous about your tournament, Joy?" Allison asked.

"A little."

"You've played in them before, though, right?"

"Yes. I won state."

"I've never played a tournament, except the end-of-the-summer ones here at Taylor Park."

"You'll play good," Joy told her.

"I don't know. There is a lot more pressure playing tournaments than just playing a few sets."

"You're a good player."

"Thanks. So are you."

"Thanks," Joy smiled. "We go to Iowa tomorrow."

"Yes, I know."

"Grandma is coming."

"Wow, that's neat. Where does she live?"

"With us."

"Oh, in your home?"

"Yes. She cooks for us."

"My grandmothers and my grandfather live in Minnesota."

"Oh."

"That's just the next state over. It takes about five hours to get there by car."

"Oh."

"Is Michael coming to watch you today?"

"I don't know. He makes mom nervous."

"All boys make moms and dads nervous if they have daughters."

"Huh?"

"Parents of girls always want to protect them. They think all boys are bad influences."

"Oh. Michael's nice."

"He certainly seems nice."

"And he's funny, too. He makes jokes sometimes…do you have a boyfriend?"

"No," Allison replied. "There are some boys in my class I like, but we're just friends, not boyfriend and girlfriend. Do you know what I mean?"

"Yes."

While the girls chatted, their mothers talked, too.

"Did you go to the team practice?" Brenda asked Cheryl.

"I did. They have some nice players."

"Yes, they do."

"Have most of them always lived in Oakbrook?"

"A lot of them have."

"From what I understand, the league is run by the community? Is that right?"

"Actually, the county."

"So, it's not USTA sponsored?"

"No, the United States Tennis Association does not organize play. Jefferson County does."

"OK."

"Who did you play with?"

"A few of the women. Sorry, I'm not very good with names. But I did play a couple of sets with Sadie, their captain. I told her about Allison and Joy working out together. She said a lot of positive things about Joy, but she also said something that troubled me."

"Really? What was that."

"Well, she said it was great that Joy was going to play in the Special Olympics USA Games, and she commended you for getting her out at an early age to play. She mentioned that your son was helpful, too."

"Ricky was and still is."

"Sadie also credited Henry's athleticism for Joy's success. And, of course she praised Coach Carrabas for his involvement. But what she said that bugged me was that she didn't think it was a good idea for Joy to play on the high school tennis team."

"Why was that?"

"She thought, you know—it might make some kids feel, uncomfortable competing against her for a position on the team."

"Hmm. That's interesting, because no one has even discussed the idea of Joy playing on the high school team."

"Do Sadie's kids play tennis?"

"No, they don't. Neither of her older kids is athletic, and the little one is only nine months old."

"Well, I'm surprised she said that—I mean, it obviously doesn't impact her or her kids. Don't you think that's strange?"

Brenda wanted to tell Cheryl that Sadie's remarks weren't strange at all. They were the kind of statements Sadie had been making her whole life. Instead of divulging the contempt she felt, Brenda calmly replied, "Lots of people don't understand about kids with special needs. It's a constant struggle to have them mainstreamed in school and given a chance to accomplish what they are really capable of doing. Out of curiosity, were there other women around when Sadie made that comment?"

"I think a couple were, but nobody else said anything."

"Interesting."

"I told them how much Allison has enjoyed playing with Joy and how good the matches have been."

"I really appreciate that."

"Well, I think you are doing an incredible job with Joy."

"Thanks, Cheryl, but you and Allison are helping us a lot, and I'm really grateful to both of you."

"When do you leave for Iowa?"

"Tomorrow."

"Wow."

"We arrive tomorrow night. Saturday and Sunday, judges assess each participant's ability in individual sports and each team's ability in team sports. On Sunday night, the athletes have a parade before the games begin on Monday. It should be really exciting. Some famous Iowans will be welcoming the athletes, then Hootie and the Blowfish will perform for them."

"Fantastic."

"It really is. And what people don't realize is that the athletes range in age from eight up to older adults. Special Olympics isn't just for kids."

"Yes, I read about that when I was on the internet, and Tom was talking about it the other day, too."

Brenda and Cheryl looked up to see Tom's students exiting the courts. Joy and Allison returned to their mothers and waited for Coach Carrabas. As usual, he gave his pupils a short sermon before they left the park. And as usual, it began with a question. "How can we tell when someone at your level or even at the professional level is feeling pressure and starts to choke?"

"They miss a lot of shots," a girl suggested.

"Correct, and that's a result of pressure or choking. What do they do that causes them to mishit their shots?"

"Take their eye off the ball?" responded a boy. "They don't watch it."

"Yes. When players get nervous, they don't watch the ball as carefully. True. What else do we notice...? Anyone...? Well, they don't move their feet. They stand still like their feet are imbedded in concrete. If you don't move your feet and get in position to hit the ball, chances are greater for a mishit. You can feel it happening to yourself sometimes. And if you watch your opponents, you can see it happening to them when they're tight, too. And, how do we take advantage of an opponent who is tight?"

"Make them run."

"Good suggestion," Coach acknowledged. "How about hitting to their weaker side," he added, "which is usually the backhand. Or, another strategy is to hit the ball right at them. If they aren't moving their feet, they will have more trouble with that shot than making them move for a shot...so, once again, how does choking on the court relate to choking in other things. First, what other things are you doing when you choke?" he asked.

"Taking a test in school," someone blurted out.

"Or getting your driver's license."

"Going out on a date," one boy divulged to the amusement of the rest. "Are you suggesting we need to move our feet more then, too, Coach?"

Coach laughed. "Moving your feet is good on the tennis court," he said. "What can you do when you're tense about an Algebra test or getting your driver's license...? C'mon," he encouraged, but no one said anything. "How about preparing better, so you're not so nervous. It will decrease the amount of times you choke. But say you do choke, what can you do?" Still, no one volunteered. "You can actually calm yourself by imaging things that relax you, and you can practice it before you actually need it. For example, I love to think about the water on Pierce Lake lapping against rocks. I find that sound peaceful. Sometimes, I just imagine the sound in my mind when I'm alone. Then when I'm in a match or doing something that makes me tight, I conjure up the image and sound of the lake in my mind and it helps relax me. The key is that you have to practice it when you are relaxed before you can use it when you are tight. OK...? It's one of the most important lessons I ever learned.

"As I mentioned after our last session, I will be gone this Saturday and won't be back until late the following Saturday. In the meantime, practice your tennis and your imaging."

A few students had questions, and Coach stayed to answer them before greeting Allison, Joy, and their mothers. "Where is Ricky this evening?" he asked.

"He's home helping his dad fix the water softener."

"Well tell him I asked for him, please...OK, girls, tonight we are going to do something a little different. As usual you will warm up, then I am going to go on the court with you. You will alternate serves, and at the end of *every* point we will discuss what you did."

"Oh, oh," Joy said.

"It's really like we always do, Joy, only instead of waiting for your set to end to talk, I will talk to you at the end of each point. So, go ahead out and warm up, and I'll be over in a few minutes."

Tom excused himself and walked down to the shelter. As he watched the rough water and felt the chilly evening breeze, he considered what advice he could deliver to Joy during this last teaching session. He had already conceived the format, discussing each point separately, but he had to remember not to make too many suggestions during his lesson. Tom believed lots of coaches and teachers confused students by overwhelming them with facts. And Joy thrived on repetition. Whether it was learning something Tom repeated multiple times, like "turn your body sideways on your volleys," or hitting the same shot over and over, like the lob to her opponent's backhand, the more Joy heard advice or practiced strokes, the better she performed.

After using the facilities, Tom returned to Joy and Allison, who were still practicing groundstrokes. "Let's warm up your serves, now, then I'll have you play out points." He watched them serve and struggle with the wind. Despite wind screens on some fences, their balls blew forward or backward when they tossed them in the air, floating into the net or out of the service boxes after they hit them. Coach decided to take advantage of the conditions. He had played a tournament in Ames, and Iowa State's courts were open and very breezy. "So just toss the ball in the air and watch what the wind does to it. Good. You can see that on this side, it blows forward, right? To compensate, you have to toss the ball a little behind where you usually toss it. By compensate, I mean adjust the toss to get it where you want it. Give it a try," he encouraged the girls. "Keep doing it until you feel comfortable." Once they understood what Coach meant and practiced it, he moved them to the opposite side where the wind was in their faces and blew the ball backward. Again, he had them repeat their tosses several times. After working on their tosses, he taught them how to hit serves into the wind and with the wind. "This is where coming over the top of the ball is extremely important, especially with a wind at your back," Tom directed, then he demonstrated what he meant. "See how I hit over it? OK, now you try. Before each serve, remind yourself where the wind is coming from."

Tom watched his pupils and acknowledged their progress, "Nice. You guys are definitely getting it…now, Joy, go to the other side and serve a ball, then Allison will serve from this side to you. I'll have you switch sides shortly."

After Joy served and the girls played out their first point, Tom brought them to the net to discuss it. "How did the wind affect your lob, Allison?"

"It blew it out."

"Right. It is really difficult to lob when wind is at your back, especially when it's blowing this hard, unless you have topspin. Joy, your serve into the wind was fine. You adjusted your ball toss and stroke perfectly."

As instructed, the girls alternated serves and discussed every point with Coach Carrabas. Joy became frustrated when serving with the wind behind her. Her ball toss was exactly where she wanted it, but she overhit her serves causing them to land behind the service line. Remembering his first encounters with Joy, Tom suggested she hit her serves underhanded from the court's north side. Joy was skeptical, but it worked. As a matter of fact, Allison had trouble returning Joy's serves, because the wind caused the ball to spin more. Coach reassured Joy that underhanded serves were not only legal, but they could be very effective. It was another weapon in her arsenal—another shot she could use.

Finally, they worked on lobs facing the wind, and learned how to hit shots deeper than usual while allowing currents to bring the ball back on the court. All in all, the last practice was a success. Tom was pleased.

As he went back to the oak trees to talk to both mothers, he thought about Joy's influence on his ability to teach and how his relationship with her made him a better communicator—a more effective coach. Sure, he always taught groups of students in classrooms and on the courts, but she taught him to look at the individual within the group. Teaching masses of students was efficient; teaching individuals allowed his students to reach their potentials.

His tennis teams had won numerous titles over the years. He had garnered so many trophies, Oakbrook High had to build a special showcase to house them. But even more rewarding was working with students like Joy, guiding them to achieve the maximum they were capable of achieving.

"Well," he began, talking to both mothers, "we had another productive evening. We learned how to harness the wind tonight. We learned how to serve with the wind in our faces and at our backs, and we learned how to lob into the wind. Conditions tonight were difficult but not unlike those Joy could face in Iowa."

"Thank you, Tom. We really appreciate the special time you've given our girls," Brenda said.

"It's been my pleasure, but I'm also going to reap some rewards. I want both girls to try out for our tennis team this fall. They're good players and would be an asset to Oakbrook's program."

"Thank you," Cheryl replied proudly.

Brenda felt overwhelmed but concerned. "Believe it or not, we just had this conversation, didn't we, Cheryl— what, maybe ten minutes ago? We know for a fact some people in the community don't want Joy to play on the high school team."

"I heard one mom say something, but her kids don't even play tennis," Cheryl corroborated.

"I'm not surprised," Tom smiled. "Even in a close-knit village like ours, there are prejudices."

"Please, don't allow Joy on the team if she doesn't deserve to be there, Tom" Brenda pleaded.

"I promise you that I won't, but I have no doubt that she will make it, because she's good enough to play for us."

Brenda was jubilant. "Wow! I never pictured this happening. To me, it's almost more exciting than nationals."

Tom sat down on a bench. "I understand. I really do."

"People are going to say she's a good player, because of the special attention you paid to her, you know."

"I will respond by simply saying that any youngster who wants more of my time as a student or as a tennis player simply has to ask for it. I have always been willing to help kids who need extra time or help, providing they are willing to put forth effort. To her credit, Joy has always done that."

Neither Joy nor Allison heard the adult conversation. They had gathered their tennis gear and were lollygagging back to the oaks.

C H A P T E R   2 6

— ⚜ —

Friday, August 15, 1975

BRENDA BARELY LEFT her room the day following Derek's accident. She had no idea how to answer questions people would ultimately ask. What happened? Where is your father now? Did he go to jail? How is Derek? Surely no one would ask how she was, but maybe that wasn't important.

Rally wouldn't leave her side. Even when she went to the bathroom, he followed Brenda to the door, then back to her room again to lie down beside her. He dragged her outside a few times to relieve himself, but he seemed to understand her need for seclusion and made his outings as infrequent as possible.

Mrs. Nelson called Derek's mother and learned about his surgery and cast. Their conversation was brief and tense, which made Ellen feel worse. Working at the library the following day, she learned that Ralph had been released from jail after an overnight stay and would be charged with drunken driving, endangering a life, leaving the scene of an accident, etc., etc., etc.

"You need to get ready for tennis, Brenda," her mother warned entering her bedroom. "Come on. You haven't been out of this room since Wednesday."

239

"I can't go to the park. I don't want to see anybody."

"Brenda, we both have to face the community. You and I didn't do anything wrong. Your father did."

"I know, but he's my father, and everyone will judge me, too, for what he did."

"Look, it's no different for me. I was married to him. Not only that, but I was the one who suggested he pick you up at the park. I'm going to have to face people who know what happened all day long."

"I will, too," interrupted John.

"At least you'll be home, John," Brenda tendered.

"The sooner you face everyone and deal with things, the faster you can leave it behind you."

When Brenda covered her head with a pillow, her mother walked over and sat down beside her on the bed. "I know this isn't easy…look, I'll drop you off and stay awhile to make sure you're OK. Will that help?"

"I don't know."

"Come on. Get up and get dressed. I'll make you a little breakfast, and we can go to Taylor Park together."

When Brenda arrived with her mother, she noticed fewer kids were on the courts than usual. She wondered where the others were.

Al and Carrie greeted them. "It's so nice to see you again, Mrs. Nelson. Hi Brenda," Carrie said.

"Hello," Al added. "I'm glad you came to watch her tournament."

"Tournament?" asked Brenda's mother.

"Yes. Today is round one. Novices play, with the winner advancing to the main draw tomorrow."

Al explained, "Brenda, you will play Philip first. The winner will play the winner of Jamie and Kelly's match."

"With everything that's going on, I forgot," Brenda admitted.

"It's OK. You're here now. Here are the balls. You play on Court One. You guys get a ten minute warm up, then play the best of three sets."

Brenda fidgeted with her racquet, "I wondered where the rest of the kids were."

"They'll all be here tomorrow," Al assured her.

"Al," Mrs. Nelson began, "I want to thank you for taking the kids and Rally home Wednesday."

"It was no problem at all."

As Brenda left for her match, Mrs. Nelson confided in the teens, "This experience has really impacted Brenda. She didn't get out of bed at all yesterday. I really had to prod her to get her here today. Please keep an eye on her for me."

"Absolutely," Carrie said. "But if you have time, I know she would appreciate your watching her play a little. I don't think the match will take very long."

"I'm sure that would be a good idea. I guess the library won't miss me if I stay for a short time."

Ellen Nelson sat down on a secluded bench to watch her daughter's match. She thought about Ralph, remembering their first encounter at her college library in Chicago. He had recently returned from Korea, was attending school on the G.I. Bill, and still wore his army uniform. She found him handsome and polite. He told her he was studying psychology with the intention of seeking a career in Intelligence in the service. Ellen worked behind the desk at the time and vividly remembered Ralph needed to read an article in *The American Journal of Psychology* on phobias. She knew it was a ploy when he asked her to show him exactly where the journals were stored, but she indulged him, because she was attracted to him immediately.

Before going out with Ralph, Ellen had dated sporadically. Early on, she adopted the role of stereotypical librarian, replete with glasses, frumpy long dresses, and hair in a bun. She avoided socializing, preferring the fantasies of novels to the realities of life.

Ralph changed her profile and her self-image. Beneath the façade of intellectual, he discovered an exciting partner, who liked to have fun. He took her to Wrigley Field, restaurants, the movies, even night clubs. Ellen, who hadn't spent time alone with a man before, was austere; Ralph, who was much more experienced, ably eased her into intimacy.

During their courtship, Ellen saw little to foreshadow what would happen to them later on. It wasn't until they were married that she noticed Ralph was drinking more in addition to staying out later than he used to. Work was not as rewarding for him, so he left the army without securing another position. For a time, he drove semis to supplement the family income. After their children were born, he became more aloof, drank even more, and gave Ellen reason to doubt his fidelity. When she confronted him about their deteriorating relationship, he blamed his problems on his stint in Korea, explaining he was having nightmares and flashbacks about his tour there. At a therapist's they saw together, Ralph admitted to an affair he had been having for a couple of years. For Ellen, that was the last straw, she reclaimed her librarian persona and initiated divorce proceedings.

In the end, she promised not to ask for financial assistance for the children if he agreed not to see them without her permission. He acquiesced, and she held him at bay until recently, when she thought he was sober and ready to be a parent again.

While Ellen was thinking about Ralph, Al drifted over to watch Brenda's match with her. "She's doing great, isn't she," he remarked.

"What's the score?"

"I think she is up 4-0."

"I'm afraid I've been letting my mind wander."

"When you first came today, you told us Brenda was having a hard time," Al reminded her.

"That's right. She has been bullied by some girls here at the park. She's afraid this recent episode will provide more fodder for them."

"I've seen the bullying. I haven't interfered, because I wanted Brenda to stick up for herself."

"It's very difficult for her. She claims those girls are older, plus she doesn't have a support system like they have."

"She's right. They're older, and they're united."

"Brenda is a lot like me. She is more of a recluse—somewhat introverted; she doesn't have a lot of friends."

"I think tennis is good for her," Al said. "She's playing very well for someone who never played matches before. I've noticed she is more confident."

"She certainly loves the game, and she is terribly fond of you and Carrie."

"We think she's a great kid. We're glad we've gotten to know her better this summer," Al said looking up at the court. "Looks like she won the first set 6-0. I'm not surprised. Can you stay for the second set?"

"Yes, I'm going to."

"I'm sure Brenda appreciates your support," continued Al, before walking towards Court One.

Ellen leaned back on the bench. She began berating herself for not being a more attentive mother. She hadn't talked to her daughter about a lot of issues she should have. There was little conversation about periods when Brenda had her first one a year ago. They hadn't had a proper talk about sex, either. Nor had they spoken about difficulties girls and women have with peers who become foes overnight. In addition, she had hidden lots of information about her relationship with Ralph that Brenda was old enough to understand. In reality, she thought, once she divorced Ralph she went back into her shell. Her kids needed and should receive more from her. Supporting Brenda at this tournament could be a first step towards that goal.

Ellen concentrated on the match. She never realized how skilled her daughter was. Brenda won point after point against a boy her own age. In addition, she hit the ball so much harder than he did. Ellen watched them switch sides as Brenda called out the score, "3-love." This little girl, who wasn't a little girl anymore was her daughter. Abandoning Ralph did not mean she had to abandon love. Loving someone did not mean you left yourself open to have your heart broken—well, not all the time.

After Brenda won the second set, she ran over to her mother. "I won 6-0, 6-0, Mom."

"He didn't win any games in two sets?" her mother asked.

"Nope."

"Nice going. I'm very proud of you. When do you play next?"

"Just as soon as Jamie and Kelly are finished. I play the winner."

"Would you like me to stay?"

"Yes. Very much. Can you?"

"Is there a payphone at the shelter?"

"Yes."

"Let me call the library to tell them I'm going to be late."

Jamie beat Kelly and received permission from Carrie to go to the shelter before playing the novice finals.

Brenda sat at the bench her mother had occupied waiting for her to return. As Ellen approached, Brenda asked if she was able to stay.

"I am," she informed her.

Uncharacteristically, Brenda stood up to kiss her mother on the cheek. "Thank you, Mom," she said.

Uncharacteristically, her mother hugged Brenda. Returning her kiss, she replied, "You're welcome, dear… I think I just saw the boy you're going to play at the shelter. Is his mother here?"

"I don't know what she looks like, but I don't think so. The lady who was sitting over there was Kelly's mom. I think they left already."

"Oh."

"You know, if I win this match, I come back tomorrow and play against the older kids."

"Yes, that's what Al said…it looks like your opponent… um…"

"Jamie."

"Yes, Jamie—is back. Good luck. Play well."

"I'm gonna try, Mom."

As Brenda jogged to the court, Carrie handed her a new can of balls and talked to both players briefly before sitting down next to Mrs. Nelson. "Are you nervous?"

"A little. I think Brenda is excited about playing this match."

"They've played before—a few days ago—Brenda won. But there's more pressure on her now."

"This is all so new to me. When I was a child, sometimes I played tennis with friends, but it wasn't organized or nearly as competitive as it is now."

"I don't know if that's a good or a bad thing," Carrie responded.

"They sure play better now than we did."

"Probably. But are they having as much fun?"

"I guess I don't know. It must be fun to be as proficient as they are."

"Of course it is. Competing is fun, too. But so is playing for the heck of it. For me, sometimes those fun matches are the best matches of all."

"I guess they're ready," Mrs. Nelson said, pointing to the court.

Al stood by the fence as Brenda served the first point. The ball passed back and forth multiple times before Brenda hit it into the net. "Nice point, guys," Al encouraged. The second rally was shorter, as Brenda netted a ball again. Down love-30, she looked unsure of her shots. A double fault put her behind love-40. Brenda took a deep breath before serving the fourth point of the game. Again, she missed her first serve and was forced to hit a second. When her ball fell short in the service box, Jamie nailed it for a winner. Game over, Jamie led 1-0.

Before they switched sides, they took swigs of water from their bottles and toweled off. It was comfortable sitting under the oaks but very hot on the court.

Jamie won his serve easily to go ahead 2-0. Before Brenda served to begin the third game, she grabbed a ball, turned around and belted it into the fence behind her, disgustedly.

Al moved from the fence to join Carrie and Mrs. Nelson under the oak trees. "She's a little tight," he remarked to no one in particular. "She'll be OK. I'm sure she'll loosen up."

"Isn't that bad sportsmanship?" Brenda's mother asked.

"I suppose it is," Al replied. "I try to teach players not to lose their cool on the court and certainly not to take their anger out on their opponents. Smashing a ball at the person you are playing against is prohibited. But, there are a few players who seem to compete better after they let off some steam by yelling or pounding a ball against the fence like Brenda did."

After the brief outburst, Brenda played better, not only winning her serve but winning the next game, too. At 2-all, Brenda served again and double faulted the first point of the fifth game. However, that was her last double fault, and she didn't lose another game, either, winning the initial set 6-2.

"OK, you two. It's hot out. Why don't you take a break between sets today," Al suggested. "If you want, you can go to the shelter and wash up."

"Good idea," Carrie concurred.

Al smiled, "Thank you."

"Well, I'm glad you moved away from the fence, because I think you were giving her bad karma," Carrie teased.

"I wouldn't do that."

Mrs. Nelson chuckled at the teens' goofiness.

Before Brenda and Jamie returned to the court, three girls drove into the parking lot on their bicycles. Carrie and Al stiffened noticeably, recognizing Sadie, Dee Dee, and Rachel. The girls skidded to a stop on the gravel before walking their bikes toward the courts. "Where are the kids? Who's playing?" Sadie asked.

"Brenda and Jamie are in the finals. They're taking a break," Al answered.

"Have they begun to play yet?"

"Yes, they already played the first set."

"Who won?" Dee Dee asked.

"Brenda, 6-3."

"6-2," Carrie corrected Al.

"That's too bad," said Sadie sorrowfully. "I was hoping Jamie was going to kick her butt."

"Me, too," said Rachel.

As Al stood up and moved, the girls noticed Brenda's mother hidden behind him. "Do you girls know Mrs. Nelson, Brenda's mother?" Al asked serenely. I'm sure you've seen her at the library, haven't you?" he pressed. "Stay away from the players, please."

The girls waved shyly to Brenda's mother, then walked their bicycles back to the parking lot and left unobtrusively.

Returning from the shelter, Brenda and Jamie saw them leave. "What were they doing here?" Brenda asked.

"I think they wanted to scout your match."

"Ha. Ha," Brenda laughed. "I know what that is, Al."

"I know you do," he said patting her on the shoulder. "By the way, did you finish the book?"

"I did."

"Did you love it?"

"Yes, it was great."

"I agree."

"Do you two have a secret I don't know about?" Carrie asked lightly.

"You could call it that," Al replied.

"Hmmm," Carrie muttered.

"All right. Let's get back and play another set. Both of you played a great first one. Keep up the good work," Al directed.

Between Al joking with her and witnessing the departure of her tormenters, Brenda eased into the second set confidently. At the end of three games, she led 3-0. "It looks like she's in the groove again," Al said to Mrs. Nelson.

"Yes," she responded. "Those girls, are they the ones who bother her?"

"Yes," Carrie answered.

"I've seen them before, but what's the girl's name with the red hair?"

"Dee Dee."

"Oh, yes. She just moved here a couple of years ago," Mrs. Nelson remembered. "And the other one is Rachel, right?"

"Right."

"I used to know girls like them when I went to school."

Carrie agreed, "I think we all did."

"It's really sad," Mrs. Nelson continued, "Sadie's father is so nice, and he has done so much for the community—starting the emergency medical service and all. You wonder how a child turns out like that coming from a good family."

"Carrie thinks she has anorexia," Al said.

"She looks thinner every time I see her. I suspect Carrie is right," Mrs. Nelson agreed.

Silently, Carrie, Al and Mrs. Nelson watched the match. Brenda continued to play well, overpowering Jamie 6-1 in the second set. They shook hands at the net after the match and chatted before returning to the oaks.

"She's too tough for me," Jamie grinned.

"You are a great sport, Jamie, and your tennis improves every time you play," Carrie complimented him.

Jamie placed his hands on his hips, "You better win tomorrow, Brenda. I'm rooting for you. What time does she play?"

"I don't know," Al said. "I think Carrie has the draw sheet—Carrie, what time does Brenda play tomorrow?"

"Early. Nine o'clock. She's the first one out there."

"Who does she play?"

"Rachel."

As mother and daughter entered the car to go home, Ellen told Brenda she was very proud of her and extremely impressed with her tennis game. She also described her encounter with the three girls and how Al effectively humiliated them.

"Do you understand why I call her Sadistic Sadie, now?" Brenda asked.

"Yes, I do."

"Can you come back tomorrow and watch my match?"

"Absolutely. I'm going to drop you off at home and go to work. I'll arrange for someone to cover me tomorrow, so I can see you play."

"Thanks, Mom. I love you."

"I love you, too."

CHAPTER 27

———— ❖ ————

Saturday, August 16, 1975

BRENDA AND HER entourage—her mother, brother and Rally—arrived fifteen minutes early for the match with Rachel. Family support eased Brenda's anxiety some. Her heart rate slowed and her stomach, which had growled almost as loudly as Rally, finally quieted. She brought some used balls onto the court to practice serves. John stood across the net to retrieve them.

The air was calm, the sky cloudy. Perfect weather for serving. No wind to blow her ball toss and no sun to blind her when she looked up. She thought about the double faults in her matches the previous day, then recalled what Carrie taught her—if you're hitting the ball into the net on your serve, keep your left arm up longer after you toss the ball in the air. She needed to remember that today.

She wore a different outfit for the match—a lavender top with matching socks—a white visor and white shorts. She had bought the clothes with her mother months ago in Madison, but she had buried them deep in a drawer. Today, she felt like wearing something brighter. When she examined herself in the mirror, she felt good about what she saw—first, her complexion looked so much better; second, lavender was the perfect color for her. She even smiled at her reflected image, wondering for a second what Jamie would think.

Her practice serves went deep into the service box with good pace. John tried to catch them after they bounced, encouraging her, "Perfect! Right where you want it." They switched sides of the net, and Brenda served a few more times. As she hit her last ball, she saw Carrie approaching the court.

"Hey, Brenda. How are you doing?"

"Fine. I was just hitting a few serves."

"Good for you…hi," Carrie addressed John. "It's nice of you to help your sister."

"Hi. She was really hitting good serves. They were hard. Some of them I couldn't even catch…I'm going to learn to play tennis, too. My mom is going to get me my own racquet and tennis shoes and a tennis hat or visor. Just like Brenda has. How old do I have to be before I can have lessons at the park?"

"You have to be going into seventh grade. What grade are you going into?"

"Fourth," he said dejectedly.

"Well, you have a little while yet, but I bet Brenda will hit with you."

"Will you?" John asked his sister.

"Sure, as soon as Mom gets you a racquet. You didn't seem interested before."

"Well, I am now!" he insisted.

"Brenda, you and Rachel are going to play on Court One," Carrie instructed. "Here is a can of new balls for your match. Just like yesterday, you have ten minutes to warm up. Do you want to take a break before Rachel comes?"

"Sure."

As Brenda left the court with John, she heard the familiar "Ka-ka-ka-ka" announcing Sadie's arrival with Rachel and Dee Dee. Brenda had prepared herself for this inevitability. Her plan was to ignore them for as long as she could. Casually, she sat down next to her mother to drink some water.

As the triumvirate approached the courts, Al intercepted them. "Only the players are allowed beyond the benches and tables…Rachel, you play Brenda on Court One. Carrie gave her a new can of balls. Are you ready?"

"Yes," Rachel answered.

"Pretty snazzy outfit she has on. Don't you think?" Sadie sneered, loud enough for everyone to hear.

"OK, girls. Start warming-up. I'll tell you when you have two minutes left so you can practice serves. Good luck to both of you. You play two out of three sets. Regular scoring. Carrie and I will be around if you have any questions."

Rachel was nervous. She had trouble initiating a rally, repeatedly hitting her feeds into the net. When Brenda hit to her backhand, Rachel's returns sailed out of play. She even struck her volleys poorly, missing some altogether. Al gave them two more minutes to warm up their serves before instructing them to begin the first set.

Brenda began the match by hitting her first serve into the net. She eased up on her second serve, but it fell short, too, prompting Rachel's supporters to clap and hoot. Immediately, Al went to their table to admonish them, "Please don't do that again! Cheering for a double fault is rude. It's not proper tennis etiquette. You can cheer when someone makes a good shot, but you cannot jeer when a player makes a mistake. Understood?" he asked. No one responded.

Undeterred by the double fault, Brenda kept her left arm in the air longer on her ball toss to serve out the first game convincingly. In the second game, she blasted returns to Rachel's backhand winning that one as well. There were no double faults in the third game, as Brenda continued to serve effectively. At 40-15, she took a short ball out of the air for a winner to go up 3-0 in the set.

Brenda was so focused on the match that she didn't even notice Jamie arrive to sit beside her mother and John, nor did she see Coach Carrabas enter the oak grove. The fourth game went to deuce several times, then alternated between ad-in and ad-out, before Brenda again attacked Rachel's backhand for the deciding point. The next two games were over in no time. Brenda won the first set 6-0.

As she drank from her canister, Brenda heard clapping. She turned to see Jamie standing to applaud her. The freshmen girls at the nearby table glared at him as he gave his friend a thumbs-up, too. Brenda pretended she didn't see or hear him, but glancing at the spectators, she also noticed Coach Carrabas.

Brenda was somewhat complacent at the start of the second set, losing the first two points of the initial game by hitting shots long. Then she began to feel tight, double faulting the third point. After winning the next one, she hit the final shot of the game into the net giving Rachel a 1-0 lead. Rachel won the next two games, too. Before she knew it, Brenda was losing 3-0. Sadie and Dee Dee were ecstatic.

Watching Rachel's friends celebrate brought back the disturbing memory of her first encounter with them. Brenda briefly replayed the humiliating episode in her mind, replete with wet pants and lies the threesome had told. Effectively, she stoked the fire. Unloading on Rachel's serve, she smoked a devastating forehand winner down the line. Everyone witnessed the blast but no one could utter a sound. Brenda won the next three points to capture the fourth game, easily. The return she nailed was the turning point of the match; the momentum had shifted. After six games, the score was tied, 3-all.

Pundits profess the seventh game of a set is the most crucial. Some might argue with that generalization, but no one would argue about its importance when the score is tied 3-3.

With Brenda serving, all eyes were glued to Court One. Al and Carrie, who were still recovering from Brenda's explosive return of serve in the fourth game, sat down with Coach Carrabas. John clutched himself, because he had to pee so badly. Anxiety immobilized Mrs. Nelson and Jamie, too. By that time, almost the entire summer group had arrived for their pending contests, but even they were focused on Brenda and Rachel. Unquestionably, everyone knew the score—on both accounts. The tension could not have been higher if the match had been a final.

Brenda served the first point and followed Rachel's return with a shot to the backhand. To everyone's surprise, Rachel hit a soaring lob over Brenda's head. Brenda retreated quickly, allowed the ball to bounce, then hit an overhead winner for the first point. The onlookers applauded both players. Brenda won the next two points with her serves; although she didn't ace Rachel, she placed both shots deep in the service boxes, into her opponent's body. Rachel won the fourth point of the game by lobbing Brenda again, but Brenda won the game hitting a strong crosscourt forehand for the final point.

Down 3-4, having lost four games in a row, Rachel became tentative and allowed Brenda to hit winners from all corners of the court. The next two games were over in short order. Brenda won the match 6-0, 6-3. After shaking hands, the girls left the court together, acknowledging the cheers.

First to congratulate Brenda was John, still holding himself. "Way to go, Brenda. That was awesome."

"John, for god's sake, go to the bathroom, please!" Brenda instructed. John needed no convincing and ran off to the shelter.

Jamie was next in line, "Well you did it again. Nice going."

"Thanks for coming, Jamie."

"I wouldn't have missed it for anything. That was sweet."

"Nice playing, dear," her mother said admiringly, as she hugged her daughter.

"Thanks, Mom."

"Congratulations, but you're just getting started, Brenda," said Al. "You're due back here at one this afternoon for your next match."

"She plays again?" her mother asked.

"She certainly does," Carrie assured her. "She plays the winner of the match on Court Three…didn't she play great today?"

"How old are those kids?" Mrs. Nelson asked looking over at Brenda's potential opponents. "I don't recognize them in their tennis garb."

"Fourteen. They're freshmen."

"They look so big to me. And you mean she has to play another boy?" Brenda's mother observed.

"Yes," Carrie answered. "We don't separate boys and girls in this tournament."

"So, how is Rally doing?" Al asked.

"He's great." Mrs. Nelson answered. "He loves the kids. Sleeps mostly with Brenda but sleeps with John, too."

"Have you ever met Coach Carrabas?" Al asked Mrs. Nelson as Tom approached.

"No, I haven't. It's nice to meet you. I'm Brenda's mother, Ellen."

"Yes, I just met Brenda the other day. It's so nice to meet you. Your daughter is quite a tennis player for just learning the game. I was very impressed with her today." Then turning toward Brenda he said, "Nice match, young lady. That was a fine effort. Congratulations."

"Thank you for watching," Brenda replied.

"Good luck in your next one," Coach said.

After John returned from the shelter, the Nelsons walked to the parking lot. Near the bike rack, they noticed Sadie and Dee Dee. They were comforting Rachel, who was obviously crying. Sadie looked up at Brenda ready to say something, when seemingly she changed her mind and said nothing at all.

After an early lunch at home followed by a short nap with Rally, Brenda returned to Taylor Park with her mother, John, and the puppy for her quarter-final match. She did not change outfits, because she felt the lavender top brought her good luck.

"Are you going to practice your serve, Brenda?" John asked. "I'll chase down the balls again for you if you want me to."

"No, not now. Thanks."

"Then I'll take Rally for a walk. C'mon, boy," he called. "Let's go to the lake." Eagerly, the dog followed John to his favorite spot on the beach, then plunged into the water to hunt minnows.

Like the morning, the afternoon was slightly overcast, but a mild wind began to blow off the lake. By the cemetery on the hillside opposite the park, some sumacs had begun to redden and a lone maple tree displayed a handful of yellow leaves.

Carrie, clipboard in hand, walked over to the Nelsons. "Hi everyone. Brenda, you play Tyler Haugen in the quarter-finals. He came early and is warming up with a friend on Court Three, where you two will be playing your match. He already has a new can of balls. Good luck."

"What time is it?" Brenda inquired.

Carrie answered, "Five 'til one,"

"Thanks," Brenda said, then turning to her mother she continued, "see you shortly."

"Play well, dear."

Tyler Haugen was the first seed and favored to win the tournament. At age fourteen, he stood almost six feet tall and weighed at least one hundred and eighty pounds. While he loved playing tennis, his primary sports were football and basketball. He was aloof when Brenda walked onto the court, mumbling to his hitting partner.

Brenda felt uncomfortable. The sensation increased as the two boys slapped each other on the back and laughed. So, this is how David felt when he saw Goliath, Brenda mused.

Brenda and Tyler had met a number of times over the course of the summer, but facing him one-on-one in a singles match, made him appear more ominous than she remembered. He wore a black tee shirt with "Led Zeppelin" emblazoned on the front, gray gym shorts, and a white visor. Looking away from Brenda, he opened the new can of balls. "Are you ready?" he asked curtly.

"Yes," she replied.

They warmed up—that is Brenda tried to warm up, but Tyler hit winners off her feeds instead of allowing her to practice her shots. To salvage some respect, Brenda smacked a few hard forehands at Tyler when he approached the net to hit his volleys, too. And she surprised him a few times. Tyler's serve, however, took her breath away. She had never tried to return a serve with that much steam on it. Remembering Coach Carrabas's comments to the older kids after the Ashe-Connors match, she thought about trying to take some pace off the ball to throw Tyler's timing off. Unfortunately, she had never practiced that tactic before, and it wasn't easy to slow shots down while keeping the ball deep in your opponent's court.

Brenda won the toss, deciding to serve. Tyler's attempts to intimidate her by pounding back returns failed; he overhit four shots in a row. The first two landed in the net—the next two were beyond the baseline. At 1-0, they switched sides, and Brenda began to gain some confidence. However, in the second game, she was unable to get a racquet on Tyler's first serves, and there was enough spin on his second serves to make it difficult for her to return those, too. With the score tied 1-1, Brenda served again. This time her opponent let up on his returns and they rallied longer, but Brenda could not keep the ball away from Tyler's long arms. He outdueled her to lead 2-1. He won his serve again in the fourth game, then broke Brenda in the fifth. Serving at 4-1, Tyler struggled with his first serves. Brenda became more patient with his second serves and started lobbing her returns deep in his court. Unused to this tactic, Tyler whaled on his overheads hitting most of them out. The score was 4-2, but that was the last game Brenda would win in the set. Tyler's first serves started to come in consistently, and they were just too fast for Brenda to control.

Watching the match from the sidelines, Al approached Court Three to tell the players they could have a five-minute break. Tyler said he was ready to play right now, but Brenda wanted a breather and walked to the oaks to sit with her mother.

"I didn't see Jamie. Was he here?" she asked.

"No. I haven't seen him this afternoon."

"Is John still at the lake?"

"He came back and watched a little of your match. As usual, he got antsy and wandered off with Rally again."

"Tyler is really good," Brenda confessed, taking a drink from her canister. "He hits the heck out of the ball, and I can't get anything past him."

"He's really big, too," her mother smiled. "I think you're playing really well, all things considered."

"I'm not quitting. I'll tell you that."

Ellen didn't know how to respond. The whole scenario—the tournament, the competition, playing against boys—it was all foreign to her. She may have played a little tennis when she was younger, but she never played against a six-foot boy. That was for sure!

Brenda stood up and returned to the court. Tyler was waiting and handed her two balls. "It's your serve," he said more congenially, looking her in the eye. Brenda was shocked by the change in his demeanor.

In the first game of the new set, Brenda hit her serves well, but Tyler's returns were more effective. She lost it without winning a point. In the second game, Tyler's first serves were still too hot to handle. She tried lobbing the ball when she got a second serve, but the wind off the lake had picked up, and she had difficulty keeping her shots on the court. Down 0-2, Brenda decided to take pace off her serves. She hoped that Tyler, with the wind at his back, would start to hit his returns out, and he did. She won the third game easily. As the wind continued to pick up, however, Tyler adjusted his shots and won the next four games in a row. Brenda never gave up, but her opponent's game was just too much for her. When the match ended 6-2, 6-1, Tyler sprinted to the net and shook Brenda's hand. "You really played well," he praised her. "You're a very smart player."

"Thank you," Brenda responded. "Nice match. Good luck tomorrow."

Despite the score, Brenda was pleased with herself and her play. As she came off the court with Tyler, Al and Carrie congratulated both of them.

"She's a crafty one, isn't she?" Al asked Tyler.

"I told her that," Tyler admitted. "She tried everything out there today."

Al shook both their hands, "Yes, she did."

Carrie gave Brenda a hug, "Nice going. You did very well."

Brenda's mom and brother hugged her, too, and Rally placed two muddy paw prints on her new white shorts.

"Don't worry," her mother advised, "it all comes out in the wash."

"That's an aphorism, isn't it?" Al queried Mrs. Nelson.

"Indeed it is. Very good! I'm quite impressed, Al... Coach Carrabas's influence, no doubt?"

"But, of course," Al smiled.

CHAPTER 28

─────── ✤ ───────

Friday morning, June 30, 2006

BEFORE BRENDA LEFT for Iowa, she decided to finish up a few odds and ends at work. She went to Few Hours A Day Nursery before the rest of her family was up and wasn't at her desk more than fifteen minutes when her phone rang.

"Hello," she answered.

"Hi. Is this Mrs. Bjorkman?"

"Yes."

"Hi, Brenda. Charlie Wasson. I hoped you'd be at work early today. Glad I called the nursery first."

"Oh, hello, Charlie," she said to the police chief. "What's up?"

"I'd like you to come to the station. There's someone here who'd like to see you."

"Who is that?" she asked nervously.

"Come on down to see for yourself," he answered. "We caught the crooks who broke into your nursery, and I've got one of them locked up."

"Really?"

"Yup. C'mon to my office. I'll bring you to him."

"Why does he want to see me?"

"Oh, I don't want to spoil it for you."

"Mmm. OK. I'll be there shortly."

Brenda's anxiety level was off the charts. Tension around nationals was substantial, but this new wrinkle made it ten times worse. Charlie said they captured one of the thieves who stole from the nursery, but why did he want to see her? Had he seen the video? Was he going to blackmail her? She would accommodate him and drop all charges—she would do anything to make sure her abuse of Ellie didn't become public. Panicking, she almost drove through a stop sign and into an oncoming truck on her way to the station.

She left her car and walked the steps to Charlie's office. He was sitting behind his desk writing. "You aren't going to believe this," he said to her shaking his head. "Come on with me, Brenda."

She followed him down a windowless hallway to an area she had never visited before. From a few yards away, she could make out bars and behind those bars someone was sitting on a cot. "I'll leave you two alone," Charlie said as he turned around. Brenda wanted to leave with him. She squinted as she got closer to the cell, trying to recognize who was there.

"Hi," said a raspy and familiar voice behind a gray beard.

"Hi," Brenda answered back. "What are you doing here?"

"What do you mean? Chief told you, didn't he?"

"I guess he did, but I didn't expect to see *you*."

"Ya, it's been awhile, hasn't it, Brenda?"

"Does Mom know you're around?"

"Nope. I haven't spoken to your mother in years. Heard she was living with you and the plumber though. I saw your daughter at the park a couple of times playing tennis. She's really good. Read the article about Special Olympics in *The Oakbrook Current*, too. When are you leaving, anyway?"

"This afternoon…did you ever speak to her?"

"No, I didn't want to frighten her. I'm not sure I'd know what to say to her anyhow."

"Mmm."

"Ah, well, I guess I caught you just in the nick of time."

"Why did you take our equipment, Ralph?" she asked.

"Needed money."

"Did you rob those other places, too?"

"I was probably involved in some."

"How did you know we had equipment worth taking?"

"I saw Williams's truck outside your place."

"Have you been hanging around town?"

"I have a sort-of friend who lives nearby. I stay with her occasionally."

"Is she involved in all this?"

"Nope. Didn't have a thing to do with it."

"Really. So, how did they catch you?"

"Fingerprints. Matched the ones from that bike accident years ago."

"Oh, my god."

"Yup."

"Why did you take my old computer, too?"

"To make it look more real. If I left it, they'd wonder why I didn't take it."

"So, why did you want to see me?"

"Oh, I suppose to do something helpful as a father for once in my life."

"What do you mean helpful?"

"I saw the video of you and that kid, Brenda. You know, the one in the highchair…you're not saying very much… what in hell did you smack her hand for? You, a nursery school teacher!"

"It's a long story, Ralph. It goes way back to when I was in middle school."

"Well, whatever the reason. How could you do it with video cameras around? Are you stupid? I knew it was you even with the shades drawn…"

"I didn't know a camera was there. The point is I should never have hurt Ellie."

"Whose kid is she?"

"Sadie Appel's."

"That Winetraub girl? That little bitch that used to harass you all the time?"

"Same one."

"Oh. Now I understand…still doesn't give you an excuse to hurt her kid."

"No, it doesn't. I regretted it immediately…so, where's the disc now?"

"Gone. That's what I wanted to tell you. I broke it with the heel of my boot, so no one could get their paws on it."

"How did you happen to see it anyway?"

"I thought I'd sell the discs, because they are re-writeable. First, I wanted to make sure there were no recognizable recordings. If there were, people would know where I stole them from. When I saw you and that kid on one, I destroyed it."

"Thank you."

"You're welcome. Look, I know I've been a real burden to you and your mother, even though I haven't been around much. That time at the park—I'm sure you took a lot of crap after I backed into your friend in the parking lot."

"And got shot at!" Brenda amplified.

"Ya. That, too."

"During my first week of high school," Brenda recalled, "when I went to the Girls' locker room to change into my tennis clothes, Sadie had stuck 'Wanted' posters with fake pictures of you on every locker. And hanging beside mine was a black and white striped shirt with an inmate number taped to the front."

"That's sick," her father replied.

"Sure is. And there are a lot more stories I could tell you…but you've helped put an end to this nightmare, and I'm grateful. Billy Williams and his team lost the CD. They kept looking for it but couldn't find it, thank heavens. Where was it anyhow?"

"In the utility closet under the cover for the video player."

"Unbelievable."

"Well, good. I'm glad it's over. Now you can focus on Joy."

"So, what can I do for you?" Brenda asked.

"Nothing. I called those lawyers."

"The Femrites?"

"Yes. They weren't in their office yet."

"Do you need money to hire them?"

"Probably wouldn't hurt."

"I'll see what I can do before I leave for Iowa."

"Thanks."

"Ya. Thank you, too."

———— ⚜ ————

CHAPTER 29

Friday afternoon, June 30, 2006

BRENDA WENT HOME after leaving the police station. She thought about telling her mother and Henry the whole story—the episode with Ellie, the video cameras, the CD—all of it. What a relief to unload her burden once and for all. But she was still so ashamed, she couldn't say anything.

So, when she greeted her mother in the kitchen, she told her about Ralph but excluded the part about Ellie. Ellen was mildly amused by the story.

"Have you seen him around town recently?" Brenda asked.

"No, I haven't."

"Did you know he was hanging around Oakbrook?"

"A week or two ago, I overheard a couple of women at the library talking, but I couldn't pick up the whole conversation, and I haven't spoken to him myself in ages."

"Apparently, he has a lady friend close by."

"I'm not surprised."

"He claims he's seen Joy."

"Really? And talked to her?"

"No, he actually said he didn't talk to her."

"And Ricky?"

"He didn't mention Ricky."

"That's interesting…do you want something to eat?" her mother asked.

"That would be great. I'm just going to talk to Henry for a second, and I'll be right down."

"Eggs OK?"

"Fine. Thanks, Mom."

"The kids are in their rooms getting dressed. I started to help Joy pack, so you wouldn't have to do everything."

"I really appreciate it."

Upstairs, Brenda repeated the story again for Henry, minus the CD. She explained that Ralph might need some money to hire a lawyer. More concerned about his wife than Ralph, Henry asked how she was doing.

"I'm OK. It was a bit of a shock to see him like that, but I'm OK," she repeated.

"Good. How do you feel about loaning or giving him money?"

"I don't know. He's getting older. I'd hate to see him go to prison for a third time at his age. Besides, all the items he stole have been rounded up, so we don't have to press charges."

"True, but you aren't the only one he stole from."

"I know."

"I just don't want to make it look like we're in cahoots with him, by giving him money so he can hire a lawyer," Henry suggested.

"Do you think it would look that way?" asked Brenda.

"It could, but if you want to help him, I would never stand in your way. When push comes to shove, he's still your father."

"I guess."

"Brenda," her mother called. "Breakfast is ready."

"Did you tell Mom?" Henry inquired.

"Yes, I did."

As soon as Joy and Ricky heard their mother's name, they left their bedrooms to sit with Brenda while she ate. Both were very excited about the trip, so Brenda elected to table any discussion about Ralph and focus on Iowa instead.

Ricky faced his mother. "What time do we leave?"

"We're going to pick Coach and Mrs. Carrabas up around noon and have lunch on the road at a McDonald's or something," Brenda reported.

"McDonald's!" Joy chimed in.

"Yes, I know you love it. That's why we're going there," Brenda told her. "But first, we need to get packed. Who needs help?"

"I do, Mom," Joy said. "Grandma and I started. I remembered my red Wisconsin outfit for the parade."

"Good girl," her mother responded.

"Why don't you go up and help her, dear," Ellen suggested, "and I'll finish cleaning up here."

"Ricky, could you dry the pots for Grandma?"

"But I'm not packed yet."

"We've still got a couple of hours before we leave. You've got lots of time to pack," Brenda said.

When the family was finally ready to leave, Henry arranged the back of the van carefully with suitcases, tennis gear, water canisters, umbrellas, and folding chairs. Ricky had decorated the luggage rack with red and white crepe paper streamers and written "Nationals" on the rear window with a thick magic marker.

"How are you planning on going, Henry?" Brenda asked as her family entered the van.

"I'm going to head towards Dubuque, pick up 380, then take 35 into Ames. It should take us five hours of travel time—maybe six with a stop for lunch," was his response. "Kids, when we pick up the Carrabases, I want you to sit in the way back, so Grandma, Coach and his wife can sit in the middle seat. OK?"

"Don't forget, it's a holiday weekend, so there may be more traffic than usual," Brenda warned Henry.

"You're right. The fourth is Tuesday, isn't it."

Tom and Nancy were waiting by their driveway with their luggage. Tom wore a white Wisconsin tee shirt, and Nancy had on a red hat with a "W" over the visor. Henry helped them place their belongings on the decorated roof rack, and the kids shifted seats to accommodate the new passengers."

"All aboard," Henry called out. "Anyone forget anything?"

"I hope not," Brenda sighed.

Silent at first, as the van travelled towards the beltline, passengers began to talk about their favorite topic—tennis.

"They've played two rounds at Wimbledon, already. Blake and Andy Roddick are still in it. I think they play their third round today and so does Venus," Tom announced.

"Who do they play?" Brenda asked.

"Roddick plays Andy Murray, and James Blake plays Max Miryni. I think Venus Williams plays Jelena Janković."

"Tough matches for a third round," Ricky piped in.

"I saw you play a tough match a few days ago, Ricky. How are you enjoying your lessons?"

"They're great."

"The high school kids do a good job of teaching, don't they?

"Yes, they do. I really like them. They've taught me a lot."

"Some of your shots remind me of your mother's."

"Really?"

"I certainly recall that forehand," Tom enthused. "Did I tell you guys the first time she tried out for the high school team when she was a freshman?"

"I don't think so," Ricky answered.

Coach told the story of their mom's challenge matches against JV and varsity players. He recalled the tension, because a number of upperclassmen felt threatened. Most had played with Brenda during their summer clinics and knew how good she was.

Brenda won her first two matches easily against a couple of JV players. She challenged a varsity player, Dee Dee next. The event was a big deal, and Dee Dee's supporters lined the fences around the court before the match even began. Several freshmen sat at benches and tables under the oak trees to root for their classmate, too.

"A war of words broke out," Tom reminisced.

"It was a war," agreed Brenda. "All the juniors were there shouting insults."

Tom adjusted his cap. "It was extremely intense."

"Wow!" exclaimed Ricky. "So, what happened?"

Tom explained the shouting ceased once the match began. He recalled feeling surprised at how well-behaved both sides were. After Brenda won, however, there was pandemonium. The freshmen surrounded her and literally lifted her off the ground.

"Way to go, Mom," Joy said proudly.

Henry changed the subject, "Anyone hungry? We're closing in on a McDonald's, and I know one young lady who is very excited about it."

"That's me!" exclaimed Joy.

Ricky leaned forward in his seat. "Were you there, Grandma Ellen? When Mom tried out for the team?"

"I don't think so. I don't think I went to the tryouts, but John and I were at almost all Mom's home matches once she made the team."

"Uncle John?" questioned Ricky.

"Yes, Uncle John. He was so supportive of your mom when she played tennis. Of course, she was a wonderful big sister, too. It's sad what happened."

"He was killed in the war, wasn't he?" Ricky recalled.

"That's right, Son," acknowledged his father. "In Desert Storm."

"Who?" questioned Joy.

Her father answered, "Your mom's brother. We've talked about him before. His name was John. He passed away in Iraq in 1991—the year you were born. We actually named you after him, Joy."

"Oh, I didn't know."

Brenda reached an arm around the back of her seat and squeezed Ellen's hand.

"Here we are," Henry remarked.

"McDonalds!" said Joy, cheerfully.

Her father looked out his window. "It looks like the drive-through lane is clogged. Why don't I go inside with the kids, and we'll bring the food and drinks out to everybody. What would you like?"

Leaving Coach and the three women in the car, Henry left with the youngsters.

Ellen brought up Sadie. "I didn't want to say anything in front of the children, but I'll bet Sadie was the ringleader when you had to play Dee Dee, Brenda."

"Of course."

"She was so disruptive," her mother continued. "Any time there was an argument, she was always in the middle of it. On the tennis court. In the library. It didn't matter."

Tom recounted the two Milwaukee high schools that banned Sadie from playing on their courts because of her behavior. "Some of her line calls were egregious. Then, of course, she would dispute her opponents' calls, too. It wasn't easy being her coach."

"How about the foreign exchange student from Japan, who played on the team one year?" Nancy reminisced, recalling how she almost left Oakbrook because of Sadie. Katsumi Tomori was from Yokohama and a very good tennis player. The Carrabases were her host family, and their twins loved her. After one of the early practices, she came home to Nancy crying. Katsumi had caught Sadie making fun of her speech and appearance behind her back.

"I put an end to that in a hurry," Tom divulged. "I think I made Sadie sit out some of the early matches."

"Sadie also stole Katsumi's math homework once, erased Katsumi's name, and put her own name on it instead," Brenda remembered.

Tom leaned forward and looked at Brenda, "I don't think I heard about that."

"Because Katsumi figured out what happened and put her own name back on the paper before the teacher collected all of them."

"Wow."

"And I told you what Sadie said about Joy playing for the high school team, Tom."

"You said something about that to me. It was Sadie who made a remark to Allison's mother?"

"Yes. She hasn't changed much over the years."

"Lunchtime!" Ellen announced, as Henry, Joy and Ricky returned to the van with paper bags, napkins, straws, and drinks.

After lunch Henry put on the air conditioner, as the day was warming. "Would you like to hear some music? I brought some CDs to play."

Ricky adjusted his seat belt. "I want to hear more stories about Mom, Coach" Ricky said.

"Me, too," Joy agreed.

"You guys!" Brenda interrupted. "Whenever I bring this topic up you always tell me you heard it before."

"We've never heard Coach's version before," Ricky smiled.

"Well, to make a long story short, your mom played for the varsity all four years and went to state in singles her junior and senior years. She always played excellent tennis and was a great captain, too."

Joy leaned forward, "You went to state like me?"

"Yes, Joy. Both of us went to state. Isn't that neat?"

"I hope I get to go some day," Ricky sighed.

"You will, buddy," encouraged Henry. "You're a fine athlete, just like your mom and sister, and you work hard."

"You know what you didn't mention, none of you, and I'm surprised," Nancy recounted to Tom, Brenda, and Ellen. "The team mascot."

"Oh, jeez, how could we forget Rally. He was at every home match," Brenda said.

"Yes, he was, and John and I were responsible for holding on to him," Ellen piped in. "I remember the expressions on some of those player's faces when they saw him for the first time. It was very funny."

"He was huge," Tom mused.

"But gentle as the wind," Brenda boasted. "I still miss him."

Henry tapped her on the shoulder, "Wasn't he your prom date senior year, Brenda?"

"I wish, but they couldn't find a tux big enough to fit him, and he didn't dance very well, either," Brenda chided.

Joy leaned forward, "Are we there yet, Dad?"

"Almost, honey. It won't be long now. Why don't you sit back and try to nap."

"Are you getting excited?" her mom asked.

"Yes, I am."

———— ✤ ————

CHAPTER 30

Friday evening, June 30 and Saturday morning, July 1, 2006

IT WAS STILL light outside when Henry pulled into the motel. Both families registered and brought their luggage and gear to their rooms. Once settled, Tom borrowed the van to drive to Special Olympics headquarters at the Iowa State campus. He signed in, retrieved several packets of information, and studied the bulletin board for messages. The other three Wisconsin tennis players elected to stay in dormitories with their families. Tom checked to see if they had picked up their instruction folders, and they had.

Prior to leaving Oakbrook, Tom had spoken with everyone involved with the team and scheduled a meeting for Saturday morning at the outdoor tennis complex. There, doubles teams representing their states would play multiple tiebreaks allowing judges to place them in the various draws based on their levels of competence. Following the doubles assessment, a similar process would be repeated for singles players. Tom was required to be at every match his athletes played. Sunday would be used to complete the singles evaluation, and Sunday night was the parade and lighting of the Flame of Hope.

Henry dropped Tom off at the courts early Saturday morning so he could find out where and when his doubles teams played. There, he met his counterparts from other states, and they shared stories and advice while waiting for their players to appear. Some coaches had to supervise other venues besides tennis. The Massachusetts coach was in charge of a few athletes running track in addition to following tennis players.

When all four Wisconsin players and their families arrived, Tom assembled them to explain the format. The three women from the Milwaukee area, Maureen, Becca, and Shelley were in their late twenties to mid-thirties, the age range of most female tennis players from other states. Joy was one of the youngest, if not the youngest participant.

Since no one else was using the courts, Tom ushered his team out to warm up. The foursome looked sharp in their white sleeveless tops and red skirts and visors. They had played several matches against each other over the months leading up to nationals and seemed comfortable interacting.

While his team prepared, Coach assembled their families. "It's very important that we practice appropriate tennis etiquette. The directors made it very clear to the coaches that we need to respect our players' opponents like we expect them to respect us.

"As excited as we are, we should not boo, make negative comments, argue with line calls, or confront other parents. I know I've spoken to all of you before about this issue when we met in Oshkosh, but I want to remind you again. Please allow me to do the coaching. It's difficult for participants to listen to more than one advisor when they are playing. Most of all, have fun this week. I'm sure you're very proud of all four players—I know I am."

"Good luck, Coach," a parent called, "and thanks."

"You're welcome. Thank you for coming and allowing me to coach your athletes."

While the Wisconsin players worked out on their court, judges posted a schedule. Coach Carrabas copied it and gathered everyone to explain the timetable. "Joy, you, Maureen, and your opponents will be the third group on Court Four. Shelley and Becca will be the sixth group to play on Court One. The format is a ten-point tiebreak. You need ten points to win, and you have to win by two points. As I told you before, these matches do not count towards medals. These tiebreaks allow judges to place each doubles team in its appropriate draw. That means that there are a number of gold medals for doubles and singles, too. Not just one."

By this time, the courts were surrounded by multiple women in tennis garb and fans with programs and portable chairs. Iowa State University had over three thousand Special Olympics athletes competing on their campus and like the tennis players, all were being assessed by judges to create parity among teams and individuals competing in each event. Competition for medals would begin after the opening ceremonies.

Waiting to play, the Wisconsin team sat down together. Maureen and Shelley were more talkative than Becca, who was rather quiet. Joy participated in the conversation but rarely initiated it.

"I didn't think there would be so many people," Maureen admitted.

"Me either," Shelley agreed.

"Coach said not every state has a women's team," Maureen announced.

Shelley's eyes squinted. "Wisconsin doesn't have a men's tennis team, but most of the other states do."

"Why not?" Joy asked.

"I don't know," Maureen said. "Ask Coach. He's coming now... Coach!" she yelled to Tom.

"Hi ladies. What's up?"

"How come we don't have a men's tennis team?"

"Wisconsin, like most states, tries to have as many men as women on our Special Olympics team. This year the men play softball and have a lot of players. To even things out, we have women playing events that men aren't playing, and tennis is one of them."

"I'm hungry," Shelley confessed.

"Did you have breakfast?" Coach asked.

"A little."

"I have some bananas. Who would like one?" Tom inquired.

Shelley and Joy raised their hands.

"Here," Tom said, handing them out. "Do any of you need to go to the bathroom before we play our tiebreaks?"

Becca raised her hand, and Tom pointed to the portable facilities.

"Should we drink our water now?" Joy asked.

"Great idea, Joy," Tom commended. "It's going to be a warm afternoon, and you want to stay hydrated. Why don't all of you take some swallows before you play."

There was a lot of excitement as the first teams went on the eight outdoor courts to warm up and play tiebreaks. Within half an hour, Maureen and Joy were called. Tom stayed by the fence, coaching them when they changed sides after every six points. They played a doubles team from Nebraska and won 10-3.

A short time later, Tom told the other Wisconsin doubles team that they were going to play two women from New Hampshire on Court Five. Shelley grabbed her tennis bag excitedly, but Becca crossed her arms over her chest, stomped the ground, and puckered her lips. Coach thought she was going to cry. "Hey, Becca, what's up?" he inquired.

She maintained her posture and sniffed but didn't reply.

"Are you OK?"

Becca scuffed the grass and looked away. She began to shake her head vigorously, finally spitting out, "No!"

"What's going on?" Tom questioned.

She held up her hand and spread her fingers.

"Five? Yes, you and Shelley play on Court Five."

"No," she shouted. "Not five! Not five! You told us we were playing on Court One!"

"That's where the judges reassigned you," Coach instructed, as Becca kicked her tennis bag. "I know you would rather play on a different court. I get it. I know you don't like Court Five, but judges won't let you change. Shelley needs a partner and she wants you."

Becca turned her head away.

"I'll tell you a little story," Tom continued. "When I played a tournament here, I had to play on Court Five, too, and I wasn't sure I wanted to. But it became my lucky court. I won a couple of matches on five. Do you think it could be Shelley's and your lucky court, too?"

Becca shrugged.

"Let's go," Shelley said to her partner. "I want to play. Please play with me."

"Good luck you two," Coach encouraged. "Play well and have fun."

To Tom's relief, Becca picked up her tennis bag and followed Shelley to Court Five. As soon as the foursome began to warm up, Becca's anxiety seemed to diminish. The tiebreak was closely contested, but the Wisconsin duo eventually beat their New Hampshire counterparts 10-8.

After the initial tiebreaks, judges updated schedules based on results from previous rounds, and as the day progressed, the Wisconsin doubles teams each played six ten-point tiebreaks. Saturday afternoon and evening men's and boy's doubles teams played tiebreaks, and Sunday, using the same format, the singles draws for both sexes were established.

⚜

CHAPTER 31

Sunday evening, July 2 and Monday, July 3, 2006

DESPITE AN EARLY morning thunder storm, Sunday evening was beautiful with temperatures around 70. Native Iowan, Tom Arnold, hosted the opening ceremonies at Hilton Coliseum. The large oval arena was filled to capacity. Athletes representing all fifty states plus the District of Columbia marched to vintage Olympic music and applause from over ten thousand fans, twelve hundred coaches, and eight thousand volunteers. Tears flowed as Joy, Maureen, Becca, and Shelley, wearing their Wisconsin uniforms, followed their state flag. Hootie and the Blowfish serenaded everyone with multiple songs including *Hold My Hand*, *Time*, and *Only Wanna Be with You*.

The highlight of the evening was athlete, Rolla Lucas of Davenport, lighting the Flame of Hope. All stood to cheer as the blaze soared, calling an end to the ceremony and a real beginning of the games.

After athletes and fans left, Tom, along with other coaches, attended a meeting at the Coliseum. There they received draw sheets for their events. At a prearranged breakfast Monday morning, Coach Carrabas relayed that information to his tennis players and their families. "We play doubles first. Maureen and Joy are in the same draw as Shelley and Becca. You are at opposite ends of the sheet, so hopefully you will meet in the finals," he said with a smile.

"On Wisconsin!" a parent hollered.

Another yelled, "Way to go, girls!"

"Wisconsin's first match is at 10 o'clock. Joy and Maureen play against a doubles team from Kansas," Coach directed. "We won't know court assignments until each match is called. Shelley, you and Becca play an Illinois team, but we don't know times yet." Looking at his watch, Tom said, "I've got 8:30. Let's meet up at the courts at quarter past nine. Incidentally, all of you play two sets and a ten-point tiebreak to decide matches if necessary. All scoring is no-ad. That means if you are tied in a game, 3-3, you do not play deuce or ad points. Receivers choose which player the serve goes to, and you play one final point for the game. I know that's complicated. I will be nearby to help if you need me. I can't coach you when you are playing games, but I can when you change sides, just like I did Saturday and Sunday."

Both Wisconsin doubles teams won their opening matches, and after lunch, they played their second round. Facing a tough team from California, Becca and Shelley lost 6-3, 6-3. A little after two o'clock, Joy and Maureen took the court against a team from Arizona. Their match was very close with long points. Wisconsin won the initial set 6-4 and was up 5-4 in the second, when the Arizona women won three games in a row to win the set 7-5. Before playing a tiebreak, Tom coached his players. As was his style, he initiated the conversation with a question.

"You guys won that first set and you were winning the second. Can you tell me what they did differently?"

Joy looked up at the sky, "They lobbed."

"Yes, they did, Joy," Tom agreed. "When did they lob you?"

"I don't know," Joy responded.

"They lobbed you on their service returns," Coach reminded them.

Maureen clapped, "Right!"

"So, what do you do?" Tom asked them. Both were quiet. "How about having the net person stand back on the service line instead of close to the net." Tom suggested. "That will make it more difficult for their receivers to lob over your heads."

"Should we both do that?" Maureen pondered.

"I would," answered Tom.

"You're playing good, Joy," Maureen announced.

"So, are you," Joy responded. "Your serves are really good."

"I agree," Tom piped in. "Why don't you let Maureen serve first for our team. Remember to switch sides after every six points like you did in the tiebreaks you played before. Come over to me at those times, because I am allowed to coach you during crossovers."

The Wisconsin team served first. When the players changed sides, the score was tied at 3-all. Tom huddled with his twosome, "I had a thought," he said. "What if we started to lob them on our returns? They're playing close to the net. Do you want to try it?"

"Sure," Joy said. "I'll try on this point."

Maureen chimed in, "OK."

The Arizona server went to Joy's backhand, and Joy lofted a beautiful shot over the net person for a winner. Up 4-3, Maureen served again, and Joy moved back to prevent her opponent's lob. Confused, the returner hit a short ball that Joy volleyed for a winner. On the next point, Maureen served hard into her opponent's body to put her team up 6-3. Arizona won the following three points, however, and they changed sides at 6-6. Joy had one more serve, and again the Arizona returner, trying to lob, hit a ball short. This time Maureen put it away with an overhead. The tie-break lead went back and forth between both teams. Up 10-9 with Joy serving, the Arizona women played back. Seeing a vacated forecourt, Joy hit a soft shot off the return that neither opponent could reach, allowing Wisconsin to win the tiebreak and the match.

Exuberant fans cheered and crowded around the win-ners when they came off their court. As Maureen hugged Joy, her first question to coach was, "When do we play again?"

"Tomorrow. Let's meet at the restaurant at 8 o'clock for breakfast like we did this morning. All four of you played really well today. I'm very proud of you. Have a good night and get some sleep."

"When do singles matches begin, Coach?" a parent inquired.

"Thursday."

Once Tom, Nancy, and the Bjorkmans were in the van, Coach asked Joy how she felt about winning two matches at nationals.

"I was nervous in the tiebreak," she confessed.

"You didn't show it," Coach countered. "You played very well. That last shot, where you dropped it short, was brilliant, Joy."

"She's hit those against me a couple of times," Ricky said.

Joy wrapped her arms around herself, "Maureen was nice. I like to play with her."

"She obviously likes playing with you, too," Tom added.

"Well, I was really impressed with you, Joy," her father began, looking at her through the rearview mirror. "I know how tense a situation like a tiebreak can be. You handled it like the athlete you are. You played smart, sweetheart. How about you pick where we eat tonight."

"Pizza!"

Henry agreed, "Pizza it is."

CHAPTER 32

Wednesday, July 5, 2006

JOY AND MAUREEN advanced to the semi-finals on Tuesday, beating some good doubles teams along the way. To celebrate, the entire Wisconsin contingent watched Fourth of July fireworks at Cyclone Stadium and went out for ice cream afterwards.

Wednesday morning breakfast was quieter than usual, because Shelley and her family were absent. At seven o'clock that morning, Shelley's parents had called Tom to say she was not feeling well. Shelley had been up most of the night vomiting, and today she had diarrhea, too. Her mother suspected food poisoning, but no other family member was ill. Both parents wondered if she was going to be able to play singles on Thursday.

Joy and Maureen's match began a little after eleven o'clock under clear skies with temperatures in the low 70s. Tom prepared his team well, as the California duo they were playing was the same twosome who beat Shelley and Becca in the second round. "One woman is really tall," Tom told them. "Do you remember her? And she loves being up at the net. However, when she poaches, she always stands in the middle of the court. Both alleys are usually wide open. Tall people at the net are intimidating—you know what that means—it's frightening to see them up there—but they have a harder time bending down than shorter people. Hitting a ball right at their bellybuttons is very effective."

Joy and Maureen started to laugh.

"Seriously," Coach offered. "That's where you want to hit it, or down the alleys. OK?"

"Did Shelley and Becca try that?" Maureen asked.

"Good question. Yes, they did, but they had trouble placing their shots. The tall woman was able to pick a lot of them off, because they were in the middle of the court instead of the alleys, or at her shoulders instead of her waist."

Since most doubles teams had been eliminated, crowds watching the semis were smaller, but tension was far greater than the initial matches. Players who won this round were guaranteed silver or gold medals, and everyone on and off the courts knew it.

Once warm-ups began, the tall Californian looked even taller. Her arms seemed to stretch the full length of the net. Her partner was no slouch either, hitting nice slices on her forehand and backhand sides.

"What do you think, Tom?" Brenda asked as Coach strayed from the court towards the fans.

"They're tough. Did you see much of Shelley and Becca's match with them on Monday?"

"I saw quite a bit of it."

"They beat them pretty easily, but our team had trouble with slices and were beaten at the net. I've hit slices to Joy over the years, and I think she can handle them. I don't know about Maureen."

The Wisconsin team opened strong, while the California women seemed to shy away from the net. Joy dealt with slices well; Maureen had more difficulty and netted shots she normally returned with ease. On the changeover, Joy and Maureen were up 2-1.

Coach Carrabas corralled them. "I don't think these women are going to stay back much longer. I expect to see JoAnn, that's the taller woman, begin to play her usual game by knocking shots off at the net. Let's see if we can prevent it. I want you to send up lobs to keep them back in the court. And what do you do if JoAnn comes up to net?"

"Aim for her bellybutton," Joy laughed.

"Or hit it down the alley," Maureen added.

Tom nodded, "Right, but first, let's see if we can keep them deep."

After hitting the first serve of the fourth game, both Californians came to net as Tom predicted, and Joy sent a great lob over their heads for a winner. On the next point, Maureen lobbed her return, too, and their advancing opponents were forced back to the baseline to retrieve it. The match's longest rally ensued, and when JoAnn finally approached the middle of the net, Joy won the point by sending a perfect shot down her alley. Up 3-1, Maureen served well, adjusted to sliced shots, and allowed Joy to volley winners off returns. During one point in the fifth game, JoAnn again tried to rush the net, but before reaching it, Maureen hit another winning lob. Frustrated, both Californians began to overhit their shots. Joy and Maureen won the first set 6-3.

The wind blew harder when their second set began. Gusts reached almost twenty miles per hour, and both teams had difficulty controlling their shots. In particular, JoAnn and Joy had trouble serving with the wind at their backs. By the end of seven games, Joy and Maureen were down 4-3. At the changeover, Coach made a few suggestions. "Joy?" he asked. "Do you remember the last practice we had at Taylor Park?"

"Yes."

"Do you remember the wind that evening?"

"Yes."

"What did you do when you had trouble keeping your serve in with the wind at your back?"

"I served underhand."

"Exactly. Do you think you can serve underhanded again?"

"Yes."

"Maureen, be ready at the net. Joy's serve is going to take some funny bounces, and your opponents aren't going to be able to control their returns very well, so you may see some bounces you weren't expecting. OK?"

"OK."

"With the wind behind you," Coach added, "it's going to be much more difficult to lob, especially on the side Joy is serving from. So, when you are on that side, like right now, I would not try to lob."

Joy began the eighth game double faulting her first underhanded attempt. Undiscouraged, she found her range on the ensuing serves. The Californians tried slicing returns but failed to control their shots. Most balls fell into the net; a few were long, and Joy won her serve without difficulty.

At 4-all, JoAnn's partner served with the wind in her face. Unused to the conditions, she struggled, losing the game at love.

Changing sides and up 5 games to 4, Maureen began the tenth game. JoAnn tried to lob a return, but the wind carried it out. On the next point, the same thing happened to her partner. The Californians won the next two points by slicing returns and keeping the ball low. On the fifth point, JoAnn sliced her return again. Joy poached, but the ball suddenly dipped causing her to mishit it into the net. The Californians again tried a lob on the next point. Despite the wind, the shot stayed in for a game winner. Again, the game score was tied.

With the wind at her back, JoAnn was up next. When her underhanded attempts failed, she resorted to her usual service motion. Unable to control her ball toss, she lost four consecutive points and the game.

"What's the set score?" Joy asked Coach Carrabas as players changed sides. "5-4?" she questioned.

"No, it's actually 6-5. Where is the wind going to be now that you are switching?" Tom asked.

"At our backs," Maureen answered.

"Right," Tom agreed. "Can we lob?"

"They did," Maureen said, "but we shouldn't. Right?"

"Right," Coach agreed. "They were fortunate that last lob was good."

Joy grinned, "And if that woman comes to net I can hit her bellybutton."

"You're too much, Joy Bjorkman!" Coach smiled. "Go get 'em, ladies! But be patient."

Maureen gave Joy a pat on her shoulder as they went out to play the twelfth game of the set, and Joy patted her partner back.

Joy took a deep breath and looked around the court before serving. Her underhanded shot took a wicked bounce before sliding away untouched. She glanced at Coach, who, trying to contain his emotions, smiled at her. Maureen lost the next point, unable to volley a return after another good serve. Seemingly unfazed, Joy calmly hit two more underhanded winners. With game and match on her racquet, she hit a regular serve. JoAnn hit a strong forehand. Approaching the net, Joy hit a volley that barely grazed the tape. When JoAnn tried to hit it, the ball struck the frame of her racquet then bounced into the fence at the back of the court.

Joy and Maureen raised their racquets in the air and rushed to shake hands with the Californians. Wisconsin fans, who had been reserved throughout most of the contest, ran to embrace the victors and Coach Carrabas. "Thanks," Coach responded, "but we have more tennis to play. Let's not celebrate too soon. While we are assured of medals, I would prefer gold to silver. During your semis, ladies," he addressed Joy and Maureen, "I was watching the teams on Court Six. You play the winner in the finals."

"Where are they from?" someone asked.

"The women in beige are from New Mexico. The blue team is from North Carolina. Your finals are scheduled for two-thirty, so let's grab some lunch."

"How's Shelley doing?" Henry asked. "Have you spoken to her family?"

"I have," Tom reported. "She is still having problems. I'm going to withdraw her from the singles competition. I've received information from other coaches that more tennis players and athletes at other venues have reported a similar illness, so I want every one of you to wash your hands carefully before eating. OK?"

By two-thirty, the wind had died down making playing conditions easier. It was clear from the onset of the match that Carolina's team was not nearly as proficient as California's. In an anti-climactic final, Joy and Maureen easily won the gold 6-1, 6-3. Celebrations after the match, however, were more boisterous and went on longer than those following the semi-finals.

In late afternoon, Wisconsin players and families, minus Shelley and her parents, went to Cyclone stadium for the medal ceremony. Standing on the middle and tall-est of the three-tiered platform, Joy and Maureen received gold pendants suspended by red, white and blue ribbons. Coach Carrabas was close by to congratulate them first. "I am so proud of you two. You played great and deserve the medals you won."

"It was the bellybutton shot that won it," Joy smiled.

"You and your bellybuttons, Joy!" Tom said.

"I only have one."

"Yes, I know. It's the same for all of us."

CHAPTER 33

Friday, July 7 and Saturday, July 8, 2006

THURSDAY WAS A red letter day for Wisconsin's tennis team. The three entrants—Becca, Maureen, and Joy—each won two singles matches. Together with their families at breakfast on Friday, however, the mood was somber. Joy had been up most of the night with nausea and vomiting; she looked pale and lethargic. Tom informed everyone that Shelley had been moved to the rec center, where a hundred and forty cots had been set up for sick athletes. The health department suspected norovirus and had increased the number of medical volunteers.

"Are you sure you want to play, Joy?" Tom asked sympathetically.

"Yes. Please," she begged.

"What do you think Henry? Brenda?" Coach questioned.

"I don't know," Brenda sighed thoughtfully. "If she wants to, I don't see any harm in trying. What do you think, Henry?"

"I think she looks tired. You need to drink, Joy. How about a Seven Up?"

"I'll try," Joy responded.

"I don't know," her grandmother intervened. "I think she looks like she doesn't feel well. I would be inclined not to push her."

Henry placed his hands on his hips. "Here's what I think—you can try to play, but if you don't feel well, you have to come off the court. Understood?"

"Yes," Joy replied.

"She plays at ten?" asked Brenda.

"Yes," Tom acknowledged. "Why don't you try to drink some liquids, and we'll drive up to the courts at nine-thirty."

Joy drank some Seven Up, and it stayed down. Unfortunately, she developed diarrhea and had to use the bathroom three times before she left for her match. Since her nausea and vomiting were less, she felt a little better. Her parents and Coach were more optimistic about her chances of playing.

Joy's opponent, Samantha, was from Delaware. Tom had not seen her play before. After talking to other coaches who had observed her, he strategized with his student. "This is a good time to use that high lob to the backhand," he suggested. "Remember what you do after that?"

"Yes, I come to net."

"Right, Joy, you hit the approach shot. You need to win points faster than usual, because you're not feeling one hundred percent. Hopefully, using the lob and approach will help. How are you doing?"

"OK."

"Do you still want to play?"

"Yes, I do. I want to."

Becca and Maureen's matches were later, so Tom stayed by Joy's court as she warmed up with her opponent. Joy won the toss, electing to serve. She played a flawless first game with accurate serves plus strong groundstrokes. As instructed, she lobbed to her opponent's backhand and followed up with approach shots. Checking in with Coach at the changeover, she smiled, seemingly upbeat.

She broke Samantha's serve for the second game, then won her own serve again to go up 3-0. As she changed sides again, she told Coach she needed to go to the bathroom. Tom explained Joy's situation to the Delaware coach, then showed Joy where the portable potties were. He waited nearby, and when she exited, inquired how she was doing.

"I'm OK. I just feel a little tired."

"Do you think we ought to stop the match?"

"No. Please don't," she insisted.

They walked together back to the courts, and when Joy entered, Tom called to her, "Joy, you're going to the wrong side." Joy nodded absentmindedly and walked to the other end. Before serving, she bent down to tie a shoelace. Abruptly, she toppled onto her back. Eyes closed, her legs stiffened, and her arms began to jerk involuntarily.

"Oh my god!" Brenda yelled. "She's having a seizure!" Both Bjorkmans ran towards the court. "Didn't she get her pill this morning?" Brenda asked Henry.

"I think she did, but she may have thrown it up."

Before they could reach their daughter, a referee ran to her, followed by a woman in a short white jacket carrying a medical bag. The referee kept onlookers away from Joy. "Please stay where you are," he instructed. "We have a physician right here." When the Bjorkmans explained to him they were Joy's parents, he waived them onto the court.

Kneeling down beside Joy, the doctor placed a towel under her head, and held her arms, so that Joy wouldn't injure them. When Brenda and Henry arrived, she introduced herself without looking up. "Hi, I'm Doctor Arnold. Are you this young lady's parents?" she inquired calmly.

"Yes," Brenda answered.

"Has she had seizures before?"

"She used to, but she hasn't had one for a year now."

"Is she still on medication for them?"

"Yes, Dilantin."

"And do you know if she received her meds today and in the past few days?"

"We think she got her pill today, but she's been vomiting, and it might have come up."

"Has she had diarrhea, too?"

"Yes," Brenda replied. "She went to the bathroom a few times this morning and again a couple of minutes ago."

The doctor asked several more questions before reassuring the Bjorkmans, "She's going to be fine. I have injectable lorazepam in my bag, and I am going to draw some up in a syringe now. If the seizure doesn't stop, I will give it to her."

Removing her cellphone, Dr. Arnold dialed a number and began speaking. "I need an ambulance at the tennis courts, please. I have a patient who's having a seizure. Thank you."

Talking to Brenda while ministering to Joy, she said, "Once it stops, we're going to need to get some lab tests."

"Why do you think she's seizing?" Brenda inquired.

"It could be because she vomited her meds, but it could also be from loss of electrolytes through vomiting, diarrhea, and sweating. She's a little dehydrated. Notice how dry her tongue is, and her eyes look a little sunken to me. Kids who have a seizure disorder need less of a stimulus to have a seizure."

Brenda was frightened. "When is it going to stop? They never used to go on this long."

"I'm going to try to stop it now, because it doesn't seem to be abating on its own…Sir," she said to Henry, "will you hold your daughter's right arm for me as best you can. I need to tie a tourniquet around the upper part. This medicine works best if given IV."

Accessing a vein, Dr. Arnold slowly injected the lorazepam intravenously, and in less than a minute, Joy's seizure stopped.

"Oh, thank you, Doctor," Brenda said looking directly at Dr. Arnold for the first time. Her face was familiar and searching, she noticed a faded red birth mark on the doctor's right temple. "I'm so glad you were here…I…good gosh. I don't believe it…Carrie? Carrie Archibald?"

"It's actually Carrie Arnold now," the doctor smiled. "And, you're Brenda. From Oakbrook. Right?"

"Yes…Dr. Carrie Arnold," Brenda cried, as she wrapped an arm around her tennis mentor and friend. "Oh, my god, it's good to see you."

"And you, too, Brenda. Look at you, a mother. What a wonderful job you've done with this young athlete. Competing in the Special Olympics USA National Games. How awesome is that!"

"Can you come to the hospital with us, Carrie?"

"Absolutely. Here comes the ambulance now. We'll let the EMTs do their thing then go to the E.R. at St. Francis with them."

"Henry," Brenda said, "I'm going to ride in the ambulance with Joy. Please drive to St. Francis Hospital with Mom and Ricky. Meet us in the Emergency Room."

On the way to the hospital, Joy began to awaken, asking what happened. Her mother told her she had had a seizure, but she was going to be fine. Then she introduced Joy to Carrie. "This is my friend, Carrie Arnold. She taught me to play tennis when I was a little girl. She's a doctor now and is taking care of you."

After her family arrived at the hospital, Brenda brought Carrie to meet her husband and son and to see her mother again.

"What a thrill this is," Ellen enthused.

"For me, too, Mrs. Nelson," replied Carrie, "to see you both again and to meet your family."

"I take it you live in Iowa? Did you return after college?" Brenda inquired.

"Yes. You remember my dad was teaching at Colonial. So, after college, I went to med school at Iowa and did my residency in Pediatrics at Minnesota. Because my folks were in Iowa, I returned here to find a position at a clinic in Oskaloosa. My parents live just half an hour away. Dad is retired now."

"Do you have kids?" Brenda asked.

"Yes, I have two and my husband has two."

"So, I have to ask you—do you see Al at all?"

"Actually, Brenda, I bumped into him a couple of times in the twin cities when I was doing my residency."

"How was he?"

"Great as usual. He was teaching and coaching basketball and tennis. He seemed very happy. I'm hoping to see him at a reunion one of these years."

"I'm glad to hear that," Brenda smiled. "I loved that guy."

"So did I," Carrie admitted. "So did I."

Tom stayed for Maureen's and Becca's matches after the ambulance left. Both women lost, however, so he and Nancy found a ride to the hospital with another coach. Joy was still in the ER receiving IV fluids in a cubicle, surrounded by her family and physician. Tom recognized Carrie immediately and gave her a big hug. "That was you on the court in the white coat!" he exclaimed. "I still think of you as a high school student. How are you, Carrie?"

"Great, Coach. How about you?"

"Fine. You remember my wife, Nancy."

"Of course. Nice to see you again, Mrs. Carrabas."

"You, too," Nancy replied.

"How come I didn't see you by the courts before?" Tom asked.

"I was at some of the other venues—softball and swimming."

Tom walked over to the cot. "So, tell me how your patient is doing?"

"She's a bit drowsy from her seizure and from the medication I gave her, but she's going to be fine, aren't you Joy?"

"Yes," Joy agreed through half-opened eyes.

"We're giving her some fluid. She was a little dry."

"Have you seen her lab tests yet?" Brenda asked.

"We're waiting for the Dilantin level, but all the other values were normal, and that's good news, Brenda."

"Do you think she needs to stay overnight?"

"I don't think so. We can probably give her a dose of Dilantin and send her back to the motel with you. Her vomiting has stopped, and she hasn't had diarrhea for a couple of hours. But remember, she's contagious. Make sure to wash your hands frequently when you're around her. You need to wash your hands, too, Joy. OK?"

"OK," Joy mumbled.

"Well, let's keep the fluid going and see how you look after this bag is finished." Turning to Tom, Carrie said, "I haven't seen you since graduation. Are you still playing tournaments?"

"A few. When I have time."

"Do you still teach tennis in the summer?"

"I do. In addition to lessons at the park, I've been coaching Joy since she was ten."

"That's really special."

"Joy will be going out for our high school team. Won't you?"

"Yes," Joy answered.

"How neat is that—to have coached mother and daughter?" asked Carrie.

"It's the best," Tom admitted. "It doesn't get any better."

"And you're obviously in excellent shape."

"I feel really great for a sixty-six-year-old senior citizen."

"Well, no one would believe you're a day over fifty," Carrie remarked, "and you seem to have the same level of energy you had when I was in high school."

While the gathering waited for the IV to finish, they retold stories about the old days in Oakbrook—most tales involved tennis, of course. When the Bjorkmans finally left the hospital late Friday night with Joy, Ellen, Coach, and Nancy, they thanked Carrie and begged her to stay with them the next time she was in town.

Joy spent most of Saturday morning and afternoon at the motel, where she slept with her gold medal around her neck. By evening, both Joy and Shelley felt well enough to attend the closing ceremonies along with the other Wisconsinites. Kurt Warner, MVP quarterback of the Arizona Cardinals, a native of Iowa, was master of ceremonies. After the flag was lowered, the athletes, families, fans, and volunteers began their treks home.

CHAPTER 34

Saturday night, July 8 and Sunday, July 9, 2006

JOY HAD NOT recovered completely from the previous day's ordeal, and the closing ceremonies had tired her out. She was withdrawn and slept most of the way back to Wisconsin.

When the Bjorkman van approached Oakbrook around midnight, fire engines and police cars greeted them, their sirens blaring, lights flashing. Kids and adults lined the sidewalks of Main Street waving Wisconsin pennants and yelling, "Joy! Joy! Joy!" The fifteen-year-old awakened and was overwhelmed, as were her parents, grandmother, and brother. Tom, who engineered the celebration with Nancy, smiled as he waved to onlookers, too.

As the escort arrived at Village Hall, Mr. Appel, the newly-elected village president came outside to greet Joy and her entourage. He invited them onto the front steps where he presented Joy with a large bouquet of red roses. A photographer for *The Oakbrook Current* chronicled the event for the newspaper.

The Bjorkmans hugged each other, weeping openly as the crowd clapped for their gold medal champion. Joy shyly sidled up to her parents, while Ricky, Ellen, and the Carrabases remained close by.

"I'd like to say a few words," Stan Appel said into a loud speaker as the crowd continued to buzz. "May I have your attention, please. This is a special day for Oakbrook. Never in the history of our village have we had an Olympian. Joy is our first one. Not only did she win a gold medal in tennis for doubles, but she made it past the first few rounds in singles as well. Congratulations, Joy," he finished looking at her proudly.

As the crowd clapped, Tom took the microphone from Stan. "May I?" Tom asked. "I know Joy joins me in thanking all of you for coming out tonight. In a community like ours, a victory for one is a victory for all. In addition to congratulating Joy, I would also like to congratulate her parents, Henry and Brenda and her brother, Ricky for their relentless support of all Joy's endeavors."

Again, the gathering applauded, shouting Joy's name, as her family alongside the Carrabases descended Village Hall steps to embrace them. Even Michael and his mother, Sally were there, as were Allison and her mother, Cheryl. The Bjorkmans were deeply touched.

"Hi, Joy," Michael said.

"Hi, Michael," Joy responded, bashfully holding her bouquet.

"Nice going...can I see your medal?"

"Sure," and she removed it from her neck.

"Is it real gold?" he inquired.

"I think so."

"Don't forget about our bowling date, Michael," Brenda smiled.

"Don't worry about that, Brenda," Sally laughed. "That's all he talks about."

"Congratulations, Joy," Allison said hugging her friend. "Those flowers are beautiful."

"Thanks," Joy replied, "but you shouldn't hug me."

"Why not?"

"I've been sick."

Allison backed away. "Sorry."

"It's OK, Allison," Brenda interjected. "She had a stomach bug and is contagious. Just make sure you wash your hands when you get home. That goes for you, too, Michael."

After another half hour of mingling with the crowd, the Bjorkmans, Carrabases and Ellen made their way back to the van. Henry drove Tom and Nancy home. As he accompanied them to their door with Brenda, Henry said, "I don't know how to say thank you, Tom, and you, too Nancy, for all you have done for our family. None of this would have happened without you."

"It was a privilege," replied Tom, as Nancy nodded her head. "It takes special kids to participate in Special Olympics, and Joy is really special."

"She sure is," Brenda agreed. "Thank you."

The Bjorkmans and Ellen slept soundly Saturday night, grateful to be home again. Brenda awoke early Sunday morning and lay in bed thinking about the Iowa trip. Watching

Joy parade around the track in her red outfit was incredible, especially remembering she barely weighed two pounds the day she was born. The matches were fun to see, too, but they were stressful. Winning the medal was surreal. Then the seizure… and Carrie. Last night was the icing on the cake, she thought. There were at least a hundred people at Village Hall to welcome them home and congratulate Joy.

Brenda yawned and thought about all the work awaiting her at Few Hours A Day Nursery. She had been gone over a week and undoubtedly had piles of bills to pay plus all the children's logs to update. If she went to work this morning when no one else was around, she could catch up and wouldn't be as swamped Monday.

Brenda arose quietly, washed, dressed, and drove to the daycare. She walked into Room One unburdened for the first time in three weeks. She took a deep breath as she looked at the corner crib. Glancing up at the video camera above the cubbyholes, she shook her head apologetically then wandered off to her office. She sat down at her desk and opened the computer to access her emails. One in particular caught her eye.

To: B.Bjorkman@minutes.com
From: oddsandends@vintage.com
Subject: You and me

Congrats on Joy. Thanks for the money. Am back home. Be down in 3 weeks. R

Epilogue

ONE WEEK AFTER they returned from Iowa, Joy and Brenda met Michael and Sally at Two Lanes Bar. As they entered the facility, patrons clapped. Michael, proud of his friend, took Joy's hand and raised it over her head with his. By the second game, Joy caught on to bowling, even making a strike. Michael proved to be an excellent and patient teacher, while reveling in the role. Like most boys, he also enjoyed performing in front of his "girlfriend." He bowled a 138 and 144. With encouragement from Brenda, Sally promised to enter Michael in Special Olympics events.

When Joy turned sixteen, her parents threw a birthday party for her. Classmates with their parents attended, as did her tennis teammates. As she opened her presents, a small white puppy bounded towards her. When Joy saw it (actually, saw her), she screamed with delight, but the pup turned tail, skidding away frightened. Brenda caught and brought her back to Joy, who placed the dog gently on her lap. She was thrilled and without deliberation named her "Happy." A pure-bred Great Pyrenees, Happy weighed over ninety pounds when she was full-grown.

2006 would not be the last Special Olympics USA National Games for Joy or Maureen. In 2010 they competed in Lincoln, Nebraska, and in 2014, they played in New Jersey. They won gold again for doubles in Nebraska, and Joy won gold for singles in Nebraska and New Jersey. Tom, of course, coached his players at both events.

Joy also played varsity singles and doubles for Coach Carrabas at Oakbrook High. With Allison as her partner, she won their conference title at number two doubles her last two years. In 2015, Joy was inducted into the Oakbrook Sports Hall of Fame along with Tom Carrabas for their achievements at Special Olympics.

Ricky made varsity as a freshman and played number one singles and doubles for Oakbrook's tennis team three out of his four years. In addition, he won a few rounds at state after winning his conference title as a junior and senior. A National Merit finalist, he was accepted to the U on a full academic scholarship to study social work.

Ralph had to serve time again for theft and was incarcerated for six months. After his release, he and Brenda and Ellen, too, seemed to reconcile their relationships. Both Ricky and Joy loved their new-found grandfather, as he was uncharacteristically warm and playful with them. Despite his disparaging remarks years ago about women's tennis, he happily went to the Special Olympics USA National Games in 2010 and 2014 to watch his granddaughter compete. He remained sober for the rest of his life. In January, 2015, he had a massive heart attack and passed away. Brenda's secret died with him. The Bjorkmans bought him a plot in the Oakbrook cemetery overlooking Pierce Lake and visit his gravesite a few times a year.

Sadie was Sadie. She didn't accompany her husband when he presented the bouquet of roses to Joy. And when Joy played for the high school team, Sadie never called Tom's decision into question, but she did not attend any of Joy's matches either. Sadie's weight continued to increase but her standing in the community diminished, as did her circle of friends. In 2008, when the ladies' team voted her out as captain, Sadie stopped playing tennis altogether. Her oldest daughter, Molly, married a computer programmer from California. Sandy ran away from home at seventeen and has been in and out of rehab since. Ellie is doing well in elementary school.

Al and Carrie saw each other again in 2011 at their thirty-fifth high school reunion. Both were productive and seemed happy with their lives. Al loved teaching and coaching. He tried to impact his students as Coach Carrabas had influenced him. Carrie loved medicine. In addition to volunteering for Special Olympics, she worked in a free clinic one night a week. She also kept her embalmed appendix on an office shelf to help inspire patients who were interested in becoming physicians.

Henry, Brenda, Ellen, Joy, and Happy continued to live in the same home after Ricky went off to college. Joy missed her brother and looked forward to seeing him when he returned for holidays and summers.

The economic recession of 2008, affected lots of businesses, but Few Hours A Day Nursery survived as did Henry's plumbing shop, where Joy continued to work after high school.

And the city of Oakbrook endured, too, despite road construction through the center of town—so did Taylor Park and Pierce Lake. As for the grove of trees near the tennis courts, new generations assembled to converse, and the oaks heard them all.

Acknowledgements

SINCE I AM sure my acknowledgements are incomplete, I would like to thank everyone who inspired, encouraged, read, edited and critiqued my book. In particular, the readers: Kathy Karofsky, Cindy Benzon, John and Joy Newman, Maynard Poland, Jean Hopp, and Ed Bonkowsi; and the editors: Amy Karofsky, Sherri Newes, Janie Heck, Jon Fons, and Fran and Kay McGuire. Thanks to Bob Whitehead, who taught me about SONA coaching requirements, selection of the athletes, and the tennis format used in Special Olympics events. Lastly, a special thanks to Logan Karofsky for designing the cover for my novel.

About the Author

PETER KAROFSKY IS a pediatrician and professor emeritus of the University of Wisconsin School of Medicine and Public Health. He resides with his wife, Kathy, in Middleton, Wisconsin and Fort Myers, Florida. His email address is: andtheoaks@gmail.com

References for Special Olympics USA National Games, 2006

Cedar Rapids Gazette; July 3 and July 8, 2006.

Oskaloosa Herald; July 5 and July 10, 2006.

http://www.soky.org/features/tang_0702.htm#.VlUrDYSMCt8 (Team Kentucky)

http://www.nchpad.org/395/2169/Special~Olympics~Makes~Its~Mark~in~Ames~~Iowa (History of Special Olympics)

http://www.iowastatedaily.com/news/article_6c7e42ff-7801-56e4-a25f-7b7890e03ca0.html (*Iowa State Daily*)

http://www.wunderground.com/history/airport/KAMW/2006/7/5/DailyHistory.html?req_city=&req_state=&req_statename=&reqdb.zip=&reqdb.magic=&reqdb.wmo= (Ames weather)

Made in the USA
Lexington, KY
18 November 2016